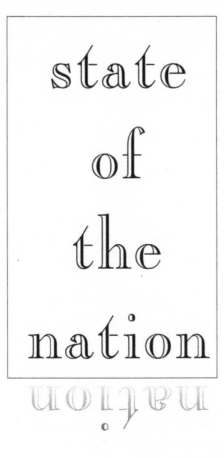

state

of

the

nation

DAVID JACKSON AMBROSE

THE TMG FIRM

New York

The TMG Firm, LLC
112 W. 34th Street
17th and 18th Floors
New York, NY 10120
www.thetmgfirm.com

State of the Nation
Copyright © 2018 David Jackson Ambrose
Published by The TMG Firm, LLC

For more information about special discounts for bulk purchase, please contact The TMG Firm at 1-888-984-3864 ext 12 or publishing@thetmgfirm.com

ISBN: 978-0-99879-939-1
Library of Congress Control Number: 2018903215
All rights reserved

First The TMG Firm Trade Paperback Edition April 2018
Printed in the United States of America

Cover created by Brittani Williams for TSPub Creative, LLC.

"esē diaspora en pasais basileias tēs gēs ..."

"thou shalt be a dispersion in all kingdoms of the earth."

-Deuteronomy 28:25

Author's Note

I would like to thank Joan Mellen, whose unwavering honesty and encouragement was an invaluable impetus to see this project through to completion.

This book is also dedicated to my mother, Carolann Ambrose. The road that she was destined to travel by her God was also the road that permitted me to reconnect with my creative self.

I would also like to thank Ann Green, Tenaya Darlington, and the English Department of St. Joseph's University, who fostered an atmosphere of mutual respect and creative imagination. They allowed me to heal from the microaggressions of corporate America and to reconnect with my pre-traumatized soul.

Also to all those quieted voices on the periphery. Don't ever stop dreaming big. Always believe in yourself, and remember to pass along what you learn to those you encounter on your path. Light.

Prologue

Through the quivering grasses of a long overlooked field, a stagnant breeze carried the scent of daffodil. The night was a sheet of pitch opacity, erupted by intermittently winking stars flashing above. A distant blast from a ship was the only sound he could hear other than the ragged breathing that tore through his lungs, and the blood clotting through his ear canal, amplified by the rapid beating of his heart.

Distractedly, he marveled at the anomaly of a ship sounding this close to Atlanta. Then he marveled that he was able to give consideration to the thought. He wondered if the abstracted movement of his mind and the rapid beating of his heart were a response to the chemicals coursing through his veins, or if the loss of oxygen was the culprit. Crouching in the knee-high grass, he reached a lean brown arm toward the garroted lesions on his neck. He remembered the rasp of the cord as it had torn the skin from his pulsing larynx, bracing tightly against his jawbone as it had closed the airway to his lungs. He had struggled weakly against the tightening cord, and against the body that straddled above him on the cool concrete floor, but the drugs he had been given had left him poorly equipped for fighting back. He could only remember the way that his vision, rather than snuffing out, had seemed to do a slow spherical fade, diminishing the peripheral first, narrowing into a pinpoint of sepia before total blackness.

He had awakened on an influx of air, rigidly contorting as the memory of the strangulation had rushed back into his head with the ferocious immediacy. Consciousness had brought him to an awareness that a weighted object inhibited the movements of his body. After a flash of terror, he had calmed himself so that he could determine the physical predicament his body was in. His wrists were bound. His ankles were immobile. He assumed: good scenario, they were also bound, worst case; he had no ankles. The object covering his face and body smelled of mildew. Concentrating on the texture of the object and the easy maneuverability of the object when he shrugged his shoulders, he concluded that a rug covered, rather than encased him.

He could hear tinny radio music somewhere above, Springsteen insisting everyone had a hungry heart. Beyond that, he heard the low growl of an eight-cylinder engine and smelled the distinct blend of leaded gasoline, motor oil, and metal. A smell familiar to his burgeoning sexuality of late night trysts in vans and pickup trucks. Getting free from the binds on his wrist had been no problem. Adults always calculated parameters of such things by their own measure of familiarity, so they never had an accurate gauge of the thinness of young boys, nor their flexibility. This misjudgment had enabled him to extricate himself from attempts at physical domination since the age of five. Once free, he had slid the carpet slowly aside to find that he was on the floor of a small passenger van. A soiled mattress lay beside him, its ticking barely discernible through the Rorschach of blood that seeped in an undulation from the inanimate body spread-eagled upon it. The eyes from the body stared, wide and glassy, a permanent tableau of horror etched upon it.

The boy stared, the face of the corpse nudging a minute compartment of his memory, but he was too overcome by the immediacy of his own circumstance to give it much consideration. He pushed the carpet aside and quickly untied the binds on his feet while looking toward the drivers' bay of the van. Through dirty faille curtains, he could make out a dim shape rocking back and forth with the motion of the vehicle.

A pitch in the road jarred him back to the present. He crawled toward the moonlight that cast a glow through the window of the rear bay doors. With shaking hands, he located the latch and gave a twist. He had not been expecting the doors to be unlocked, but they were, and his unpreparedness had allowed both doors to rapidly swing open, creating a loud influx of air that roared through the van and smacked the back of the driver's head.

The vehicle careened sideways as its brake pads ground into the drums, throwing the boy back into the belly of the van, onto the blood smeared mattress. The bay doors clanged shut against the steel beam that divided them, pitching the interior into darkness. Through the cacophony of images that assaulted his brain, the boy scrambled to gain footing, dimly noting the temperature of the body as his arms flailed to find purchase amidst the sickly, viscous stickiness of the saturated mattress. He crab-walked toward the moonlight and lunged toward the door, falling with a thud onto the hard dirt, cracking his jaw in the motion. He grunted past the pain and quickly rose, spitting out teeth and blood as he looked to find his bearings. Beyond a fence, he saw a field of waist-high brown grass dotted with Black-eyed Susans. He looked behind him and saw a shadow looming along the side of the van, gravel being kicked up by large thudding boots. He darted toward the fence and leaped at it with a blood-choked scream. He scrambled up the length of the fence. It gave a jarring counter-motion as his pursuer hurled his weight against it and grabbed the boy's ragged Adidas.

The boy grunted as he was tugged downward, but he did not let go of the fence. His laces were untied. The shell-top shoe easily slipped from his foot, and he kept climbing toward the top. The jagged ridge of barbed wire seared heat through his palms, and he pulled himself over and landed on the other side with a thud, too scared to savor the small victory. He looked back to the fence. The shadow lurched back to the van and began to rummage around in the interior. The boy crouched into the camouflage of lemongrass and ran.

The moan of the ship horn blared again, pitching him from his nanosecond reverie and back to the present. He didn't know what drugs he had been given. His vision was blurry. The light seemed to have a shimmering, gossamer quality, trailing itself with an aura. Sounds produced a reverberation, making it hard to trust his instincts. As the immediate panic of waking from the coma waned, the endorphins that had given his senses an edge began to be subsumed by the chemicals in his body. His sense of space was unreliable. The sounds of night whispered soothingly, comforting him. Humid air caressed the sweat that beaded along his back, cooling his overheated body. Slowly, he rose, moving beyond the lemongrass that tickled his face. He stood tall and regal amidst the pitch of night, his height belying his age. Through the white noise ringing in his ears, he turned toward the whispering grass, almost serene as he absently turned his head and descended into the trajectory of the machete arcing through the air, slicing cleanly into his smooth brown throat with a metallic song. His hands flung out in front of him, graceful and luminous in the blue moonlight, and raised toward the lip of blood that began a crescendo, spurting crimson liquid through the night as the boy's spine curved backward and tumbled into the daffodils.

The ship horn rang low and somber.

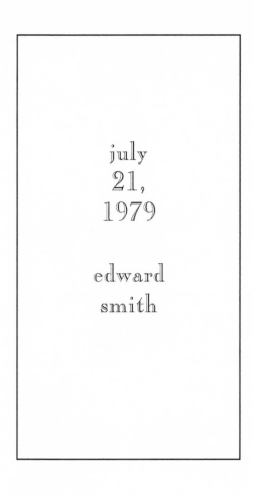

july
21,
1979

edward
smith

JULY 21, 1979

SANTOS

It could laughingly be called a bedroom. It was barely long enough to accommodate the metal cot and low slung, three drawer dresser that furnished it. It had once served as a mudroom that adjoined the kitchen of the shotgun house in which it was contained. A jagged shard of mirror leaned from the dresser onto the slats of whitewashed walls that were equal part sheetrock and stucco patchwork. The only adornment boasted was a lone poster of Marilyn Monroe hanging by two rusted thumbtacks.

An outsized boom box dominated the space, twitching on its precarious perch of the dresser as it bobbed in time to the bass that pitched from its woofers. Narrow hips clad in Jordache denim rocked in time to the Teutonic blips of Kraftwerk.

Santos grabbed the dirty oversized T-shirt from the cot and shoved his arms through the sleeves as he mumbled, "Tour de France, Tour de France."

The shard of mirror reflected large eyes set deep in skin like melted chocolate, chemically curled hair and a thin wisp of hair above full brown lips. He adjusted a few strands of hair as if these minute adjustments made a discernible difference in the image that glared back at him. He noticed a shadow of movement tug at the corner of the mirror and muted the animation of his hips.

Turning fractionally, he glanced briefly at the woman standing in the doorway that led to the kitchen. He turned back to the mirror and began to fuss with his hair, noting that the woman was wearing her cleaning scrubs under a battered linen trench. One hand held the strap of an oversized duffel that was slung over her shoulder. Her other held his brother's grubby fist, who was sucking his thumb and drooling a spool of saliva onto his bib overalls.

His eyes pinned hers through the mirror as she made a quick, impatient click with her tongue. "When you gwan feed 'im?"

"He done et already. Him had two patties. Wasn't nathan for drink so 'im had water."

She pulled her arm forward, moving the moaning young boy into the room. Santos flicked his eyes at Jonas as he lumbered to the cot and flopped on it, his eyes watching the ceiling. Gloria shrugged the duffel on her shoulder and looked pointedly at imaginary lint on her trench. "I need you tek him wid you. I got to atten' to some business..."

Santos' narrow wrist flicked the volume button on the boom box and tsked pointedly. "I can' do that right now. I got an appointment."

His mother's eyes narrowed, and she thrust out a hip to rest her fist on. "What appointment you got, you can' tek yu brudda?"

Frustration etched his voice, "Got a doctor's appointment!"

"Well, you gwan' need tek him. I gotta go." Gloria turned on well worn, sensible heels and left both boys in the room.

A worm of uneasiness lurched in Santos' belly. He briefly rubbed his hand over Jonas' head before exiting the room and trailing Gloria through the narrow, dark kitchen, and sparsely furnished living room. Santos heard the crumbly sound of plastic casters on the wooden floors, justifying the unease in his belly. He neared the door leading to the porch and watched his mother's hunched shoulders as she descended the stairs, pulling a small valise behind her. He walked onto the porch and let the metal screen door bang shut, knowing how much it annoyed Gloria.

Gloria cringed and stopped in her tracks, turning slightly to look back at him.

"How long yuh be gone this time?"

She fumbled in her purse for a lighter for the cigarette clutched between her grim lips, eyeing him inventorially. "Don' know. Be awhile, got a cleaning job up in Cleveland. Soon's a get settled and get me first check, I'll send money."

His heart was racing, but he managed to keep his voice devoid of the panic he felt. "What we gone do in the meantime?"

"I lef' fifty dolla under the toaster." She looked at him one last time, blew out a puff of smoke and headed off down the narrow lane.

Hand on his hip, he watched as her form grew smaller. "Fifty fucking dollars," he muttered. "Cunt."

He turned back into the house and let the door bang shut.

The Pennsylvania Regional Health Initiative operated from a small Tudor building on the grounds of a long-abandoned steelworks factory. It was nestled between two postmodern medical buildings, all standing out in stark relief from the large matte black buildings in various states of decay that surrounded it; silent evidence of the state of disrepair of the town, formerly full of prosperous, well paid steelworkers during the economic boom of the first half of twentith century America. Shaded by willow trees, the stately portico managed to imbue a sense of awe and grandeur even 100 years after its construction.

While the exterior denoted historical opulence, the interior of PRHI was all clinical modernity. Santos loved the austere minimalism of the waiting room. The clean lines of waiting rooms were so unlike anything he was familiar with that they almost acted as the antithesis to the squalor and chaos that defined his home life. He found a degree of comfort in the absence of emotion and sensory stimulation offered by the stark design. The subliminal scent of disinfectant and lemon wood cleaner instead of fried fish and TJ Swann liquor had a therapeutic effect on him. The gleaming maple floors reflected the light of the sun beaming through long narrow windows hung with metallic blinds. The modular seating of pale avocado faced a sturdy chunk of maple, which, held an array of fashion magazines, one of which Santos picked up as he flopped onto the sofa. Jonas pushed the magazine aside and nudged himself onto Santos' lap. Sighing, he wiped the drool unfurling from the younger child's mouth with his shirt sleeve, then opened the magazine so that Jonas could look at the pictures while he read and dreamed of Kim Alexis doing a photo shoot in some exotic locale.

The receptionist desk was unmanned, which was the norm here. Usually, there were only two people manning the office, Dr. Levitz and the intake coordinator, Miss Purchase. Every now and then, the doctor would have an assisting nurse, but it was not a constant.

Ordelia Purchase stepped from her tiny office lodged behind the receptionist desk, her low slung sturdy frame the picture of homespun efficiency. She adjusted the large red Cazals on the bridge of her nose and beamed a benevolent smile. "Hello Santos, right on time."

He glanced over her shoulder absently, preferring the Vogue pictorial to Ordelia Purchase. "Hey, Miss P."

Ordelia approached with a swish of nylon and thigh fat and rocked before him on gleaming white shoes. "And who do we have here? You know the doctor does not permit nonpatients..."

"Sorry. This is my brother. I'm watching him. My ma is out of town working, so I had to bring him. He's fine with me. He won't be no problem."

Ordelia looked at the boy. A section of her brain locked into place as she calculated the possibility of the child's suitability to be added to the agenda of PRHI. Her actions, however, did not show this minute calculation. Instead, they demonstrated the skills that had allowed this eleventh grade drop out to acquire the rare opportunity to obtain a well-paying, respectable job as Health Initiatives Coordinator for a federally funded research project. She beamed that beneficent smile that maintained a 100 percent retention rate and knelt so that she was eye level with Jonas. "Hello, sweetie. What's your name?"

A quick assessment showed that the boy had some sort of intellectual deficit. His eyes were glassy and unfocused. He did not make eye contact with her but instead looked up at the cherubs and dragons of the crown molded ceiling. She judged his age to be around ten. Beneath the squalor of ashy skin and uncombed hair, she noted the glow of good health.

Santos rubbed Jonas' head and smiled down at him. "He don't talk. He used to. But he ain't talked for 'bout two, three, years now. Don't know why. Kinda weird. But Jo always been a little strange, right Jo?"

Jonas smiled and made a sound low in his throat, rubbing his head against Santos' chest.

"Who's his primary care physician?"

"Don't have one. He ain't ever been sick."

"Well, he's here. Don't you think we should take a look at him? Can't hurt. Besides, I can double the stipend you receive if we add him as a patient..."

Santos pictured the fifty-dollar bill Gloria had lodged under the toaster, which was now lodged into the coin pocket of his snug jeans. "Sure."

Ordelia struggled triumphantly to her feet. "Good. You two just sit tight, and I'll get the paperwork together, then I'll see you. Doctor's not in today, but I think you and I can handle things on our own, right? Won't be the first time."

Santos nodded as he watched Ordelia walk back to her office. He smirked at the swish-swish her whites made when she walked, acrylic spread to maximum capacity, the bulk of her ass looking like a busted can of Pillsbury Grands biscuits.

The assault of noise emanating from the television was pre-empted, as the screen illuminated the prefabbed image of an aerosoled talking head.

Late last night Atlanta police located another missing child. The body, 14-year-old Alfred Evans was found in the outer marshlands by a citizen, who came across the strangled body while he was duck hunting. This makes the second child found, the first being that of Edward Smith, found washed up on the banks of the Chattahoochee River by a group of fishermen last month. Police are hesitant to define the deaths as serial killings despite the similarities in the manner of death.

Whether police call these deaths serial killings or not, however, is of little consequence at this point. Parents and children, particularly in local black communities are demanding government intervention, as they allege that local efforts to stem further occurrences are minimal at best. New York rabble-rouser Reverend Al Sharpton is scheduled to conduct a press conference later this afternoon. Given his reputation for fanning the fires of unrest, pundits have hypothesized that he will be pointing an accusatory finger at Georgia's history of racism as the reason that little revenue has been invested in probes into these occurrences...

The screen suddenly went black. Santos turned quizzically and saw Miss Purchase standing at the receptionist desk with a remote aimed at the TV. She shook her head and went back into her office with a tsking voice. "Such sad news; why can't they focus on something more uplifting...?"

Her door closed with a minute click. Santos stood, moving Jonas to the seat beside him. "Gotta go to the bathroom. You sit here. Be right back."

Stepping into the bathroom, Santos quietly locked the door and removed his shirt. He ran water in the vast enamel sink and dislodged a wad of paper towels from the dispenser. Whenever he visited the medical center he used the bathroom to wash up. The clean, Spartan environment, with its pearlescent liquid soap, smelling luxuriously indulgent, was almost as compelling a reason for his regularly scheduled appointments as was the fifty-dollar stipend he received. Fifty bucks. It usually took him the entire weekend to make fifty dollars. And this way was by far the preferable money-making endeavor. He had been allowing men to go down on him for five dollars a pop for the past two years. When one of the many 'uncles' his mother had sporadically brought home had taken advantage of one of the times that Gloria was out of the house, he had been made to understand the value of his body as a commodity. One that could be used to provide things that his mother had not been able to. He had quickly become adept at gauging the level of interest the adult gaze contained. There were minute signals that telegraphed parental...perfunctory...predatory.

The soap gave off the scent of pine, and he dabbed at the sparse hair under the hollow of his armpit. He inhaled deeply. The smell was as calming as smoking a joint. He unclasped the button of his jeans and applied a warm paper towel to his groin.

There was a sudden, loud boom beyond the solid wooden door, then a muffled yell. He quickly put his T-shirt back on and rushed back into the lobby. The chair he had left Jonas sitting in was empty. He looked around frantically. A high pitched yell came from behind the desk. Santos ran into Miss Purchase's office, to find his brother standing still as death, in the center of the room, rigid and erect. Next to him, a floor lamp lay on its side, a chair dangling precariously along its length. Papers and books were scattered on the floor, some caught beneath the desk and were slanted askew against the wall. Cowering in the corner, behind the desk, Miss Purchase crouched amongst a bay of filing cabinets. Her glasses hung from her nose, and stray strands of hair sprouted out from her previously unmolested bun.

Santos walked over to Jonas, placed a palm against the back of his head and pressed him into his torso while murmuring. "Hey. It's me. Everything's all right. It's me, Jo."

Jonas jumped at the initial contact, then, realizing it was his brother, he allowed himself to be pulled closer, the scent of his brother calming him. Miss Purchase stood and began to slide her desk back to where it had been. "I don't know what happened. I just brought him into the office to do some diagnostics, and he just made this ... this...howl. He... he was sitting in that chair, and then he jumped up and... sort of pushed out and knocked all this stuff over, he just kept screaming. Like he was being hurt. I hadn't even touched him..."

Santos cut her off. "Yeah. He gets like that sometimes. He's kinda funny about being made to do things. Sometimes he has tantrums. Uh, maybe we should come back. I should take him out to calm down. Otherwise, it will only get worse. Let me take him out. We'll come back after I get him calmed down."

Ordelia could think of nothing she wanted more than to get Jonas out of her office.

"Yes. Yes, that would be fine. Go."

He paused, resting his fists on his denim-clad hips. "I'm going to need my payment, though. Or we can just wait here until you finish with me..."

She eyed him knowingly, squinting down at him. "Sit tight out in the waiting area for a second. I'll bring your payment out. You can call me to reschedule."

Santos rubbed Jonas' head, smiling craftily.

SWINGING JACK'S BARBER SHOP

Swinging Jack's could be said to be the hub of the small enclave of shotgun houses that made up the community that included the house where Santos lived. Long-standing residents stopped by as regularly as they did Dirty Frank's Bar or even their own living rooms. In addition to the regular tightening up of fades or dreadlocks, one could keep up to date on the most recently released films, buy dresses and perfumes. Or if one was in the know, pick up some potent ganja from the dark room out back. If one waited around long enough, they would be able to buy some of the best oxtail soup in the state, if Lou Bates was out hauling around his creaky cart.

The blare of the radio mixed with a droning TV program and loud baritone voices booming with testosterone.

Chicago stood in the eye of the storm honing the edges of a beard, the stub of a Cuban clenched between full brown lips. One eye narrowed as he gauged minute levels of asymmetry and descended upon them with the buzzing razor. The razor stopped in mid-flight as the bell above the door jangled, and a round hip flagged the periphery of his sight.

Chicago flashed teeth as brilliant as tombstones and spread his arms expansively. "Ah, here she go. All late. But smelling good enough to eat."

Yasmine flicked a dismissive wrist loaded with wooded bangles as she entered the shop. She usually stopped by Swinging Jack's twice weekly to set up a small post at the rear to sell perfumes and oils. She only had to break off twenty percent of profit to Swinging Jack, as her already established, mostly female clientele stopping by was sure to create an uptick in Jack's profit base, as local horndogs stopped by to get a rap along with their fade. Yasmine was all undulation and obsession, her curves swathed in a deep crimson jersey that seemed to descend into the molten bronze of her skin.

Walking to the back of the room, she turned up the volume of the TV and turned off the radio. The local update, featuring that fine ass Jared Scott, the first black area news anchor had just come on. She shushed everyone and put her hands on her hip to emphasize her point.

While certainly too soon to describe these incidents the work of a serial killer, per se, the murders of two youth in such close proximity, and found within a month's span is certainly a reason for alarm.

Former congressman and current grand wizard for the local chapter of the Ku Klux Klan, Lucas Toliver, while not overtly taking credit for the murders, has expressed that they are just the beginning of an agenda to cleanse the area of what he calls "a contaminant of civilization." Let's take a look at his recent public address...

The soothing contours of Jared Scott shifted into the gaunt, sharp features of a middle-aged white man with straight flaxen hair above a furrowed brow and close-set eyes. A phalanx of microphones were pushing toward his grimly pursed lips as questions were hurled at him by a gaggle of onlookers.

He ran a large hand across his hair and nodded at a question.

"Sure. I will take credit for it. I don't mind being the figurehead for a movement, if you will. There is a segment of society that is draining our resources. Where most of us are working hard and adding to the strengths of our economy, political realm, gene pool, there are others who lay about waiting to victimize hard working citizens. Those who prefer robbing and plundering to a hard day's work. Who engage in sexual acts that condemn them to hell. Who drain government revenues. Those lives lost are not of value. They do not create a deficit to society. The two missing are just a warning of what will follow.

Jared Scott briefly reappeared.

"While no physical evidence has been found to link Toliver to the crimes, authorities have him under surveillance, in part due to the death threats that have been made against Toliver in light of his outrageous and highly inflammatory statements.

Chicago shook his immaculately clipped afro and grunted. "Ain't that some bullshit. Two murders. The beginning of a crime wave…"

Yasmine closed her eyes for a second, wiping a tear from her rouged cheek. "Like only two babies been killed. Killing black babies ain't nothing new. It's been going on since before I was a baby, and it will be going on long after I'm dead and gone."

"News ain't news till white folks say it's news. A body must have been found out on some white man's property down there in Atlanta."

"You think the KKK did it?"

The man being attended to in Chicago's chair chimed in. "Don't matter if he did or didn't. He ain't going to do no time for it. Why you think his dumb ass is on TV saying all that bullshit? 'Cause he knows that not a damn thing's gonna be done to him. Unless the nigga is on tape cutting a motherfucker up and throwing the body in the river, he ain't gonna do no time. And if he do, it's gonna be for littering the mu'fucking river."

Chicago banged him on the back, laughing riotously. "You got that shit right!"

Yasmine laughed too, but then felt guilty for laughing in the presence of the ghosts of black children, and walked to the back of the shop with a sob.

MISS PURCHASE

Ordelia uprighted the two drawer file cabinet and pushed it flush against the wall. A bead of sweat coursed down her broad forehead, stinging her eye. She wiped absently and surveyed the narrow confines of her office to make sure everything was as it had been before the boy had blacked out.

Satisfied that things were as they should be, she nodded and wiped her meaty hands on the hips of her uniform. It seemed that all those old wives' tales about the supernatural strength of retards and crazy people turned out to be true. That, or she needed a damn day off. She had been working far in excess of her normal hours lately, so she knew she was a bit off her game. Since Dr. Manderlay had informed her that they would be closing down the Norristown operation, she had been coming into the office after hours to dispose of the voluminous files that had been acquired over the seven years that the program had been running. Though the documentation was prolific, it paled in comparison to the documents she'd had to dispose of when the Tuskegee project was shuttered a few years back.

She shuddered just thinking about that; the apologies to the participants, the payouts, the explanations.

She found it odd that instead of outsourcing a company to box up and catalog the old files it had been ordered that she shred them. First, that the extensive medical data on local teen boys would not be saved to draw comparisons to other trials seemed odd to her. Second, that Doctor would not permit her to hire a temp to do the tedious shredding involved really chapped her ass.

Not to the point that she would create a fuss over it, she knew she had a great set up here, but it was odd all the same. Not the first odd occurrence she had encountered while working for the Pennsylvania Regional Health Initiative, which had first been called the Federal Project for Farmworker Health, back in the 1930s, down in Tennessee. She'd had a pretty comfortable living working as a federal employee, the first colored woman in her county back then to have a job with such prestige. A pretty cushy job, where she collected data on sexually transmitted diseases and charted the course of progress and response to treatment. There had been many occasions of patients acting uncharacteristically: hallucinations, or confabulating. Of irate parents who had been unaware that their child had been sexually active, or under a doctor's care.

But this kid; the retard that the Pettifore boy had brought in with him. Ordelia shook her head at the memory. She would call Dr. Manderlay as soon as she ended her shift tonight to request a day off. She needed it. She was clearly running on fumes.

When the Pettifore kid had gone into the bathroom, Ordelia had thought it would be an advantageous time to draw a baseline sample and perhaps even introduce a small specimen into the host.

She had put on her most officious and maternal aura of approachability before descending on the boy and coaxing him into her office. He had drooled and looked off at the ceiling but allowed her to take his hand and guide him back into her inner sanctum. A swift sensation of disgust had washed over her at the feeling of slick phlegm that adhered from his hand to hers, but she quickly subverted it and remained on task.

After depositing the moaning form into a chair, she walked to her desk and searched for a towelette and alcohol to wipe the filth from her palm. She had briefly looked up from her drawer at the boy. Had she managed to keep disgust from registering on her face? She thought she had. But she could not really recall.

Next, the moaning had abruptly stopped. It seemed that all sound had stopped. She no longer heard the muted drone from the radio or the whippoorwills singing beyond the window. The boy was still curled up in the chair, but he looked up and made eye contact. The look of vacancy that had been on his face before was gone. In his eyes was total awareness. He seemed to know who she was. Then, the look vanished. The boy stood up and gave a piercing scream, stretching his long arms out in front of him.

Ordelia instinctively covered her ears. While the boy did not seem to move, when he stretched out his splayed palms, the desk in front of her had seemed to shift. The lamp beside the kid toppled over, and papers from her desk suddenly hurled as if blown by a tsunami. The desk quivered and pushed against Ordelia's thighs as she rose from her chair and backed against the wall.

Next, the older kid had burst into the room, and the wailing stopped as abruptly as it had begun. Everything had happened in a split second; so fast that Ordelia was not quite sure what she had actually seen and what she had thought she saw.

She had been glad to get rid of him. Well, the doctor had not yet returned her call, but she no longer needed his input. That kid was not worth the trouble of adding to the clinical trial. Besides, he was only about nine or ten; he certainly couldn't be sexually active at this point.

JONAS

The fat lady was yellow. Yellow is not red. But it is still bad. Red is bad. Bad things happen to red people. But it's better than no light. People with no light do bad things to people. White is good. If I look at my hands sometimes I can see white; but sometimes not. I wonder why San can't see the fat lady's light. He should stay away from her; she's not good. Maybe San cannot tell the fat lady is not good because San lost the white light. He changed. Maybe that's why he can't see the fat lady's yellow.

Gloria is yellow too. But her yellow goes lighter when she finds an uncle to live with us. But when she looks at me or when she looks at San her yellow goes dark, the same yellow of the fat lady.

San's light was white like mine, but that was a long time ago when I still used my voice; before Uncle Nash went away. When Uncle Nash came, San's light grew dim. Then San turned grass colored. San was still good though. At least he did not turn yellow like Gloria or the fat lady. Or shut off, like Uncle Nash. I did not like Uncle Nash. He did not have no light. I stayed out of Uncle Nash's way. If he was in the front room, I stayed in San's room.

But after a while, San turned red. And I could not stop crying.

"What's wrong with you?" San asked. "Why do you keep crying Jonas? "

"'Cause you gonna die, San!"

He smacked me behind my ear and pushed me on the bed. "Stop acting like a retard. Everybody's gonna die. Knock it off!"

So I knocked it off.

SANTOS

Santos stood at the magazine racks before the great plate glass windows at the front of Woolworth's. He flipped absently through a *Fantastic Four* before picking up the thick *Vogue* lodged on the back shelf. Brooke Shields stared back, her matte berry lips slightly parted to give the allure of post-coital repose that had catapulted her to the upper echelon of haute couture. He could feel the glare of the store manager burning into his back.

"If you're not buying, no reading the magazines, kid."

Santos continued to flip through the pages, changing his stance to a wider legged, aggressive pose that prepared for battle. Jonas lurched out from the candy aisle with a Laffy Taffy in one grubby hand and Now and Laters in the other. Santos cuffed him behind the ear and tsked.

"You must've lost your mind. You know you only get one, put one back and let's get the fuck outta here." He watched Jonas lurch back into the candy aisle to return one of the items. He laughed to himself. Jonas was always pushing the envelope to see what he could get away with. People thought he was a retard, but they did not know. There was nothing slow about Jonas. You always had to be on the lookout with him, because he was always up to something, whether it was acting like he was a dimwit so some sucker would give him spare change or a free snack, or eavesdropping on adult gossip because they thought he was too addle-brained to comprehend what they were talking about.

Back when Jonas still talked, this had been a great strategy. Jonas would hear all of the neighborhood stories about who was fucking whose husband, and at night, after Gloria had gone to bed, he would keep Santos updated on everything.

After the boys paid for the Laffy Taffy, and a Coke for Santos, they went back out into the blazing summer sun, crossed the street and entered the barren, threadbare park area of the lower courtyard that banked the Montgomery County courthouse. Jonas immediately ran to the dented merry-go-round, its paint long chipped off to a warped metallic hue, and plunked himself down, dragging himself into a circular motion with his scuffed Kids.

Santos set down his Coke, ran over and grasped the rails of the equipment and began to spin it fast, faster, jumping on board as the thing spun at breakneck speed, Jonas squealing in delight. Santos stretched his head back, enjoying the breeze created by the motion, smiling expansively.

He missed the time he and Jonas used to spend together when he was still using his voice. Although they were still close, there was so much that they shared when they were both talking to one another. When Jonas still used his voice, Santos did not feel quite as alone as he did now. On the previous occasions when Gloria had skipped town, whether it had been for some job in some far off location, or to spend time with some man, it had been like the two brothers were working together to keep themselves fed and clothed, and to make sure probing adults at school and in the neighborhood did not discover that their mother was in absentia.

Now, it seemed as though every decision was his alone.

Of course, that wasn't really fair. Jonas always indicated whether something was a good idea or a bad one. If Gloria came home with an 'uncle' that would end up kicking her ass, Jonas would squeal and demonstrate his dislike, or if someone from the county was going to knock on the door, he could always tell, because Jonas would rush upstairs and hide in the cardboard trunk hidden in the closet of Gloria's room. But it was much better back when he would tell you that you needed to hide, or that Uncle DeForest had a yellow light, rather than guessing something was amiss based on his behavior.

Like with Miss Purchase. Had the moans Jonas had been making in the waiting room been some sort of signal that Santos had missed? He hadn't known there was a problem until the loud bang and rushing out to find her office in disarray. And what was the problem at the clinic anyway? Was there something really wrong there, or was it just that Jonas didn't like unfamiliar places? Santos didn't want to stop visiting the clinic. He couldn't. He needed the money that they paid him for his participation. All he had to do was give up a little blood, and bam, easy money.

He didn't like to ignore the signals his brother gave. Time had shown him that wasn't a smart thing to do. He had ignored Jonas back when he still talked. Jonas had said that he didn't like Uncle Nash. He said Uncle Nash didn't have a light. But Uncle Nash was tall, handsome and smooth talking, unlike most of the beer-swilling men that had been in place before him. Uncle Nash was free with his money, always being sure to give Santos a few dollars here and there, buying him new kicks when he needed them, and not the bobos that the other kids teased him about. Uncle Nash bought him Converse All-Stars, the best. So Santos had ignored Jonas.

That had proven to be unwise. All the gifts and money had led to waking one night with a hand over his mouth while his pajamas were yanked from his body. The pain had been unlike anything he could even put into words. And after that, it had become an almost daily occurrence. When Santos had refused and threatened to tell Gloria. Uncle Nash had leaned casually on the door frame, crossing his long legs.

"Yeah. Go on. You do, and I'll kill all of you. If you don't want to, that's fine...your brother looks pretty good too..."

So with the unspoken agreement that his sacrifice was saving his brother, Santos endured the unspeakable for months.

And although he had ignored Jonas, to his own detriment, that problem had worked itself out. After five months of sexual abuse, one day, Santos had been lying on his bed reading an Xmen comic when Jonas stepped in the doorway crying.

"What's wrong with you? Knock it off."

"You gonna die, San."

Santos had clipped him behind the ear; their signal to one another to move to another topic.

Shortly after that, Uncle Nash moved out. He stopped coming to Santos' room at night. Gloria packed up the clothing he left behind into a huge box she got from the liquor store and dragged everything out to the small patch of grass that made up their backyard. With tears streaming down her face and a Pall Mall gripped between her lips, she flung a lit match at the bundle of clothing and mumbled, "Nah good motherfucker" as the flames licked at the contents of the box with malevolent glee.

So even though Santos had ignored Jonas' warning, the problem had eventually resolved itself. The only problem was that after Uncle Nash disappeared Jonas never uttered another word.

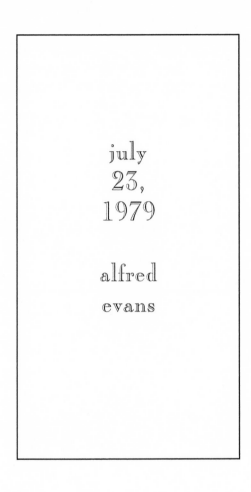

july
23,
1979

alfred
evans

THE BEAT

Lafayette Street was at its apex of activity. Traffic oozed down from Airy Street like slow-moving blood through ancient veins. The elevated trolley from Philadelphia shuttled into the transportation center with a mechanical roar. The broad iron beams that held up the tracks cast a shadow onto the dead end intersection of Lafayette and Airy, despite the lights that beamed the lures of Budweiser and Rolling Rock from the signs in the window of Joe Brown's Bar, pivotally located at the corner, across from which lay the darkened grassland and fenced off area of the Pennsylvania Railroad. The trifecta corner was a mostly unused building owned by some once grand fraternal order, its opaque windows covered with a layer of filth that had accumulated from years of accepting the soot freight trains belched into the night air.

On the steep cement stairs that led to a service entrance, a thin brown figure sat smoking a battered Newport. Torn denim shorts at one end and dingy ballet flats at the other, offered maximum exposure of long, well-formed legs, crossed at the knee. Across the street, the door to Joe Brown's Bar banged open, and music from the jukebox merged into the night sounds of car horns, shouts, and squealing tires.

Dion leaped up from the steps and began to wiggle his hips and do a quick step, singing in a loud off key voice. "You know how to love me; there's no deny...yaaaaaang..."

As Phyllis Hyman held a long note on the actual song, Dion struggled to keep apace, his voice scratching along as it lost lung capacity.

Santos rounded the corner directly into the terribly modulated singing and immediately jumped into the note, also trying to hold the note. Dion lost breath and pitched against the railing of the stairs. Santos began to laugh.

"Bitch, you know you can't sing."

"Fuck you," exclaimed Dion. He belted out another off-key note as if to prove Santos wrong. "You got a joint, bitch? I know you got a joint, bitch. So spark that bitch up, bitch."

Santos sucked his teeth. "I'm not wasting my shit letting you suck down half my shit and not paying a dime towards my nick. Bitch, please."

Santos retrieved a thin reefer from the coin pocket of his jeans and lit it with a tiny Bic lighter. Dion reached out a hand and grabbed the joint, placing it between his full lips, talking between gritted teeth.

"Damn, bitch. Could you roll this shit any tighter? I gotta suck this girl harder than Cootie's dick."

"Well bitch, give it back then. It's not like you have any problems with sucking hard."

"Uh! Well no, I don't. This shit is fierce, girl. Who you get this from, Swinging Jack?" Dion looked up the street to the head of the block and spotted a long dark vehicle rounding the corner. "Wait a minute. That looks like one of my tricks. "

He handed the joint back to Santos and walked swiftly toward the curb. "Get lost, bitch, you're bad for business."

Santos descended back into the shadows as the car slowly approached. The rear window of the car moved down, and a soda can came pitching out from the darkness. The can hit the curb and cola sprayed up at Dion's legs.

"Give the dog a bone!", a female voice screamed out from the car as it turned the corner.

Dion picked up the can and hurled it after the vehicle. "Fuck you, bitch. Your daddy didn't say that when he dropped me off an hour ago!"

"Faggot, you couldn't give it away!" The girls in the car burst into laughter and pulled off down the street.

"Uh!" Dion exclaimed. "Did you hear what those cunts said to me, chile?"

Santos came forward, laughing hysterically. "Give the dog a bone! Bitch, you are serving up canine tonight! Perhaps you need to shave before you come out to trick!"

"Wait. Fuck both of you, bitch. Y'all can't take it. Look at these legs, bitch. These motherfucking legs are OVER. Okay? Cunt would kill for these legs."

"Girl, please. Those legs are so gray I thought you fell in the alley before you hit the corner."

"Spark up that j. Those fish got my nerves all rattled. How's a hard working girl expected to function with this constant harassment from jealous bitches?"

Up at the far end of the block, a long, thin profile stood out like an exclamation point against the backdrop of streetlights.

"Hey, Luq!" Dion screamed, in order to be heard a block away.

Santos covered his ears and cringed. "Damn, bitch. That's my ear."

A battered Chevy pulled to the curb behind them. Dion looked back and then gasped. "Ooh, girl. It's one of my tricks. Time to make those dollars..."

"Or nickels." Santos murmured as Dion spun on his heels and his walk merged from his usual splay-footed gait into the hip-swaying sashay of a nubile young woman.

Santos laughed as Dion's voice rose two octaves as he hissed, "Hey Bennie, it's me; Trixie."

Santos turned as a caramel colored youth approached. His hair was chemically transformed from its usual kinky state into hard, shimmering curls, buzzed off on the sides and back. On his narrow torso, he wore a black fishnet shirt and high waist gray pants with diaphanous deep pleats on the side that billowed out like bat wings as he walked. "Hey, Luq."

"Hey. Where's he going?"

"To make a dollar. Literally."

They both laughed.

"If that," said Luqman.

Santos lit his worn joint and inhaled deeply. "That blouse is OVER. I will have to borrow it. Where did you get it?" He extended his arm to offer the smoldering joint to Luqman, who waved it away.

"This? It's a pair of stockings. I cut a hole in the crotch and put my arms through the legs."

Santos laughed. "So you're wearing a crotch on your head. Bitch, you will try anything."

"Technically, it's not on my head, but yeah."

"Bitch, you're battered! How did you get that light? You got on the war paint for the gods!"

"No, just a little powder and honey, to soak up the oil. I have oily skin. Damn, bitch. Can you get all out of my face like that? I didn't know I was going to be under investigation tonight."

Santos laughed. "There you go with those big words again." His voice changed into an exaggerated lisp as he imitated Luqman. "I didn't know I was going to be under investigation tonight."

"Eat a dick, bitch."

"Well, we know you won't be, don't we?"

At that moment, Dion sashayed around the corner, adjusting the combs holding his hair into a pile above his head. Santos burst into laughter. "Damn, bitch. That was fast. Did he spook you?"

"Chile, he wanted to fuck. He kept trying to grab my pussy. I told him I couldn't 'cause I was on my period, and that nasty motherfucker said he didn't mind the mess."

Luqman laughed and frowned. "What? Nasty! So you offered the booty instead."

"Girl, not for ten dollars. I told him I would jerk that shit off. Then, before I knew what was happening he grabbed one of my titties, and bitch, it fell out." Dion waved a dirty sock in front of his face.

"Girl, I barely escaped with my life! I had to make a run for it. I fell out of that car like Cruella Deville!"

Luqman assessed the sock. "Bitch, you used that filthy ass sock as your titty? Didn't he smell the corn chips?"

Santos fell back onto the steps with laughter. "What? No, wait. Wait, that was your titty, bitch? A dirty ass sock?"

Dion huffed angrily. "Look bitch. I was all out of water balloons, okay. A girl's gotta do what a girl's gotta do. And I did!" Dion began doing a little dance, dropping his hips low to emphasize, and drawing the laughter that he had intended.

He abruptly stopped shimmying and did an impatient click of his tongue as two girls approached. "Here comes this stank fish, trying to take my business."

The three boys drew close together. Santos and Dion smiled solicitously as Dion screamed out, "Hey Miss Ape."

Santos barked out a short burst of laughter. "White Girl Toni."

April, a large breasted red head whose milk and honey skin was marred by a spray of blemishes across her face, smiled back, although her smile looked anything but happy. "Hey girl. How's it look out here tonight?"

"Oh, girl, it's dreadful. Ain't shit jumpin' off tonight. I been out here for hours and haven't pulled a dollar."

April puffed out a plume of Newport smoke in his face and laughed. "Well, that's not unusual for you, honey. I'm sure we will do fabulously, right Tone?"

Both April and White Girl Toni wore oversized, brightly colored t-shirts, which barely covered their thighs. White Girl was the shapelier of the two. Her well-formed legs were encased in nude colored L'eggs control top pantyhose and ballet slippers. Her hair was dyed a dishwater blond and hung in loose waves to pale shoulders. She looked off down Lafayette Street, which boasted no oncoming traffic. "I don't know; looks pretty dead out here. We might do better going up the West End."

"Yes, girl. I was up there earlier. The West End is jumping tonight! I just stopped down here to see what it was like and it is tired."

"Bitch, do you think I'm stupid? First of all, if the West End was jumping for you, you would still be up there. But the other thing is, you can't do the West End, 'cause they don't deal with trannies up there. You would get your black ass shot."

Santos let out a brief, uncomfortable laugh. At that, April fixed her gaze upon him. "And you guys couldn't go up there either. You know the West End don't like niggas walking around there at night."

Luqman leaned on a railing and glared back at April. "You know. I wonder why it is that just because a white bitch gets fucked by black men, they think it gives them carte blanche to throw around the word nigga all willy nilly."

April gasped. "Oh no. I wasn't trying to be ignorant to you guys or anything. You know how fucked up they are over on the West Side, girl."

Luqman continued as if April hadn't even spoken. "And I also wonder why it is that just because a bitch associates with gay people, she thinks that it's cool to refer to them as girl..."

"I ain't no fucking tranny," mumbled Dion. "I'm a lady..."

April's vindictive smile faltered momentarily, then resurfaced. "Oh, girl, calm down."

"Particularly if said bitch does not want to get her ass kicked. Look, bitch. You better take that bullshit back where you came from..."

White Girl stepped in between the two of them and removed a piece of paper from her purse. "Hey, did you guys see this shit that's going down in Valley Forge Park this weekend..."

Luqman continued to glare at April as he read the flyer White Girl held out to him.

Luq smelled heavy marijuana fumes as Santos hovered over his shoulder reading the flyer. "Wait. Is this for real? The KKK?"

White Girl nodded. "Yeah, it's real. I took this down from the bulletin board at the transportation center."

"Valley Forge Park?" Luq read. "That's right around the corner from my house…"

Santos said, "I didn't think the KKK was still around. That was shit from the old days, back during slavery and shit."

"You serious?" said White Girl. "Of course they're still around. They just usually keep their shit undercover more than they did back then."

Luq said, "I knew they were still around. I see them on the news when they have parades and shit, but I thought they were only down south."

"Well, what do you think those skinheads down on South Street are? They might not wear sheets, but they are Neo-Nazis, and they have the same agenda," White Girl said.

Luq said, "You know what? We were the second black family to move into our neighborhood, and when we moved in, people kept setting fire to the leaves we had raked out to the curb. We thought it was this trashy white family that lived down the block, 'cause they once threw eggs at our car. My mom went over there to confront them, and the kids said they didn't burn the leaves, but we always thought it was them. But maybe it was the KKK if they are this close."

"And how about those kids that keep turning up missing down in Atlanta?" Santos asked. "How can there be no clues or explanations?"

Luq nodded. "You right. There was even some guy that said he was from the KKK. And he said he was the one doing it, and they didn't do shit about it."

White Girl flicked a finished butt into the street. "You know what? We should go to the park on this day and have a picnic."

Luq laughed. "Yeah. That would be awesome."

"Awesome, my ass," said Santos. "I'm not trying to swing from no trees on Saturday."

"Okay," agreed Dion from the corner, looking off into the distance for potential money.

"You ready, Tone?" huffed April. "This street is dead."

White Girl reached into her handbag to find a pen. She scrawled her number on a torn piece of cigarette wrapper and handed it to Luq. "If you want to go down to the rally Saturday, I'm down. Give me a call. I'll wear the shortest mini I can find."

Luq laughed. "And I'll blow out my hair so I can wear the biggest, most jungle bunny afro on the planet."

Dion watched the girls head off down Lafayette Street. "Thank god that garbage is leaving the street. How's a girl supposed to earn a decent living standing amongst all that fish?"

Santos laughed. "Girl, the only business you drummed up all night was ten girls from a trick that spooked your package."

Dion reached into his bra and withdrew a roll of money. "Lies, girl."

Luq gasped. "How much is that?"

Dion ostentatiously licked a finger and counted out the fifty dollar bills. "Three hundred dollars, chile."

Santos watched the bills, mesmerized. "Where'd it come from?"

Dion continued counting the bills, despite the fact that it had already been tallied. "Well, bitch, while boyfriend was reaching for my cootch, I was reaching into his pants pocket. And this is what was there. Now let's blow this strip. Let's go to the city, get some coke and go to Catacombs, girl."

Luq was horrified. "Like this? I need to change into club worthy clothes!"

"Oh, bitch please. You know you look fierce. Besides, we ain't waiting around for you to lay on another pound of war paint."

Santos' attention remained on the roll of bills.

Across the street, a homeless man who had been standing in the shadows of Joe Browns Bar lurched across the street. As he approached, the scent of urine merged with sweat and dirt. Dion scrunched up his nose in distaste.

The man extended a hand with long yellowed nails. "Gotta dollar?"

Santos and Dion recoiled and began to cross the street toward a waiting taxi. Luq reached into his pocket and dropped some coins into the man's palm.

"Thank you, brother. You a good man. Those two there ain't shit."

Luq smiled vaguely and began to cross the street toward the taxi, when the man reached out and grabbed his arm.

Luq looked back distractedly and pulled his arm away.

The man watched as Luq entered the loud voices that came from the taxi.

"You always giving money to bums, chile" screamed Dion. "Now Flukey Luke is gonna be following us around on the beat hustlin' for change."

"Why do you call him Flukey Luke?" Luq asked.

Santos breathed out a plume of cannabis. "'Cause he's flukey."

Dion kicked his battered shoes up onto the seat and cackled riotously.

Luq looked perplexed. "I don't know what that means..."

SANTOS

The money Gloria had lodged under the toaster did not last very long. After buying two dimes and a 40 ounce of Colt 45 each night, Santos found that there was very little left for food.

Jonas sat at the kitchen table eating a bowl of Froot Loops while Santos read a Spiderman comic. He supposed that buying comics and beer was not the smartest thing to do when funds were limited, but it was hard to listen to the voice of reason when the lure of temptation was so much louder. It wasn't that much of a problem, he figured. Santos loved Froot Loops for dinner, and he did have the money he had earned from the Health Initiative. Only, he had given that money to Luq to hold. And Luq lived way out in King of Prussia, so it was hard to get to him unless Luq came to town. He would have given the money to Dion to hold, since he lived closer, but Luq was the most trustworthy. Another reason Dion would have been easier to get the money from was because he didn't care; anytime Santos would have asked for a couple of dollars Dion would have handed it over. Luq, on the other hand, was mean. If Santos said to only give him ten dollars each week, then that was all he would get. Santos could have set himself on fire and begged for the money to pay for the ER and Luq would have reminded him in that dry, humorless voice, "but you said to only give you ten dollars every week..."

Jonas finished his cereal and reached for the box that was precariously perched atop a pile of papers and bills. Santos reached out a hand and blocked him.

"Uh, uh. We gotta make this cereal last. Save the rest for tomorrow."

Jonas looked at him with knitted brows. He pouted and began to kick his legs against his chair in fury, swinging his head back and forth and moaning. Santos grabbed the box of cereal and swung it against the boy's head.

"Knock that retard shit off!" he barked. Jonas immediately stopped and stared at him with large, solemn eyes. "That's better."

Jonas climbed out of the chair and took his bowl to the sink, piled high with a week's load of dishes. He dropped his bowl in with a clank. He then walked a few paces to Santos' bedroom and clicked on the boom box.

Linda Ronstadt was singing "Ohh Baby Baby." Jonas walked to the bed and laid on it. Santos stood up and began to sway back and forth in an imitation of Ronstadt, and began to coo along with the song. He grabbed a dirty spoon from the sink and used it as a microphone.

"Miiiiistakes...I know I...made a few...but I'm only human..." He grabbed Jonas wrist and pulled him up.

"Uh, uh. Go to your own room."

Jonas shook his head and began to cry, lying back down on the thin mattress. Santos sat beside his brother and rubbed his back, as he continued to sing. He thought about Gloria. He wondered where she was. He wondered when she would come back home. He wondered when she returned, what kind of man she would have in tow. Would he be cool or would he be a dick? Would he ignore them, or would he try to act like superdad, or something even worse? Something like Uncle Nash.

He thought about it and decided that somebody like Uncle Nash wouldn't be so bad. At least this time he would know what to expect. He would be prepared. There wouldn't be some shadow looming in the dark; heat and mass descending, before sudden, white, unbearable pain.

His empty stomach gurgled in agitation. At least Uncle Nash came with gifts. Along with the pain, there would be food, new kicks, trips to the candy store, and the latest records, with Gloria cooking meals using the stove. Some fried chicken, some curry goat, pepper rice, jerk chicken, with ice cold watermelon tea. With Gloria laughing, throwing back her head and really laughing, her brown throat pulsing from the strength of her laugh, her canines sparkling from the light. Uncle Nash is telling her to put on the red dress that he liked so much, whispering in her ear.

Reaching into his back pocket, Santos removed a package of endpapers and combined two sheets. He then crumbled a few buds from a tiny manila envelope onto the sheets and rolled it into a slender tube. He lit the joint and inhaled reflectively, taking the rich, murky smoke into his lungs. He watched as the room became shrouded in aromatic clouds. Jonas' closed eyelids fluttered dreamily as he descended into sleep.

Santos rose and turned the radio volume low. He walked out through the messy kitchen and into the darkened living room. Peering through the window, he noticed a familiar blue van with an afro Aphrodite painted along the side. He wondered why Cootie's van was parked out front. He didn't even know that Cootie knew where he lived.

He wandered onto the porch when the passenger door of the van popped open, and Dion jumped out, sashaying up onto the porch. "Hey, girl."

"What are you doing here?"

"Working, chile." Dion passed Santos and entered the house. "Bitch, I'm parched. What you got to drink?"

Santos followed Dion into the kitchen, went to the refrigerator and took out the bottle of beer.

"Now, that's what I'm talking about!" He cracked open the cap and began to drink when his gaze fell upon the stack of dishes in the sink. "What the hell is going on at the sink? That's a goddamn travesty!"

"Well, if you want to do the dishes, go right ahead."

"I'll do the dishes for a platter. Girl, I'm hungry."

"You know I don't have no food here. You do that 'food for a platter' shit at Luq's."

Dion approached the sink and began to run the water.

"Besides, didn't you just suck Cootie's dick? You should have some money."

"Girl, he didn't have no money. He's gonna pay me on Friday when he gets his check."

Santos gawked. "So you sucking dick on the installment plan? Girl, bye."

"He came around the house looking for mom. She wasn't home, so he asked me to take a ride...you think we can get something to eat from Luq's?"

"You know that stingy bitch ain't 'giving' away nothing."

"I ain't ate all day. Let's pump over there and see what she got."

LUQMAN

Luq opened the side door and looked upon Dion and Santos with a suck of his teeth. He did not seem pleased with this unexpected visit.

"Who the hell asked you two to come over here?"

Without even bothering to wait for a response, he turned on his heel and walked off. Santos followed Dion inside the dimly lit, wood-paneled recreation room.

"We came to visit. And after that long ass walk, we need refreshments," Dion cooed.

Santos looked around in awe. One wall boasted a large fireplace, with elaborate tools lining the hearth. Gold velour furniture was set along one half of the cavernous room, each piece strategically facing another to give off an aura of communal elegance. The other side of the room boasted a long bar made of cedar, with a wide variety of goblets and glasses glinting from glass shelves, resting alongside heavy bottles of liquor.

"Wow, look at all these cocktails. Let's have a drink?"

Luq arched a brow. "I don't think so. That's my mother's stuff. I'm not taking no hit for missing liquor. If you bitches want a drink, you can have a glass of fucking water."

They followed Luq up the stairs into the brightly lit kitchen.

"You stingy bitch," Dion barked. "You can at least give up some juice."

"Now you know Carol does not buy juice. The only thing in this fridge, bitch, is Crystal Light and a bevy of condiments and salad dressings." Luq opened the barren refrigerator to prove his point. The bare shelves gleamed with emptiness.

Santos mimicked Luq, "A bevy of condiments and salad dressings. Damn. I thought my fridge was bare. At least I got some milk and shit."

"Hah. We are lucky that we have electricity. We just got it turned back on this week."

Santos looked around. Even without electric, he thought that he would love to live in this big, airy house anytime.

When they all entered Luq's bedroom, Santos' eyes widened in wonder. Along every wall, and lining the ceiling, were magazine images on every bit of white space available. Dovima and the elephants stood beside David Bowie, Grace Jones growled next to Joan Crawford, Prince loomed in black bikini underwear while the Duke of Windsor and Wallace Simpson reclined in remote contemplation.

Santos approached one of the few photos that he could identify; Brooke Shields posed provocatively in Calvin Klein jeans. "Look at Brooke. That face is beat for points! Man! Where'd you get all these pictures?"

Luq sat on the narrow single bed pushed against a wall. "All over the place. Mostly from magazines. British magazines have great photography. I really love the fashion shots."

"Yeah. Brooke Shields is my favorite model."

"Yeah?" Luq seemed unimpressed. "I met her once. I worked a shift in Princeton when the store was short-staffed, and she came in to buy some things. She's got zits. Now, the model to beat is Kelly LeBrock or Andie MacDowell."

Luq walked over to the images of the models he mentioned. Vacant eyes looked back from heavily maquillaged faces. "Now, that's what I call a model."

"No, bitch," said Dion, "those girls cannot come for Miss Isabella Rosellini. Now that bitch is fierce. She gives you cheekbones that are almost as etched as mine."

"Isabella? I don't think so. That bitch ain't nothing but the poor man's Nastassja Kinski. They book that bitch 'cause Natassja is too busy acting to be bothered with Vogue."

"Who? Chile, why you always naming these obscure ass people ain't nobody heard of? Don't nobody know that chile. Miss Isabella is movie star royalty. Her mother is Miss Ingrid Bergman, honey, and they look just alike."

"Yeah," Luq countered, "like men. That's Hollywood royalty? Ingrid was a tramp. They ran her ass out of Hollywood for fucking married men."

Santos laughed while Dion posed with a hand on his hip. "Honey, a girl's gotta do what a girl's gotta do. Ingrid had bills to pay, okay? I find myself in a similar predicament all the time. I mean, I don't want to be out snatching these other hoe's men, but, shit, I gotta pay the rent, so I feel Miss Thing."

Santos silently agreed with Dion about Luq's breadth of knowledge. He knew a lot of information about celebrities that the rest of them had never heard of, but that was part of the reason Santos admired him. The two-mile distance separating primarily white and affluent neighborhood where Luq lived from the working class borough of Norristown, was, for Santos, as vast as the Atlantic Ocean. Luq's attendance at an upscale high school, where he had acquired a vast and scathing vocabulary, one far more extensive than his own, gave him a certain exotic quality. Luq listened to punk music, was well spoken, and wore clothing unlike the tight denim and brightly colored urban wear that Santos was familiar with, all of these things gave him a certain worldly air. While Dion and Santos avoided the slurs and bullying of other boys by dodging into alleys or waiting until sundown before going out, Luq walked the streets of Norristown in full regalia, ignoring the taunts of others who laughed at his experimentations with blue hair, his bondage pants, his boots that looked like duct taped paper bags.

There was a sudden shift in the room, and the boys turned as the door opened and admitted the scent of Paloma Picasso perfume.

"Hi, Aunt Carol," Dion piped.

Luq's mother entered the doorway. She was a nut brown colored woman with a firm press and curl set to her dark brown hair. She cast a calculating eye around the room, making note of where each person stood. Her nose twitched as a slight aroma signaled her olfactory senses.

"Dion, honey. The shower's calling you."

Santos stifled a gasp of laughter.

"Oh, no. I'm fine, Aunt Carol."

Not accustomed to opposition, Carol immediately countered. "No, you're not. Come on out here and let me get you a washcloth and towel.

She immediately left the room; confident her demands would be obeyed. Dion lowered his head in embarrassment as he followed. Luq and Santos looked at one another.

"Wow. Is that your mom? That is fucked up."

Luq nodded. "Well, let's face it. The bitch stinks. Walking from Norristown is a long ass walk."

"Shit, that bitch was stanking before the walk, okay? Let's be for real. She came up into my house smelling all like ass crack and Cootie's nut sack."

"Cootie? Oh god, that is so fucking gross. Why she gonna go off with that old ass man? I can't even deal with her. When she comes out of that shower, I'm going to read her viciously."

Santos laughed. "And if anyone can read viciously, bitch, we know it's you. Let that bitch have it!" As he walked over to sit on the bed, an image from an open *Jet* magazine caught his eye. He grabbed the magazine from the desk as he sat next to Luq.

"Have you heard about this shit?"

Luq glanced over absently. "What? The Missing?"

Mahogany Magazine weekly periodical date: July 21, 1979
Page Ten: (Missing children section)
Toledo, Ohio

Terrence Logan, 16 years old. Last seen by his mother July 3, at 7 pm. Mrs. Logan reports that Terrence left the house with two friends. She sent him to his grandmother's home, about two miles away, to pick up extra lights to hang in celebration of an Independence Day cookout the next day. Local authorities have designated the incident as missing persons based upon Terrence's history as a runaway and minor skirmishes with the law. Mrs. Logan denies this. His mother states that there is no way that Logan would not return home for the family tradition of

Fourth of July fireworks.   Grandmother reports that he never made it to her home to pick up the lights.

Luq leaned back against the wall, kicking one thin leg over the other. "I don't even read *Page Ten* anymore. It's too depressing. They never find anybody living. It's just an obituary."

DAVID JACKSON AMBROSE

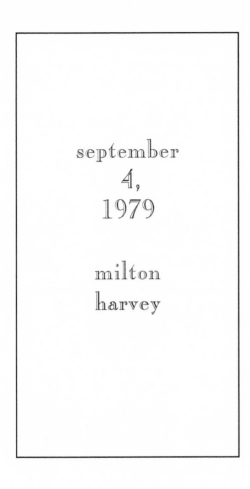

september
4,
1979

milton
harvey

THE BEAT

The humidity of the late night air hissed through the trees of the courthouse square. It clung languidly upon the leaves like dew. Far from the bright globes of light beaming on the square, the homeless man dragged his cardboard pallet into the shadows created by the thick marble slabs that gave the looming edifice of the Norristown courthouse an aura of stately grandeur.

The gaunt man spread his makeshift bed over the musty grate near the alcove of a side entrance and began to arrange himself comfortably, ignoring the minute discomforts of the metal biting through the cardboard thin and battered trench coat that served as the mattress to the box spring of the grate.

His attempts to sleep were disrupted by the clack of shoes on the flagstones and loud, raucous laughter. He pulled the trench around his head with a groan.

As the night grew older, and prospects dried up, everyone had begun to migrate from the lower corner of Lafayette Street up into the courthouse square.

Dion lounged on a graffiti carved bench, one leg resting upon the other, his large foot dangling a black ballet slipper in the air. Luq unceremoniously brushed his leg from the bench to make room so that he could sit beside his cousin. "Move, bitch."

White Girl sat on the bench across from them, her dirty blonde hair falling into heavily mascaraed eyes. As Santos walked up the stairs that led from the street into the square, he cut an eye at Dion's shoes as they slapped the pavement.

"Girl, if you are out here trying to be a cunt, why don't you wear some real shoes instead of those three dollar jobs from the Chinese store?"

Dion blew out a puff of Newport. "Chile, ain't nothing wrong with these pumps. They are very comfortable."

"And cheap," Luq added. "You know all her female accessories come from the Chinese Wig Shop. At least her titties look realistic tonight."

"Uh. Ain't nothing wrong with the Chinese store, or my Chinese slippers."

White Girl chimed in. "She's been sporting those Chinese shoes ever since I've known her."

"These chinks are lovely. I'm giving you Audrey Hepburn, chile, and you know it."

Luq barked out a laugh. "I had no idea Audrey was so damn ashy..."

"Or black" Santos added. "Which one is blacker? The pumps, or the bitch standing above them."

White Girl extended a well-formed leg, waving her red high heeled shoe. "If you wear heels, it gives your legs better shape.'

"Sweetie, I don't need to do that. Everyone knows I have the best goddam legs in the city, and those cheap ass stacks would not do anything for them."

"What's wrong with my shoes? I got them from Fayva."

Luq cast a critical eye. "Like he said: cheap. They look all kinds of plastic. You better get up onto Wild Pair. They got the heels of life! Now if you want a damn high heel, they will give it to you!"

Santos smirked. "This bitch thinks everybody got big money like him, to spend fifty dollars on a damn shoe."

"Well, I have a job, so yeah, I spend money. If I don't, my mom damn sure won't. But I make most of my own clothes."

"That's true. You do be making some shit I ain't never seen before. But for real, White Girl, if you want to bring your look up, you should be giving us Marilyn Monroe, out here. You should dye your hair platinum, and let these broke down whores have it!" Santos raked fingers through Toni's lightly curled hair. "This dishwater shade ain't getting it."

"And Aqua Net her down!" Luq added. "That way you won't look like you been blasted through a tornado at the end of the night. With Aqua Net, that mane won't move. That's how I keep my Mohawk tight."

Santos laughed again. "A tornado! Girl looks like she's been through it!"

They all laughed.

White Girl lit a cigarette retrieved from her plastic purse. "Why don't you go with me to help me pick out a pair of heels? If you make me an outfit, I can match it up with some new heels."

"Girl, if I make you an outfit, these other skunks out here will be giving you the rah-rahs! You will be jumping from car to car all night."

Santos snorted. "Bitch, please. Get over yourself. If you make her one of your get-ups, she'll look like she came from Krypton."

"That's why you always beg for my cast offs? Chile please."

Out of the shadows of the upper level of the courthouse, a thin figure descended the stairs. The group watched as a boy no more than fifteen approached them. It was clear that he was one of the scattered group of homeless people that made the courthouse their place of rest during the night. As he neared, the distinct odor of the homeless loomed in the air; dirty fabric, sweat, and the hint of excrement and urine.

"Anybody got a cigarette?"

White Girl rummaged in her purse, retrieved a cigarette and stretched out a nail-chewed hand toward the boy. "Here you go, sweetie."

The boy mumbled a thanks as he took the cigarette. "Anybody got a match?"

Dion huffed. "Damn, anything else you need? Want us to smoke it for you, too?"

"Shut up, bitch," Santos laughed. "So damn vicious."

A loud, metallic banging disrupted the revelry. A squat, black man wearing a police uniform approached, tapping his baton against a lamp post. "Move it along, people. No loitering here..."

"No loitering in the park?" Luq was incredulous.

The officer cut him off with a brusque tone. "This ain't no dialogue. I told you to move out of here. Fast."

The group collected itself and sauntered down the steps onto the sidewalk, turning right and ascending the incline up Swede Street while the cop watched them leave, continuing to knock his nightstick on the nearest object.

"Fat ass bitch," Dion mumbled.

"They ain't got nothing better to do than run around behind us." Luq huffed. "Why don't they go break up the drug dealing that happens in the alley behind the damn police station. Fuck with somebody that's actually breaking a law."

"Oh, uh uh, chile," piped Santos. "That's my weed spot, bitch. They got the banging ass weed behind the police station. If they shut that down, they fuck up my whole entire situation."

White Girl laughed. "I know that's right."

They all looked back to be sure the policeman was not still watching them, and then walked up the stairs to the upper level of the courthouse, where they spread leisurely around a marble slab overlooking the lower square.

White Girl looked at the boy that had asked for a cigarette earlier. He seemed to have made himself a part of their entourage. "What's your name, sweetie?"

Before he could answer, everyone's attention was drawn to a shadow that emerged from the courthouse interior. Flukey Luke lurched toward them, waving a finger of admonishment.

"Can't y'all youngbloods keep it down? I'm sleepin' up here."

Dion sucked his teeth. "We can tell from the smell. You want privacy, go to the George Washington Motor Lodge…"

Santos laughed.

Flukey Luke got closer. The walk that had seemed precarious before was now sure and firm. As he stood before them, he spread his feet in a stance of aggression.

"You think you funny, youngblood? You always got something to say? I could snuff you out right where you stand. You keep thinking this thing is a joke, hear? You better open your eyes and see what's in front of you. Everywhere you look somebody lookin' to take you out of here. "

"Oh shit. Let's go, girls," Dion laughed. "He's 'bout to lose it."

"Ain't nobody losing shit, my man. Y'all standing around with trash and whores, somebody gon' think that's what you are, and that's how you gon' get treated."

The man glared at Luq, then turned and walked back into the shadows.

White Girl laughed. "What the fuck?"

Dion said, "He must've been talking about you, girl, 'cause I am a lady!"

As everyone laughed, the constant, methodical banging rang out again. They looked down and saw the cop banging his stick on the concrete of the promenade below them.

He yelled up at them. "I told you motherfuckers to clear the fuck out of here. I won't tell you again."

The group snickered and walked away from the wall so that the officer could not see them from below.

"Let's just stay away from the wall so 'Licia can't see us," Dion instructed. "Y'all know her big ass is too fat to be trying to pump up those stairs to see if we still here or not."

"Don't look now, San," Luq warned as he looked over Santos's shoulder. "Here comes your husband."

Santos looked behind him as a lean, short boy approached. He sucked his teeth in disgust.

Eddie Lee was whip-thin and dark as night, with a well-groomed afro and glittering white teeth, which he flashed as he grabbed Santos' arm. "What's up?"

He didn't even acknowledge the rest of the group as he lightly tugged at Santos' arm, ignoring Santos nimbly wrenching himself free.

"Hey Eddie Lee," Dion practically screamed. "What's up?"

Eddie Lee mumbled to Santos as if he had not heard Dion. "Take this walk with me real quick."

Santos rolled his eyes and again removed his arm from Eddie Lee's persistent grasp. "Nah, I'm cool. Catch me later."

"Come on, man. It won't take long. Just five minutes."

"So we've heard," Dion chirped.

Dion and Luq muffled laughter as Santos repeated himself, "Nah. I'm good."

Eddie Lee's face began to get cloudy. "Come on, you fucking bitch."

"Girl, you better go ahead, before he beats your ass again," Dion said. Luq and White Girl looked off into the distance and tried to muffle their laughter.

Luq gasped, "I didn't know she was a battered wife."

"Yo' I got this beer…" as if by magic, Eddie Lee produced a brown paper bag in the hand that was not grabbing at Santos, in which a can of beer was nestled.

"Well, why didn't you say so." Santos reconsidered.

Just then, a flurry of noise and shadow rose on the perimeter of the landing, as two policemen ran around the wall toward them.

Dion screamed. "It's Alice, girl! Dash!"

Everyone immediately scattered in different directions, with the police quickly darting behind them.

JONAS

San been gone a long time. San always goes outside when it grows dark. After we eat, he takes me to my bed to lays down, and I close my eyes, so he thinks I'm sleep. Then I sit on the stairs and listen to him play music in his room and put on other clothes. Then he smokes ganja and go out.

This time was different. We don't eat no food. We don't got food to eat. We been eating salt sandwiches, and after two days of salt sandwiches, my tongue feels scratchy. Like licking pavement. It's sore. My belly ball up like a fist and punch me. If I drink water, maybe my belly stop fighting.

I sit up and get out my bed to go down to the faucet. I pull up a chair to the wall and climb up, then reach to click on the light switch. It clicks but no light. I forget San say no light.

Walls feel sticky. I slide my hand to feel my way, so I don't fall down steps like before. We had no lights before, when it was snow out, and I fell down steps. My arm got broke. When my arm got broke, San yells at Gloria to take me to the hospital, but she say no.

I walk better with no shoes. My toes feel the floor better. I make it downstairs. Outside I hear voices near the front door. I hope it San. But San say don't go outside if you don't want the welfare to come take you away forever and ever, so I don't go outside.

I bump into the table, and Gloria favorite ashtray fall off. Makes loud sound but don't break. In the kitchen, I make a glass of water. It don't stop my belly from making a fist, but it makes it stop growling.

I wish for San to come home. I don't like dark. I hear things. Voices say things. They laugh in the dark. They tell me bad things.

I think I can make the lights come back. If I think real hard I know how to make things happen; just like I made Uncle Nash go away.

I sit on the floor. The voices run over my head. They get faster and faster. I shut my eyes. The dark behind my eyes is better than the dark in front of my eyes. The dark behind my eyes has an orange glow. It waves up and down. I watch it really hard until the voices above my head get softer and softer. The orange glow begins to shimmer, and the voices start to go away. The voices become a hum. The hum is friendlier than the voices. It doesn't say bad things.

I have to think real hard. I watch the glow, making it grow brighter and brighter. It becomes like the sun.

LUQMAN

Sitting on the backyard step leading to Santos' house for the past hour, it began to occur to Luq that perhaps he had been the only one fleet-footed enough not to be caught by the police. He reluctantly began to muster the energy it would take to walk the two-mile trek back home. He didn't mind the walk from Norristown into the adjoining town of Bridgeport; it was at least illuminated. The stretch from Bridgeport into King of Prussia, however, had no street lights or sidewalks. In warm weather bats hurtled from the sky, pitching disconcertingly close to the stiffened spikes of his hair, and startlingly assertive skunks lunged from the underbrush with foul intentions to cast their scent at any and every one that disrupted their nocturnal appointments with suburban trashcans. In addition, random stops by police unaccustomed to lone boys of color on the streets at night, unless they were searching for an innocent white suburbanite to pillage, the walk back home was far more challenging to Luq than the walk into town.

As he gathered himself to stand, the latch to the gate leading to the alley made a metallic hiccup. Luq peered through the night as a form approached. "Hey White Girl. You made it, too, huh?"

She was smoking a cigarette. She blew out a cloud of nicotine and sat beside him, crossing her shapely legs. The nylon made a slightly alluring hiss as she crossed her legs. "Actually, my name's Toni."

"Why do they call you White Girl?"

She laughed, showing small, feral teeth and bright gums, "Seriously? "

Luq laughed along with her, "Dumb ass question, right? I just like to know the origins of nicknames. It seems like everybody out here has another name, and sometimes they make sense, sometimes not. I mean, you're not the only white girl out here, so how is it that you got the name White Girl? Like Annie. She's White. So why not her? Or April? But I admit, I so much like her being called Ape."

They both laughed, "I think it fits."

"So why you hang with her?"

"I only hang with her because I don't know anybody around here. I landed here a couple months ago when I hitched a ride from some ass wipe down Florida. He said he was driving to PA, and I figured, why not go for the ride. I had spent enough time in Orlando to see wasn't shit happening there, so why not check on P.A. So, I met April who was working the Greyhound. She let me crash, so we just be chilling."

Luq grunted a noncommittal response, "So, you didn't get nabbed by 5-0?"

Toni stretched out a leg and turned the strappy sandal a few times, "Oh, fuck yeah. In these heels? I was the first one they grabbed."

"So what happened?"

"Ah. I know the detective that works the strip. Libby. They just scooped me up in the car for a minute. He was asking me what I'm hanging around with all the faggots for. He said to get off the street for tonight. They gonna do a sweep tonight. He usually tells me and April when the cops are gonna sweep the street, and we just lay low that night."

Luq was impressed, but not really. "Libby? You fucked him?'

Toni leaned back on the step casually and shook her head. "Nah. I don't fuck out here. They don't pay enough for that. I do head. That's it. Fifty bucks a pop."

"Fifty? They don't come up off of more than a twenty spot down the way."

"Oh yeah, I know. That's why I don't go with the black guys. Only the white men; they pay it. Black guys always trying to talk you the fuck down to twenty. Fuck that. Besides, they always trying to get rough and try to get some ass even when you told them only head, so I only go with white guys. The older, the better, so you can try to slip the rest of their money out of their pockets when they ain't paying attention."

Just then, from behind them, they heard a loud off pitch wailing. They both looked back toward the door from which the wailing seemed to be coming. The wailing turned into a scream. Both of them stood up.

Luq tried the doorknob, which turned beneath his hand. He pushed the door open and peered in, with Toni standing on her toes to try to see over his shoulder. The noise grew louder, and Luq walked into the darkened room that he knew served as Santos' bedroom. From the darkened room, a sputtering light danced in the doorway on the opposite wall. He reached along the wall and flipped the light switch, but nothing happened. Luq pitched himself into the dimly lit interior. Instinctively, Toni grabbed his arm and was tugged along with him.

They entered the dark kitchen almost as one entity. The only light emanated from a fire on the stove in the corner of the room, and a little boy is flailing about in the center. Toni gasped at the sight of the boy moaning and flinging an arm that was ablaze with a small flame.

Luq brushed Toni's hand from his arm and removed the backpack from his shoulders. He reached inside and came out with a flashlight. He turned it on and set in on the floor, its meager light allowing them to see a narrow path of the room. He then turned back into the bedroom, where he snatched the threadbare blanket from the bed, rushed back into the kitchen and quickly wrapped the blanket around the flailing child, enveloping him in his arms to stop the movement, and falling onto his butt so that he could cradle the moaning boy and keep him immobile. He looked up at Toni with large eyes.

"The stove!" he barked. Toni looked at the small flame dancing on the burner of the narrow gas stove in the corner of the kitchen. She pulled the thin drape from the window and began to fling it at the fire, over and over, until it began to peter out.

Beneath the blanket in Luq's arms, Jonas began to calm down. He pitched back into the Luq's chest, feeling the heat from his body. Luq lifted the blanket and looked to be sure the flame was extinguished. He lifted the arm that had been ablaze and saw that it had not done any damage to the child, only the hem of his sleeve had been singed.

"That wasn't all that bad. He's not burned or anything."

Luq stood the boy up and brushed him off. At the stove, Toni took the charred pan to the sink towering with dirty dishes. She made a face at the swarm of roaches crawling over food remnants. "Guess the kid was trying to cook something. How old is he anyway?"

"Jonas is like seven or something, I think. Too young to be at the stove that's for sure." Luq got on his knees, smiling at the child. "You hungry? See what's in the fridge..."

Toni opened the door and peered at the bare contents. Luq looked over Jonas' shoulder while the boy moaned and hummed. "Ooh, girl. That fridge is bald headed. There ain't even mold to eat. What the fuck Miss Santos doing buying fucking forty ounces and weed every night when there ain't shit here for this boy to eat? That's what I call some nigga ass shit."

Toni slammed the door shut. "Why's he making those noises? Is he a retard or something?"

Luq laughed. "Oh my God. You know he can hear you, right?"

"What? I'm just asking."

Luq stood. Well, these bitches haven't gotten back in all this time. They probably got popped. I'ma have to take him home with me. At least I can get him something to eat."

"Where do you live? Maybe I can go with you."

"I live in King of Prussia. And it would take us all fucking night to get there with you in them heels."

"I'll pay for a cab."

"Seriously? That's awfully generous. But that won't fly. My folks would piss bricks if I tried to bring some white girl up in my house to spend the night. Anyway, somebody should stay here just in case they let Santos out and he wonders where his brother's at. Their mom isn't around, so you could probably crash here."

"Cool." Toni reached into her purse and handed Luq a ten-dollar bill.

"What's this?"

"For the cab."

"You're still going to give me money to take a cab?"

"Why not?"

"That's awfully nice. Thanks a lot."

"Not a problem. What's money for, if not to spend?"

Mahogany Magazine weekly periodical date: September 4, 1979
Page Ten: (Missing children section)
Atlanta, GA:
Thomas V. The State, 245 Ga. 688

Donald Wayne Thomas, the appellant, was convicted in Fulton County Superior Court of the April 19, 1979, murder of Dewey Baugus, a nine-year-old child. He was sentenced to death, and this is his appeal.

From the evidence introduced at trial, the jury was authorized to find the following facts:

On April 11, 1979, Dewey Baugus and a playmate left his mother's home on Primrose Circle in Atlanta to go to a ball game. After the game, the two children separated to return to their respective homes in the early evening darkness. This was the last time the victim was seen alive.

The appellant, a 19-year-old male, lived at a rooming house on Primrose Circle. Linda Cook, the appellant's girlfriend had, stayed with him for approximately a week during the time in question. The appellant had kept her locked in the room when he was not there, with a bucket he provided as her only toilet facility. Linda Cook testified that when the appellant returned to the room on Friday, April 13, she noticed that he had a lot of blood on the front of his pants. The appellant took her to the railroad tracks behind Primrose Circle and showed her the body of the victim, lying face down, and told her that he had killed the child by beating him with a stick and choking him. In her presence, the appellant rolled the body over. Telling her that he had to make sure that he was dead, the appellant then jumped on the neck of the victim. Thereafter, he threw the victim's body in the bushes. Thereafter, they returned to the room, where the appellant removed his pants and hid them behind the house. That same day, the appellant, again in Linda Cook's presence, admitted the murder to his stepfather, Enzor Lowe. However, his stepfather testified that he did not believe him because the appellant was grinning about it.

On April 19, 1979, Calvin Banks discovered the body of the victim when he took a shortcut on his way back from applying for a job at the Dolly Madison Cake Co. when the body was discovered, it was partially decomposed, and the pants the victim was wearing were pulled down to mid-thigh level.

Sometime later, after she had stopped staying with the appellant, Linda Cook contacted the authorities and related what had occurred. She was charged with concealing a death and placed in juvenile detention. She pointed out to the authorities where the appellant had discarded his pants, and they were recovered. Crime laboratory tests confirmed that the blood on the appellant's pants was human, International Type B. The blood type of the victim could not be established due to decay.

Autopsy results showed the cause of death as asphyxiation, and that numerous post- and antemortem bruises were on the body.

LUQMAN

Luq was pretty sure he would be able to sneak the kid into his room without his mother or stepfather catching on. Most times they were not in the common areas of the house. They both worked during the day and spent most of their time at home in their master suite, on the uppermost floor of the bi-level house, with the door closed, insulated from the sounds created by their three children. As for the children, they tended to be off on their own projects. There was an unspoken agreement between the siblings: you mind your own business, and I will mind mine.

Although the downstairs lights were all out when Luq approached the house, he let go of Jonas' hand outside the door and knelt down to face him. The vacant look seemed to vacate his eyes, and Jonas looked at him as if he was really seeing him for the first time.

"Now, I need you to be quiet, okay? You can stay here for as long as you need to, but you're going to have to keep quiet, like a little mouse..."

Inside, there was a distant drone from some far off radio as they entered the shadowy rec room. The smell of lemon Pledge and cool air hit Jonas' face as the thin soles of his sneakers rested on springy shag carpet.

The experience was a sensory overload for Jonas. He smelled furniture polish and bleach. His eyes touched upon gleaming chrome lamps and cedar-scented fixtures. The kitchen was a large white space, boasting grandly scaled appliances, with pans seemingly floating in the air. His eyes widened in wonder when entering the bedroom. There were thousands of people there. Ladies with large round eyes and big tall hair. Ladies crouching like panthers, or springing in the air, looking straight at him, while men looked off into the distance, pretending that he wasn't there, flexing large muscles, their bare chests slippery with oil.

When Luq flicked on the lamp, the people all retreated into their pictures and watched with remote hauteur. Jonas felt safe with all of these people watching over him, even though they were white. They weren't like the white people that he saw every day, with ugly, sweaty, faces and snarled hair, that yelled 'hey boy, you buying that?' or 'you put that down, now' or 'you got money for that?' No. These white people looked like no other white people he had seen before. They were beautiful. They did not have frowns. Their eyes were blank. Their skin was smooth and pale, like chalk, not the red blotchy faces he usually saw. The ladies wore big hats and had hair that tumbled down their shoulders or piled in a halo. They wore tight pants so blue they hurt your eyes. And silky blouses with silver fur, which opened to reveal smooth, curved throats. The men were strong and handsome. They did not scratch their big bellies and tell you to get out of their stores. They had sparkling blue eyes and strong, broad, hands with clean, pink fingernails that rested on narrow waists, or held ballerinas aloft. Their hair swirled on their heads like oceans... Like Luq.

Luq ran a hand through his Aqua-Net held spikes and sat Jonas on the bed.

"You hungry? You wait here, and I'll go see what we have to eat. Remember, you have to be quiet now."

As he walked down the stairs, Luq mumbled, "Don't get your hopes up."

The refrigerator revealed its usual offerings: nothing. There was a pitcher of some weakly colored concoction that Luq identified to be Crystal Light, some Tupperware containers holding unidentifiable grey gelatinous contents for which Luq decided not to risk botulism. In the produce bin, he could see the familiar sack of russet potatoes. He sighed tiredly. He didn't feel like peeling potatoes, but that was the only thing available that he knew would be enjoyable. He had developed the knack for making fried potatoes that were fried to a golden hue, the crispness so precise, the onions so sweet and earthy, that everyone who had ever tasted them begged that he make them all the time. This expertise had been honed from years of experience. Salvaging a meal from the meager contents of their kitchen had been a tradition in the Ettinger household before it had become the Ettinger household.

When his mother was between her first and second marriage, she had had to work two jobs; one as a receptionist for a doctor's office, and a night job as a shipping clerk for a computer peripherals company. Those two jobs barely paid for rent on their apartment in West Chester; a tiny two bedroom, one of which was crammed with the bunk beds that Luq and his younger brother slept on while their younger sisters' pink canopy loomed on the opposite wall.

During that time there had not been a month when either: A. the electric was off; B. the hot water was off; or C. the phone was off.

Luq always had a preference for the electric being off. As the oldest, he held constant responsibility for oversight of his siblings while his mother was not home. They were not allowed, under any conditions, to be outside after dark. Since he was in charge, he needed the phone just in case of an emergency. He also called his mother every day when everyone got in from school. The hot water being off was the worst experience of his life. First off, if the hot water was out, that automatically meant there was no heat. And then you couldn't take a shower, and you needed to boil a pot of water to take a bath at the sink, on mornings so cold you could see your breath. Of course, not being able to bathe wasn't that big a deal to his younger brother and sister, but Luq also needed water to comb his hair. And combing your hair, when it's freezing cold, using cold water, putting Dixie Peach on cold wet hair, the grease just sort of nestled on top, in globs, instead of merging with the water to make the smooth, shiny waves that obliterated the thick, coarse mass lurking beneath. Standing in a pitch cold bathroom, the cold tiles eating through the protection of your socks, washing with the warm soapy cloth, and then the air makes a blast past your goosebumped skin.

Even getting out of bed in the morning was tortuous. To leave the warm, musky comfort of the blankets; thick with sweat and morning breath, to brave that first blast of air...

Just thinking of it made Luq shudder.

Being without electricity. That was a minor inconvenience compared to being without hot water. Luq didn't really watch much TV. He liked to read. So even without electricity, he had something to do that entertained him. He could get lost in other worlds. In fact, if it was dark outside, he could light a candle and read a vampire story by candlelight, imagining that he was living in Victorian England, shadows looming on the walls, with mice scratching around in darkened corners.

Luq snorted. Like the time between marriages was much different than now. There was still very little food in the house. The cabinets stayed stocked with Ramen and Cheerios, and Wheat Chex, but there was never milk to put to the Cheerios. Carol bought powdered milk and added water to make a weak facsimile that tasted worse than paste. Luq was not sure if it was a deliberate oversight or his mother's poor reading skills, but she somehow conveniently overlooked the fact that the recipe for creating 'milk' from dehydrated calcium flakes required that one add evaporated milk along with the tap water. Either way, Luq would not have touched that milk to save his life. He rethought that - not to save her life. There were still instances when the electric, phone, or water were shut off. It just seemed that the instances weren't as frequent as then.

Luq wondered if the tradeoff was worth it. Less time without utilities, but still very little food in exchange for the addition of a drunken, marginally employed stepfather, who walked around in a rage because Luq refused to call him 'dad.' It's not that Luq was being starved. Dinner was served every night (almost). The cupboards were not bare. They contained Hamburger Helper, Minute Rice, canned vegetables that Carol would cook to a limp, colorless consistency, spaghetti; most of the staples were there. Carol and Ambrose would sometimes buy cheesesteaks or hoagies and then retreat to their room to eat, leaving the children to fend for themselves, but most times dinner was left in pans on the stove for the children to eat at their leisure. Or Luq was expected to cook, as he had during the time between marriages, scrounging up some semblance of an acceptable meal from the meager contents of the cabinets.

Living in the lily white suburbs of King of Prussia was not cheap. Carol constantly reminded her children of this when they complained about not having any decent cereal, like Cap'n Crunch, or Vanilla Wafers, or ice cream, or Pepsi. Or when shivering in the heat deprived bathroom. Or not being able to learn to play the French horn. Or buy a pair of Sasson jeans. Or Nikes.

So Luq had learned to sew. And then he did not need Jordache or Vanderbilt. And he could make designer clothes of his own because Claude Montana and Issey Miyake and Norma Kamali created patterns that cost ten dollars. That was terribly expensive, much more expensive than most patterns, which were three dollars. Sometimes he would have to save up to get the patterns he liked; sometimes he would just slip one beneath his overcoat and walk out of the store.

While the shortening melted in the heating pan, Luq peeled and sliced the potatoes. He always hated the drudgery of peeling potatoes before actually doing it, but once he was on a roll, he found it rather comforting. The slightly wet sound of the skin shucking loose, revealing creamy white flesh, the repetitiveness of the motion of slicing, the starchy, earthy scent of a dirty russet.

The key to a perfectly fried potato was all in the timing. The temperature of the oil needed to be just right; when you hear the slight bubbling of the grease, you flick a fingertip of water and listen for whether it crackles back at you. If it merely murmurs, you needed to wait it out. If it was lively, almost angry, it was time. You also needed to slice your potatoes to a uniform size, on the thin side, so that they could turn a crisp golden shade.

He dropped the slices into the heat and heard a satisfying crackle and hissed. First, you cooked them on high, uncovered until the first flip, and then you removed most of the oil, lowered the heat and covered, turning frequently. This way you allowed the inside to cook to a soft, buttery consistency that was such a precise opposition to the crisp outside that it could make your eyes water. You couldn't add the onions until the last phase so that they did not overcook and burn, but rather they released a pungent sweetness to the final product, allowing a bit of stickiness, adhering some potatoes to others in a voluminous, golden mass, salt glimmering on the top.

As he put the lid on the pan, the loud crackling of the oil became a low hum. Beneath that, he heard the door to the side entrance open and close. He cursed silently. Since the house was quiet, he had assumed that Ambrose and his mother were in their room sleeping. He should have known, particularly since it was a weekend, that his stepfather had been out at some local dive drinking cheap liquor and regaling some anonymous woman with tales of a life that did not exist.

Footsteps lumbered up the stairs to the kitchen. The door banged open, and Ambrose lumbered in, his lean frame swaying in the bright fluorescents. He looked dismissively at Luq standing by the stove and continued toward the other room.

"When you gonna start combing your hair?" he slurred.

"It is combed."

Ambrose shook his head in disgust. "You need to start reading some history books. Learn some self-pride and stop this white people shit."

He continued up the stairs while Luq shook his head. Dumbass. What did a Mohawk have to do with history books? Or 'white people shit.' It was so tiring. Being called white boy in school. Being laughed at. People asking him why he talked like a white boy. Faggot. Ever since junior high school, his manner of speaking had been subject to ridicule. The taunting wasn't as common now that he was in high school when the family had moved to a predominantly white school district. In junior high, which was mostly black, the taunting had started as laughter and escalated to physical; spilled drinks in the cafeteria, thrown spitballs and paper airplanes flying at his head, a foot stuck out in the halls.

By the time the family had moved to King of Prussia, Luq had found a way to combat the jeers of his peers. The skinheads and punk rockers in *I.D.* and the *Face* magazines from London looked tough and cool and indifferent. He shaved his head and left a long swath across the center. He switched out his Pro Keds for Doc Martins. He pierced his shirts with hundreds of safety pins. He shaved off his eyebrows and lined his eyes with Wet and Wild.

He did not make any friends in his new environment. He was still an outcast. Perhaps even more so, as one of seven black kids at school, but no one called him names anymore. Nobody poured soda on his head or pushed him into lockers. Instead, the student body ignored him. They acted like he was invisible. But at least nobody accused him of trying to be white; except Ambrose.

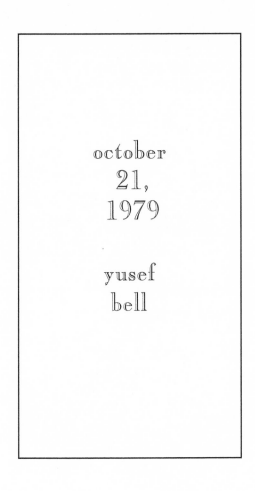

october
21,
1979

yusef
bell

ACME

White Girl finding out that he was temporarily living without a parental presence had certain advantages and certain disadvantages. As they roamed through the aisles of the Acme market, Santos couldn't help but think that this was the stand out advantage; being able eat.

Gloria usually managed to come back to the house for the weekends, during which time she would prepare meals strategized to last through the week while she would be gone. This usually consisted of stews, soups or curried something or another, meals that could be stretched, and the accoutrement for sandwich building, and some mango or pineapple punch, coconut milk, plantains, the usual staples of a Caribbean household. These were not things that any growing child had any interest in eating.

Toni breathed out carcinogenic fumes and flung ashes from the Newport dangling from her mouth as she teetered on the new stilettos that had been bought under Luq's critical supervision, flinging bottle after bottle of Pepsi into the shopping cart. Santos took the cigarette from her lips and inhaled a few tokes himself, placing an Entenmann's crumb cake into the cart.

Toni grabbed the silvery blue bag of Herr's chips and tossed them on top of two cartons of Breyers vanilla almond ice cream. "Ah. I love Entenmann's. Can you get two more?"

Santos arched an eyebrow from behind large plastic sunglasses. "Bitch, you ain't said nothing but a word."

They both cackled with delight. From the corner of his eye, Santos could see the burly security guard, who on most days stayed stationary at the front door, shadowing them. They ignored him.

"So," Santos said, "this all looks lovely, but what about some real food? We can't just eat cakes all day, can we?"

"No. Let's go get some Steakums and those Amoroso steak rolls. Hook it up with some cheese, bitch, that's all she wrote." Toni clicked past the guard as if he were nothing more than a shelf, or some other fixture.

Following, Santos mumbled. "What the fuck is he following us for? Like I'm a stick this shit down my pants."

"Well, you do have sticky fingers, 'cause you damn sure snatched my eyeliner out my bag this morning..."

Santos gasped in a poor attempt at innocence. "No, I didn't."

"Child, please. The evidence is very heavily circling your eyes behind those shades. You are serving up raccoon for points."

"Fuck you, bitch."

"Anyway, dude is probably trying to get those digits from you 'cause he's definitely in the life."

"I don't spook him as one of the children. Why you say that?"

"Because if a brother does not stare me down, I know he must be gay."

Okay. So here was one of the disadvantages. White Girl had a lot of confidence. Santos was even willing to take that further and say that she was pushy. In the short amount of time that she had been crashing at his place he had seen that the source of conversation constantly revolved around her. She was rather instructive, always suggesting what he should do, such as removing the plates of congealed food from beneath his bed and bringing them to the kitchen so that she could wash them. At least she kept the house clean. She did dishes constantly, never allowing them to pile up, as he did. The only problem was that there was always a light film of ash covering every surface of the house, as if a volcano had erupted a few weeks back and the hazmat crew had not gotten around to the cleanup.

Toni's years on this earth had shown her one thing; that black men were inexplicably drawn to her. Or so she said. She was an anomaly among white women. She was short and solidly built. Her legs were curvaceous. Her ankles were trim. Her waist was tight and svelte. But the asset she had that made men follow her off trains grabbing their crotches, with tongues wagging and licking their lips, was that she had an ass like a black woman. Round and prominent like a Georgia Peach (or 'onion,' as black men were prone to calling it) this singular asset allowed Toni a certain degree of acceptance in a group that might not have customarily welcomed someone quite so pale, with such a jarring disposition, and with a decidedly unattractive face.

First off, she was legally blind, so when she was not in public, she wore glasses that were as thick and opaque as the bottom of a Coke bottle. Added to that, she had a rather large

81

and broad forehead that she would camouflage with a swoop of teased hair. And most compelling (or as Dion noted, 'most jagged'), was a mouth that held a random display of small, discolored teeth, some present, most not, the result of a childhood of nutritionally deficient food, and an addiction to cola and candy.

That she was not a traditional beauty was a continuous source of discussion between Luq, Santos, and Dion when she was not around. Most particularly Dion, since he knew his cruel barbs concerning her missing A. teeth and/or B. beauty, would send Santos into paroxysms of laughter. "Girlfriend look like she been hit by a train going 300 miles an hour, don't she San? Don't she? I mean, her body might be sitting, and things, but bitch, that face look like 20 miles of bad road, don't it? Tell me I'm lying. Am I lying?"

Santos found these insults all the more humorous because Dion was not what could be considered attractive under any set of criteria. He was very dark, with coarse, nappy hair and an uneven hairline. For as long as Santos could remember, even before the two had become friends, he remembered kids at grade school subjecting Dion to the usual taunts that children of color pitch at those that are darker complected; black crispy critter, burnt nigga, overcooked, ugly black motherfucker, porchbunny, jigaboo.

When they became friends, and Dion had introduced him to Luq, Santos had not believed they were cousins. They were so divergent. Luq was tall and sleek to Dion's short, stout frame, Luq was quiet and reserved to Dion's loud attention-seeking demeanor. Luq was like a racehorse and Dion was like a hedgehog. Okay, more to the point, Luq was the color of burnished copper while Dion was the color of midnight. But Santos soon found out that the two complemented one another, a rapport that was more than a shared bloodline. It was a shared life; a life built upon years of summers together, of shared weekends and shared secrets, of nights chasing lightning bugs and collecting tadpoles from the creek, communal baths and shared chicken pox, going to church and laughing at Aunt Anna pretending to go into a spiritual frenzy; throwing down her cane when the spirit of the Lord descended into her body. Dion's hyperkinetic energy was tempered by his cousin's reserve. Dion's constant calling of Luq's name did not perturb him as it did Santos, it was almost as if he didn't notice it.

Santos looked at the security guard with a reconsidered glance. He was rather portly, definitely old; gray peppered the tufts of hair huffing out from beneath a too small cap, but he had nice chocolate skin that glowed with health, or sweat, Santos couldn't be sure, but the potential payoff of having the security guard from the local grocery store as a paramour was rife with possibilities. On lean days Santos could come in and pocket a can of ravioli or some Suzy Q's while the guard looked the other way, or if they hooked up on the regular, maybe the guard would bring over some things to stock the lean cabinets. Then he and Jonas could be sure that there was always something to eat, even if it were only cakes and donuts.

The infinite possibilities were abruptly cut off when they headed toward the registers, and the guard mumbled under his breath as they passed. "Fucking faggot."

While they were being rung up, Santos' breathing began to accelerate. He watched the tally window on the register as it added up item after item, the lights and bells going off as the cashier tossed each piece of merchandise down the conveyor belt. He wondered what they would do if they didn't have the money to pay for their goods. He thought about grabbing a box and just running out the door. At least it would give him something to eat.

He remembered the embarrassment of grocery trips with Gloria. There was never enough money to pay for what was on the belt. Gloria would slowly and deliberately go through the bags and take out items that they could go without for a week. After each item she would make the cashier re-tally the total, while people waited impatiently on line, huffing in frustration as Gloria interacted as if she were the sole customer in the store. Santos would slowly drift away from her, attempting to disassociate himself from the woman with the brightly hued headwrap and jangling gold hoops stretching up her arms, but Gloria would bellow, "You, bwoy! Come catch these 'tings en put em back in bag, eh? For we get on out here."

Toni reached into her tiny white clutch and dug out a roll of money, ostentatiously peeling off the requested amount and handing it to the cashier. She blew a plume of smoke toward the cashier and waited impatiently for her change, her lean arm outstretched before it needed to be.

Santos grabbed the bags from counter and rested them on his hip while Toni put her change back into the purse. They headed outside, among the curious stares of the other shoppers, her short t-shirt dress causing tsking from old ladies and crotch grabbing from young men.

A feeble ray of sun beamed between clouds on the pavement.

"Hold up." Toni stopped to rifle down the collar of her dress, reaching into her bra.

"You got more money down there? Damn, how much you got on that roll you pulled out?"

"No, chile." She took out two thin butcher wrapped packages of lunchmeat and tossed them into the bags in Santos arms. "What you get? I know you got something?"

Santos laughed and, juggling the bags, removed a pack of Newport cigarettes from his waistband. "Work, bitch!"

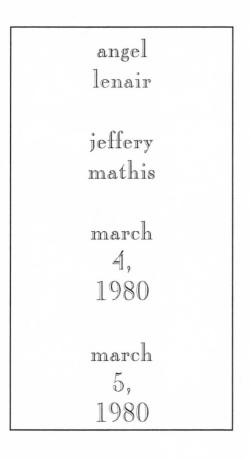

angel
lenair

jeffery
mathis

march
4,
1980

march
5,
1980

SWINGING JACK'S BARBERSHOP

Even though Wednesdays were the slowest day for making money, it was the day Chicago most enjoyed being at work. Other days were hectic, with vendors and young bucks running back and forth, deep voices disrupting the air. On Wednesdays, Chicago was able to find some peace during the lull between customers.

He'd switch off the R&B on the radio and put on a cassette with the Mills Brothers, or the Mighty Clouds of Joy, turning down the sound on the small television while "If I Didn't Care" played. He swept up tiny tumbleweeds of hair from the floor, singing to himself.

The other barber grumbled under his breath about 'old head music' while sharpening the edges of a goatee sitting in his chair. There was only one other customer in the shop, and he glared at Chicago, who was blissfully sweeping the scuffed linoleum when he could be cutting hair. The doorbell jangled as a lean young boy in too tight jeans, and dark sunglasses banged open the door with an even younger boy in tow.

The fact that the two were brothers was as clear as the identical egg yolk stains each wore on their dirty white t-shirts. The sleek, angular shapes of their heads, wild swaths of dark hair, skin as smooth as melted chocolate and large bright eyes made the younger child seem like a carbon copy of the older. The older boy pulled the boy by the hand and guided him to sit in a chair. He then looked around, not bothering to remove his sunglasses.

"Swinging Jack around?"

Chicago cocked a brow and growled around the cigar jammed in his teeth. "He stepped out to pick up some shit. He be back in a few. Whyn't you just set for a minute till he get back."

Santos grabbed a *People* magazine from the table and absentmindedly flipped through. The new configuration of Charlie's Angels starred back in all their sultry beauty. Santos pondered the image of Tanya Roberts, flanked by Kate Jackson and Jaclyn Smith. She was beautiful. She almost looked like a light-skinned black girl, with her thick, dark hair and swarthy skin. Her large eyes were made even larger with dark kohl arching up from the corners of slanted eyes toward her thin eyebrows. Her lips were made to look full and pouty with bright red lip stain that echoed the tint that swept up from hollow cheekbones. All three women wore skin-tight lycra tights in metallic hues and slingback stilettos, their long legs crossed and posed like gazelle on an African plain.

This new Angel looked promising. At least she was beautiful enough to stand alongside Chris Munro and Sabrina Duncan, not like that dog Shelly Hack. But Santos was afraid that the glory days of the Angels might be over. He wondered if that meant the same for the three of them. Luq had named them The Mannequins, after the models of the 1950s, but they had always patterned themselves after Charlie's Angels.

It had all started with Dion. Even before Santos and Dion had become friends, he could remember Dion primping around, walking through the school hallways with a paper towel over his dirty hair, rubbing it over his ears and saying "I'm Chris Monroe," or running on the playground with his finger pointed at people like a gun, and hiding behind trees, ignoring the laughter of the other children and the whispers of 'faggot' or 'sugar in his tank.'

Once the three of them became friends later, Dion would always disparage Luq for always giving his opinions and advice where they were not asked for. They would call him Lucy, from the Peanuts comic strip, who always set up a psychiatrist booth for five cents of advice, or Dion would call him Sabrina Duncan.

"Nobody asked you to solve the case, Sabrina!"

"Ain't nobody no manly ass Sabrina. She bald headed. Now Kelly Garrett? Miss Garrett is fierce."

"Yeah, Miss Kelly is cunt! And bitch be fighting! Okay?"

"And that walk. That bitch is class. Not like that skank Chris Monroe. All that bitch do is use her titties to solve the case."

"Oh, now wait, bitch. I know you not talking about me. Miss Monroe is what makes them other bitches look good. If it wasn't for my body, the trade would pay y'all dust. And I'm the blonde in the group, too? Bitch, please. Y'all know don't no man want no bitch unless she is giving you blonde mane! I am serving gold tresses, bitch, and y'all bitches can't take it."

"Bitch, you WISH you looked like Cheryl Ladd..."

"Okay, well, Miss Santos can give you Tiffany Wells. The new cunt."

"Oh hold up, bitch. Ain't nobody want to be ugly ass Shelley Hack. You done lost your mind."

"What? Miss Hack serves.... she was a huge model..."

This allegation always infuriated Luq. "Hold up. Wait a damn minute. Shelley Hack ain't nobody's model. Modeling for motherfucking Revlon used to be fierce, back when Suzy Parker and Dorian were doing it for "Cherries in The Snow," but, bitch, Charlie perfume? I don't think so. Are those commercials for drag queens, with that bitch crawling along the streets in a goddamn PANTSUIT?! That bitch must've been fucking Charles Revson, so he gave her ass a job. She is no Kelly Emberg or LeBrock..."

"Oh shit, here she go with that LeBrock shit again. Bitch, please. Let that go. Kelly is not over, with those big ass nigga lips."

"Don't do it. And look at Shelley's hair. That shit is all thick and unmanageable. It look like she is wearing a wig, all that nigga hair."

"I know, right? She do be serving up gilda."

"And them teeth? Chile, she all kinds of wrong for that hair. And all them motherfuckin' teeth. Grinnin' all hard like she black or something."

"Don't she be cheesin' like she Buckwheat?"

So, compared to Shelly Hack, this Tanya Roberts looked good. And she was tough and had big tits, so Santos was okay with taking her persona. But he just thought it was over for the Angels. They weren't doing it like they did back in the day. He hardly even watched the show anymore.

And he wondered if the same could be said for the Mannequins. Luq wasn't coming into town as much as he used to. They didn't hang out as much as before. Luq had always walked the unlit streets of King of Prussia to get to

Norristown. Now, with those murders happening in Atlanta, he sometimes got paranoid about the walk. They didn't live in Atlanta, but the black magazines, *Jet*, *The Panther*, *Mahogany*, the Philly paper put out by MOVE, all of them told about the disappearing black kids taking place all over the country. It seemed like the kids turning up missing down in Atlanta had got the attention of white people. Then, news people seemed to suddenly care about what was going on. Other than that, nobody seemed to be doing anything about the kids missing in other places.

Even the ways that they used to have fun had changed. Only last year, when CBS, NBC, and ABC first began to talk about the dead bodies in Georgia, Santos and Luq would hang out in the park all night, drinking and talking to the older guys that would wander through, or go down to Lafayette Street and trade barbs with Dion while he waited for a car to slow down and ask him to go for a quick trip. Now, even going off with strangers seemed to carry a hidden question, a threat that hadn't seemed to be there before.

Now, when Dion hopped into a car, they all wondered whether he would return. Dion wondered the same thing and kept a box cutter tucked in his underwear in the event that a transaction turned ugly.

The other people of the night that meandered through the park seemed different too. Earlier, there had been more people coming out. Now, there seemed to be less people hanging out at Miss Richie's and Joe Brown's Bar. When people did stop to talk, they did not linger as long as they used to. Previous summers had found the park filled with lively banter and laughter all through the night and into the first shimmering of daylight. Wina would come through wearing the same belted potato sack dress and cheap Payless pumps that he wore every night, seemingly oblivious to the derision he created with the smear of lipstick drawn in a clearly defined circle on the space on his face that he mistakenly assumed to be the 'apple' of his cheek. He was no longer as talkative as before. Now, seemingly more focused on getting down to Lafayette to make his money than he was on socializing.

The bums that used to sleep on the heated grates in the upper courthouse level were dwindling out. Where there used to be at least the six regulars, there now seemed to be only two or three; Flukey Luke and that young kid that was always bumming for cigarettes were the only two regulars that remained.

Things certainly seemed to have changed. And adding White Girl to the mix seemed to throw their regular dynamic off kilter.

She had gradually insinuated herself. Showing up at the courtyard or down on Lafayette without April in tow, tiny and frail, skirts alarmingly short. She'd ask Santos to walk with her or to stay close by. She said she felt safer if the cars driving by saw a black man not too far off because then it was less likely that trouble would erupt. Especially while she stood out on the street. Miss Richie's posed a constant possibility of trouble, as inebriated men came and went at random, hurling an insult or a lure at the lone blonde girl, seeming to glow against the darkness of night.

Santos felt under some obligation to make sure she was safe, he felt a sense of protectiveness for all the people hanging out downtown, and he had to admit that he felt some sort of egotism that Toni needed him. Besides, she usually broke him off some money at the end of the night.

The problem was that the mere presence of a female, let alone a white one, clearly impaired the possibilities for the rest of the group. Trade was less likely to proposition them with Toni around. Norristown was a small, insular town; the men didn't mind a casual blowjob or fucking around, but they were less inclined to do so when there were possible witnesses. Besides that, if they had the choice between getting their dicks sucked by a faggot or screwing a white girl, they would rather roll the dice and attempt to get some pussy rather than the sure thing of oral sex with a guy.

Although White Girl seemed to rely on Santos as her protector, once he had made it clear that she could not continue to crash at his house, she seemed to gravitate to Luqman. Hell, he didn't mind her crashing, he hated being by himself, and the food sure came in handy, freeing up his money for beer and weed, but that bitch tried to run the show. She thought she could direct every move he made, just because she cleaned up and provided the food. And besides, if Gloria had come home and seen some white bitch in her house, she'd go ape-shit, without a doubt. While it was unlikely that his mother would have found out Toni was there, she almost never entered his room in the limited time she was home between jobs, Santos had given Toni the impression that Gloria was the reason behind Toni being asked to roll.

Sometimes Eddie Lee from across the street would get lonely and knock on the back door late at night, and Santos didn't want Toni fucking that up. After Eddie Lee busted a nut, sometimes he would fall asleep, and wrap his sinewy arms around San, holding him close, breathing Colt 45 fumes against his neck, the bulk of his crotch warm and snug against San's back and his broad palms splayed at his clavicle, spreading a radiating warmth through his whole body.

For Santos, this was the nicest feeling in the world. Everything around quiet and musty, the only sound a light snore as Eddie Lee slept. He felt like he was floating on a cloud.

Funny thing about White Girl and her bossiness, she didn't seem to be that way with Luq. San had never seen her telling him what to do the way she did with Santos. She seemed to always ask his opinion about stuff. And her appearance seemed to change. Her skirts were still short as hell, but now, instead of t-shirts with belts around the waist, she wore actual skirts. Luq had gone through a period where he wore hoods with all his clothes. He had basically sewn tubes out of various printed strips of spandex, through which he would place his head, the cowl draping around his throat. After a few months of being laughed at and called E.T. by Dion and San, he had put the hoods on hiatus. Then, he had brought down a bag of hoods one night and given them to White Girl.

"This used to be hoods, but I think you can wear these as skirts."

They were form fitting. The bold, graphic prints made Toni stand out even more, accentuating her curves. After that, the hoods became a permanent part of her look. Whenever business lagged, or they were in a place where Toni was not getting the attention that she felt she deserved she would use the hood as a threat...

"Don't make me have to go get the hood."

It became a catchphrase for all of them. Just like Dion's, "A girl of my caliber," or "I'm a lady," and Santos', "I'll just take my nickel bag and go home," and Luq's "that's some nigga ass shit."

The bell above the door of Swinging Jack's jangled as the door opened. Santos looked up in anticipation, then his heart lurched.

Yasmin pushed a tiny cart of merchandise in before her amidst a clanking of wooden wrist cuffs and cockle shells dangling from her auburn braids.

"Hey, baby," Chicago growled. It's dead'r 'n a mutherfucker in here today."

Yasmin barely flicked her eyes at him as she undulated toward the two boys sitting against the wall. She stood before them and placed her fists on broad hips.

"What y'all doing up in here in the middle of the day?"

"Just waiting on Swinging Jack…"

Yasmin cut him off with a flick of her bangled wrist. "Uh, uh. What you got this baby in here for? Why ain't he at school? Where Miss Gloria at?"

Santos was glad that he had worn sunglasses. He felt like the sunglasses placed a wall between him and his sister in law. "His school ain't open today. They had a teacher's in-service."

"Boy, you think my head screws off? Y'all both got in service the same day? You get on out here and take that baby on to school, right now, for I call your mom! Go on, now."

Santos sucked his teeth and tugged Jonas out of the chair. "Fucking nosey ass bit…"

"You saying something!" Yasmin screamed.

He brushed past her, deliberately bumping her as he passed, grumbling, "Get your fat ass out the way, then."

He picked up his pace, his timing just right to avoid the hand that came swinging toward the back of his head.

Chicago lurched as the door slammed shut like a gunshot. He shook his head, laughing around his cigar. "Little man pissed off. Why you fucking with his get high?"

Yasmin sucked her teeth. "Get high, my ass. I don't give a shit what that boy does. He's already a lost cause. But to be carrying that baby around with him instead of taking him to school.... God knows what that boy be doing running around here like a wild animal, hanging with that other one...that, that...the town faggot..., but he don't need to be taking that baby with him, witnessing God knows what."

"Well, what you expect, child running 'round in the streets. You know his mama work hard to keep a roof over they head. She got to go where the money is. Gloria ain't never been one to lay around waitin' on no check, having the white man all up in her business."

"I know that. She could have at least told me. Asked me to check up on them, make sure the little one gets to school."

"Yeah," he arched a brow. "You could take 'em in wit' you and Nini while she gone. He working now, right?"

Yasmin sucked her teeth. "Wish I would. I got enough trouble taking care of his black ass, let alone babysitting his brothers while he out fucking his other bitch! Eh!"

Chicago shook his head in wonder.

Killing in Earnest

The lull came to a nasty end on March 4, 1980, when twelve-year-old Angel Lenair finished her homework and left her apartment in southwest Atlanta. When she didn't come home for her favorite television show, her mother, Venus Taylor, called the police. As Angel was approaching puberty, her mother worried more and more. Their home was near Fort McPherson and men were starting to take an interest in Angel.

Venus Taylor's worst fears were confirmed on March 10, 1980, when the police found Angel's body tied to a tree with an electrical cord around her neck and a pair of panties that did not belong to Angel stuffed in her mouth.

Cause of death was asphyxiation by strangulation with the electrical cord. Although Angel's hymen had been broken and there were some minor abrasions in the genital area, the medical examiner did not interpret those facts to mean evidence of sexual assault. Those findings became controversial and did not mean that Angel was not the victim of some sexual abuse.

This particular case was quite different than the previous cases, in that the victim was female and her body was found under different circumstances that the previous male victims. There were two suspects, who were eventually cleared of the murder.

The very next day after Angel's body was found, Jeffery Mathis, aged ten, had left his home to buy cigarettes for his mother in the early evening.....a few blocks away from his home. His mother Willie Mae Mathis became worried when he was gone over an hour and sent her other sons to look for him. Later that night, a patrolman told Mrs. Mathis to call the missing person's department if he did not come home by morning.

What she did not immediately understand when she contacted that department the next day is that the missing persons' department...did very little to investigate the disappearance of young people. It was assumed that children and teenagers were runaways and not the victims of foul play.

Jeffery had last been seen by a friend getting into the backseat of a blue car, possibly a Buick. Thirteen days after Mathis had gone missing, Willie Turner, who had recognized Mathis' picture from the newspaper, claimed that he saw Jeffery in a blue Nova car, driven by a white adult man. Willie Turner also told police that the man he had seen with Mathis had later in the week pulled a gun on him before taking off in his car. Police did little in response to the information given by Turner. The report was filed away and forgotten. The blue car that was earlier seen by Mathis' friend in connection with Jeffery's disappearance was very similar to the description of a car seen by an eyewitness in a later disappearance case of a boy name Aaron Wyche.

http://www.crimelibary.com/serial_killers/predators/williams/earnest_3.html

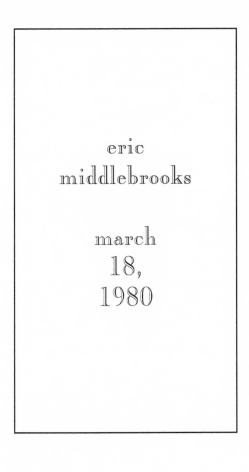

eric
middlebrooks

march
18,
1980

They got a message from the Action Man
"I'm happy, hope you're happy too
I've loved
All I've needed to love
Sordid details following"

I've never done good things
I've never done bad things
I never did anything out of the blue
Want an axe to break the ice
Wanna come down right now

Ashes to Ashes, funk to funky
We know Major Tom's a junky
Strung out in heaven's high
Hitting an all-time low

My mother said
To get things done
You'd better not mess
With Major Tom

-Ashes to Ashes by David Bowie

LUQMAN

He was bored. He just didn't know how to describe it. Bored with school, where no one bothered to teach. Where no one spoke to him, one of the seven black kids in a student body of 435. Living in a town where the only social outlets were intramural sports activities or the mall. Where nothing in his life looked like what he expected it to look like. Where clothes were cheap and garish. Where hairstyles were fluffy and voluminous, and the songs on the radio were bland and monotonous.

Nothing seemed to be the way that he dreamed of from the descriptions he read in books. The girls roaming through the malls did not look like Pat Cleveland and Wanakee. They did not wear Montana and Miyake. Their eyes were not large and sad like Joan Crawford and Bette Davis. Nobody had Bette Davis eyes. Nobody flung their hair back and blew out tufts of dramatic cigarette smoke.

People went to work in their Fiestas and Tauruses, too busy to see that their children were restless, dying. Unaware that the schools they sent them off too were war zones where the most heinous things happened.

Every now and then, a song came on the radio, or a video played on the television that hinted that there were exciting things in the world. Between a set of the same ten songs in droning rotation would come a song from David Bowie, or Madness, or The Specials that didn't sound like everything else. This music promised a world of adventure and excitement. The videos showed exotic people in faraway places, in lands that did not look like malls, where hairstyles stood out in spiky protest of the banality of everyday life, men rimmed their eyes in dark kohl. Where women flaunted bare shoulders, wore dresses with huge polka dots, and marked the hollows of their cheeks in berry stains.

The people in these videos were like aliens from another planet. They danced in a stiff, herky-jerky motion, with flailing elbows and twisted knees. They did not whisper 'dinge' when you walked past in the halls. They didn't push their tongues out against their upper lips to imitate nigger lips. Nobody talked about niggers, people just danced and sang, and lived lives where they went to clubs and drove through decimated landscapes searching for the next club or the next fashion shoot, or the next big thing.

ALICE

Coming into Norristown from King of Prussia on roller skates was no problem. It was all downhill coming off 23 East. The trip back, on the other hand, was no joke. Especially considering that the shoulder was not smoothly paved, but more gravel.

So, after skating through Bridgeport late at night, Luq removed his skates, tied the shoe strings in a knot and lugged them over his shoulder. His socks were very thick, almost like leg warmers, so even though he was not accustomed to walking barefoot, and even though it was kind of cold, he figured he'd be okay.

The skates were quite heavy across his shoulders. In addition, he carried a boom box, which he alternated from right to left when one got tired of the dragging heft. He excitedly turned to volume up as the first synth chords of "Cars" began to play. He was glad when a song he liked played during his two-mile trek back home; it made the walk go quicker.

Whenever he walked this road at night with Santos or Dion, they bitched about the darkness. Most of King of Prussia did not have street lights or sidewalks. For people accustomed to those amenities, the lack thereof could be extremely jarring. Added to that, Route 23 ran alongside railroad property, so there were lots of trees and quarries just below the stretch of partially finished highway, with the Schuylkill River garrulously murmuring in the background.

Luq felt safer on the darkened streets than the brightly lit sidewalks of Norristown. Here, at least you could silently fade into the darkness at the hint of trouble, get lost in the shadows, be less of a target. The only problem for him were the possums that meandered about and the skunks. The skunks in King of Prussia were not the kind he had learned about in school, where if you left them alone they would leave you alone. These skunks were aggressive. They would actually chase you down as if you had done them some grievous harm. There had been many instances where Luq had run screaming from a boldly spraying skunk trundling along at his feet.

There were also the bats. They would come swooping down from treetops, pitching perilously close to the Aqua Netted spikes of Luq's head, causing him to duck and swing his arms in panic. The last thing he needed was some rat with wings getting snagged in his hair.

The sound of rubber kicking up the gravel along the shoulder brought him out of his revelry, as a police squad car sped swiftly past him, swooping sideways in front of him with a short skid of brakes. Luq stopped short with a brief thought of curiosity, which quickly turned to dread as a blinding light beamed from the open window.

"Don't move!" a disembodied voice bellowed from the darkness inside.

Luq shrugged the roller-skates to a more comfortable location and turned the volume of his radio down. He walked toward the window, "I'm just walking h---"

"Do Not Move!"

There was a flourish of sounds; metal and leather clanked and squeaked as the burly squadman scrambled out of the car, his nightstick banking on the door frame as he slammed it shut behind him. "Stand back. Stand back."

The officer did a casual assessment as Luq rocked back on one heel, jutting out one narrow hip. The beam of the flashlight began a slow descent, beginning at the spiked hair, moving down to the skinny arms encased in the long sleeves of a thermal shirt. Over that was an outsized t-shirt with brightly colored flowers bordering an image of the Virgin Mary holding a bleeding baby. A large leather belt held pegged legged pants high on the waist. The pants had large sailboats scattered across them, with a large triangle of black velvet across the crotch. The kid's feet were bare except for large bright green socks that looked like the sleeves of a cable knit sweater.

"Sit."

Luq raised a bushy brow. "Huh?"

"Sit down. Spread your legs out in front of you."

Luq reluctantly lowered himself to the uncomfortable gravel.

"You wanna turn that ghetto blaster down, homes?"

"I already did," Luq replied. He turned the radio off and sat it on his lap in an attempt to obscure his pants. When he had made them, he had run a bit short of fabric, and so he added a bit of black velvet at the crotch. At the time, and earlier today, when he put them on to head into town, he had thought the idea was ingenious. Now, with the officer's flashlight looming over him, he felt a bit silly.

Luq looked off as another squadman lurched out of the car. He wondered what the hell had taken this one so long to get out of the car.

"What you doing with those skates?"

"Going home."

"Where's home?"

"King of Prussia."

"King of Prussia, huh? Where at in King of Prussia."

"Up the street..."

The officer cut him off, yelling. "Don't be a smart ass! What address do you live at!"

"One forty-one Cambridge Road..."

"Uh huh. How long you lived there?"

Luq shrugged.

"Where you coming from?"

"Norristown."

"Yeah?" the flashlight beamed on his skates. "Just thought you'd pick up some skates on your way?"

Luq was confused. "What do you mean?"

"What's with these pants?" The light scanned along his body. "What do you call that hair."

"I can't skate up this hill, so I had to walk."

"Where were you going to in Norristown?"

Luq paused. How to answer? It's not like he was really 'doing' anything when he went to Norristown. What he was 'doing,' really was nothing more than getting away from the boredom and monotony of home.

"I was at my Aunt's."

"What's her address?"

"Uh, 822 Cherry..."

"She married?"

What the fuck did he want to know that for? "Divorced"

"So you been running around here like a wild animal, stealing property from hard-working folks."

"Uh. These skates are mine. They were bought for my birthday. I skated to town, but I can't skate back home. That's why I don't have shoes!"

"Check that attitude, homes. You got any ID?"

"What kind of ID? I got my school ID..." just then, a car drove past, slowing down to observe the tableau of two cops standing with splayed legs over a young boy with no shoes sitting on the ground, before speeding away.

"Okay. Get on home. Fast. Don't let me catch you roaming around here again."

Just as Dion's Chinese slipper touched down on the asphalt of Lafayette Street, car tires squealed alarmingly close. Blue and red lights swirled past his face. He stepped back up on the curb and stealthily moved the meager wad of money from his purse to his bra as he watched the tall black man loom from the squad car. He grabbed a cigarette from his purse and lit it, trying to stop his hand from trembling as he did so.

Avery was the lone black man on Norristown's police force and had the reputation in the black community of being the worst one to have to deal with. He was six feet five inches tall and still maintained the massive build attained as a high school athlete. Dion blew out a tuft of smoke and placed the cigarette back in his mouth with a grand flourish.

Avery smacked the cigarette from his lips with a broad palm. "Put that shit out!"

He grabbed Dion by the shoulder and pushed him toward the open door of the car. Dion whined, "What? I didn't do nothing."

"Shut the fuck up." Dion quickly scooted over as Avery's crotch loomed in the doorway. "Didn't I tell you not to bring your black ass down here, harassing good folks on a Friday night."

"I'm just on my way to the Chicken Licken to get my mom a basket...."

"And if you try and bullshit me I'm a stick this club down your lying throat." He snatched the battered cloth purse out of Dion's hands and ripped it open. "What we got here? Better not be no paraphernalia or your ass gonna spend the night shivering your nuts off at the county."

"No, sir. Officer, sir. No drugs, sir."

Avery looked up from his inventory of the purse with suspicion, trying to determine if Dion was being serious or mocking him. He threw balled up tissues and a pack of Newports and a Bic lighter onto the pavement. "The fuck....?"

He raised his hand holding a small jar of Vaseline, with no lid, the soiled rim caked with lint and debris. When he realized what he was holding, he threw it down with a sound of disgust.

"You disgusting fucking..."

He removed his gun and aimed it at Dion's head. "I should blow your fucking head off... Godamn freak. Dion looked off at the other side of the window as if he were watching passing pastures from the Suburban Line railcar. Suddenly, Avery wrenched a hand into the collar of Dion's shirt, snatching money out of the bra.

"Hey!"

"Shut the fuck up!" Dion grabbed the water balloons that tumbled across the seat while Avery counted the money in his hand.

"Now get your black ass out of here before I take you to your maker, whoever that is."

"What about my mon..."

"You hear me? The fuck outta here, NOW!"

Dion scampered across the seat, sidled past Avery and dashed into the shadows of Airy Street, screaming behind him, "Black motherfucker! Some cousin!"

Santos wasn't giving much attention to the street before him. His head was bent over the latest issue of *Right On!* magazine. He was reading about the ways that Jayne and Leon Issac Kennedy kept their marriage exciting and fresh by always surprising each other with gifts and going to new places to eat. Santos added his own interpretation to the story. Judging from all the sex that took place in Leon's movies, he assumed a good deal of the magic was kept intact with a bit of dick and some freaky deaky three-way action.

The squeal of tires took his attention from the magazine to the street. A police car stopped before him.

Santos' heart skipped. While he had not done anything, he couldn't take a chance that the cops would want to contact his mother, who was not home. Not being able to reach Gloria could lead to a host of other problems, like the intrusion of Child Protective Services or Children and Youth.

After weighing the pros and cons, as the officer opened the door to the squad car, Santos spun on his Converse and sped off down Swede Street.

LUQMAN

Officer Burton looked through the glass panel of the door into interrogation room one. The bombastic voice of the chief rang in his ear as he placed a sweaty palm on the doorknob, "You get your ass in there, and you make this shit right. We don't need no trouble from the taxpayers of this township!"

He observed the tall, skinny youth pacing at the back of the room. He had shaved triangles in the sides of his head and wore a huge crimson colored sweatshirt and narrow black pants with three belts looped at his hip. Officer Burton's eyes did a cursory sweep of the black man sitting at the interrogation table; he didn't really give him much attention, other than the instinctive run through in his head to match him with black men in the area known to have warrants. Once he came to the conclusion that the man was not wanted, he was ignored.

Beside the man sat a woman with skin like warm coffee. Even from the window, Burton could see the fury flashing from large brown eyes. He entered the room and nodded as the woman placed those fiery eyes on him. "Mr. and Mrs. Ettinger. Hello. I am Officer Burton. Pleased to make your acquaintance."

Carol Ettinger crossed shapely legs with a hiss of burgundy nylon, a knee thrusting through the slit in her white wool skirt. Both she and Ambrose watched as Burton approached with a supercilious smile and stretched out a hand in greeting.

Carol made a subtle shift in her chin, flinging back tumultuous hair and deliberately crossing her arms across her ample bosom. Burton's hand wavered in the air for a moment, then Ambrose reached around his wife and shook his hand.

"How you doing, my man."

Burton could almost feel a heat emanating from the woman as he sat in the chair on the opposite side of the table. The boy standing behind them leaned against the back wall and observed with a remote expression.

Carol grimaced full berry colored lips and leaned forward, taping a darkly polished fingernail on the metal table.

"Officer.... Bird, was it?"

"Burton."

"Okay. I am late for work, so let me get right to the point." She pointed jerkily behind her shoulder. "That is my son. Luqman. This is my husband, Ambrose. We have lived here for two years now. In those two years, this department has delayed my children numerous times in their travels. Going to the school fair, going to band practice, while at the store, while walking home, while waiting on the bus. They have had to explain their presence in this neighborhood. So we are here to give you the only explanation we are going to give you as to why my black children are in this neighborhood; we live here."

"Oh no, Mrs. Ettinger, I assure you..."

Carol held up a hand. "I haven't finished; thank you. The other night, my son was stopped and accused of stealing a pair of rollerskates because he had them in his possession."

At that, Carol reached into her handbag and hurled a receipt onto the table. "This, Officer Bird, is the receipt for those skates. Please make sure that the Upper Merion Police Department are made aware that my children are not thieves. They do not steal. They all have jobs. Last year Luqman was a paperboy. One of the customers that he delivered to was the Upper Merion Police Department. Perhaps someone might remember his face if you took a look at him."

Carol stood swiftly. She moved her head imperceptively, and Ambrose rose as well. Luq walked over and followed his mother as she headed to the door.

"So I trust we will have no more issues here. Or my next visit will be down the street to my congressman's office. You have a great day."

The door slammed like a gunshot.

chris
richardson

latonya
wilson

june
9,
1980

june
22,
1980

FLUKEY LUKE

The towering walls of First Pennsylvania Bank cast a long column of shade along the alley that abutted the Norristown Post Office. The old man felt a bit of relief there in the shadows, out of the harsh glare of the midsummer day. His nose twitched at the acrid smell of garbage covering his feet. He reached for a Styrofoam container lodged beneath a heavy trash bag, opening it to find a rancid piece of meat and a partially eaten Kaiser roll. He glared with consideration at the roll, tossed aside the rest of the container and pocketed the bread in the deep pocket of his overcoat.

It was a very paltry offering, but it was too early in the day. He knew that he'd have had better luck had he waited until afternoon when the attorneys, civilians, and business workers in the downtown area finished with lunch, but he had not had any success finding a meal the previous night, so he had hoped his lucky dumpster might offer something. This was better than nothing.

He grunted at the currents of pain that shot through his knees as he clambered back onto the sidewalk. He grabbed the makeshift knapsack; an old raincoat tied with belts that held his possessions and headed up to Airy Street. He accidentally looked at his reflection as he passed a parked car and silently recoiled. He'd never get used to this. Seeing a body so out of accordance with the way that he thought of himself. A face that had once been sharp and angular now bulbous and undulating with growths. A body riddled with ailments, that used to work twelve hours cultivating Macon County soil and then another six drinking and looking for a firm young body to spend the night with.

The slowing down of his body had been a gradual one. So slow that he had not even been aware of it happening. Back home, in Georgia, the doctors had called it bad blood. Some days when he would be so fatigued that he could barely get out of bed. Other days he would be just fine.

Seemed like bad blood was something in the water or something in the soil. So many of the men back home had come down with it. So many that doctors came down from Washington, DC to take a look at things.

The old man turned left on Airy Street and turned into the upper courtyard of the municipal building. He was tired. It would be so good to be able to lay down and feel the warm air from the grate on his tired bones. But he knew better. People like him did better not to make a nuisance of themselves during business hours, lest they risk drawing attention of the police. That never led to a good outcome. The man had a missing tooth as evidence of what being visible at the wrong time could lead to.

Bad blood. That, too, had led to a bad outcome. Oh, at first things had been great. The doctors came in from

Washington with their bright white coats and shining instruments. The first colored nurse he had ever laid eyes on smiled with those pearly white teeth, her uniform sitting on her curves like foam on a wave, "this won't even hurt," she'd say, and prick you with a hypo while you looked at the swell of her bosom spilling generously against your arm.

The promises had been great: doctors looking at your health regularly, free meals on consult days, and the best thing; burial insurance. To be able to put away in style, without your family being stuck trying to scrape up the pennies to do it, that was something every sharecropper in the state could envy. But as the years had passed, it seemed like the medical attention wasn't doing much good. Instead of getting better, it seemed that things were getting worse. Small sores and lesions disappeared, only to come back later as a rash across the whole back or pustules on the hands and feet. Men that once single-handedly harvested their own crop could barely guide a mule down a trench, forgot their children's names, wandered off from home.

Soon, the men from DC were not partners, they were bosses; telling you what you could and could not do, just like the white men that owned the patch of land that you cultivated. They told you that you could not join the army because you needed to be available for examinations. You could not move, in fact, you could not leave the state to visit family without first getting approval from the nurse on site, so that your whereabouts were traceable, 'for the public good.'

The old man blamed only himself. What good had ever come from trusting a smiling white face, especially if they were giving something away?

He meandered down the steps into the lower level park, standing at the crest that cast a view of the business people making mad dashes toward the buses and trains humming at rest in their hubs.

The man began to mumble to himself, shaking his head to clear the ghosts away. But it was not ghost. It was as if the past had stepped into the present. Oh, it wasn't exactly the same, the figure wasn't as fine, the breasts weren't saluting at attention as they had been back then, but the hips still swayed the same, and the smile still illuminated the dawn.

Herwhatwasshedoingherethatfuckingbitchnursebitchnigga bitchdoingthewhitemansworkkillingherownkindshootingthem upwithdiseasewhilesherubshertittiesonyourarmfuckingbitch!

The commuters walking down the park stairs toward the trains made a wide berth around the babbling homeless man as they went about their day.

WILDING OUT

It was not often that Luq ventured into town on a Friday night before 9 pm. There was usually more time required to style his hair into a look earmarked in an international magazine, or some last minute stitches to a pair of pants. He had not taken time for additional flourishes tonight. A gigantic orange tie-dyed t-shirt over jeans with huge gashes at the knee was all he wore.

He clambered into the dirty entryway of the Norristown High Speed Line depot, sat on the steps and removed his roller-skates. He tied the laces together and hung them around his shoulders, taking a pair of Converse from a backpack and putting them on. He wiped his forehead and stood at the glass door, taking in the anemic spurts of air conditioning wheezing through the ancient vents, looking out onto the traffic on Main Street, searching for Dion or Santos to come ambling down the hill from Swede.

Instead, a very tall brown-skinned man with a well-manicured afro and a prominent nose came around the corner and stood right in front of the glass doorway, blocking Luq's line of sight. He recognized the man as Jewel Carol, whom Dion always commented upon with a reference to his much talked about, some would say legendary, penis size.

Jewel looked briefly at Luq with heavily hooded eyes, tucked his hands into his baggy pants and turned back to his surveillance of the street.

Luq still found it curious that so many men with girlfriends were always out on the prowl to have sex with other men. It almost seemed like it was done out of boredom; like jacking off or reading a comic book, you didn't have anything else to do, so what the hell. These guys were certainly not gay, in fact, they were just as likely to kick your ass as ask you to suck their dick, many times both things happened. Many times they also asked for money to get a beer or cigarettes. The straight boys were known to hang in the park just as much as the not so straight boys. Many times their presence in the park led to fights, or to the arrival of the police.

Luq smiled as White Girl walked past the doors. She wore a white satiny dress and too much makeup. Luq opened the door and hooted at her. Toni jumped, then smiled as he came out to greet her.

"I didn't see you in there."

"I know. Where's everybody at?"

Toni shrugged, rifling through her purse. Jewel turned to observe them. Luq watched his eyes do a casual perusal from her red spiked heels, rest briefly at her ass, and then complete its search. "I talked to San; he said he'd be down here around this time. You know Miss D was probably out as soon as the sun went down...hey, I'm out of cigarettes. You want to walk me down to the bar?"

"You know I can't go in there. I'll wait here."

He watched as she sashayed somewhat precariously down the slope to Joe Brown's. Jewel also watched her descent, walking over toward him and leaning somewhat drunkenly against him.

"Yo' man, you know that bitch?"

Luq moved imperceptibly, not bothering to answer, shifting the weight of the skates hanging from his neck. Although he had seen Jewel down here many times, had seen him go off with both Dion and Santos at different times, they had never conversed before, so this sudden shift in dynamic made him leery. Jewel continued talking as if the two were engaged in a conversation.

"Yeah. I seen that bitch down here before. She be banking. She probably got a wad on her right now. You get her to walk down on Lafayette? Down the back the bar where it's dark, and we can split the money. Where she got it? I bet you she got it tucked down her panties. You get her to walk with you, man. I'll take care of the rest. Then just meet me up the top of the hill, and I'll break you off."

From his perch in the upper level of the courtyard, Santos watched as Jewel gesticulated animatedly toward Luq. Santos had known that some bullshit would be going down tonight as soon as he spotted Jewel standing out on Main Street. He had decided to keep a distance away and observe for a while just to be sure how things were going to go before he headed down. Then, when he saw White Girl show up, he definitely decided to stay away. He had no intentions of babysitting tonight.

He took out a toothpick sized joint and lit it, the pungent funk a comforting addition to the humid night air undulating through the elm trees. He watched Luq walk off from Jewel, heading down the hill in the direction that Toni had gone.

Not long after that, he saw Melvin and Floyd approach. His heart pitched. Now he knew for certain that there would be some problems this night. Melvin and Floyd were two of the biggest troublemakers at school. They were the main reason that San rarely even went to school, and the reason that Dion had been transferred to the Pathway School, the same school that Jonas went to.

San hoped that Dion wasn't down on Lafayette Street, or things were about to get real ugly.

The modulated bleating of Teena Marie blared from the jukebox with metallic bombast. Even though she preferred rap or the Minneapolis sound, White Girl leaned over the cigarette machine with one arm across the top and shook her hips while she searched for her brand. She knew that she was the focal point of attention and her actions were based upon that assumption. The amber lights from the dimly lit bar shone on her hair, her dress, her skin; making her look like some sort of apparition.

The door banged open, and all eyes turned to the thin boy with shaved incisions in the side of his head.

"Hey, you can't be in here unless you got ID."

Luq stood very close to Toni, so close she could feel him trembling.

"Hey. I thought you were waiting up at the..."

"You got any money?"

"Yeah. What you need?"

"No. All your money. Where do you keep it? Is it in your bag?"

She smiled, confused. No. You crazy? I keep it in my ..."

"Let me hold it for you, all of it. Just give it here. And follow me. We're going out the back. I'll explain when we get out of here." He grabbed her arm and pulled her past the gawking celebrants, down the narrow pathway and back past the small bathrooms, reeking of urine, and to the back door. Here, he turned and held out his hand. Now both of them were shaking. She removed the cash from her bra and Luq placed it in his rolled down socks. He then pulled her toward the door and peeked out.

"Okay. Let's walk. Keep it fast, and don't look back."

"What the fuck is going on?"

He took a large skullcap from his bag and held it out to her. "Put this on, cover your hair."

And they were off. Down the narrow, dark alley, through puddles of piss, out onto Lafayette, they pitched left and ran down until they reached a narrow pass-through by the Irish Pub, up through the side entrance of the courthouse, and out onto Airy Street before tearing into an outright sprint.

At the base of the massive granite steps Toni screeched, "Wait!"

Luq stopped and looked at her. Her eyes were huge green saucers. She grabbed his shoulders, putting her weight on him and quickly kicked off her shoes. She then nodded to him, and they dashed up the steps, past the promenade and up through the pitch black of the unlit churchyard cemetery. The relative safety of the dark space allowed them to slow down to a brisk walk.

"Okay," Toni gasped, leaning on a mossy headstone, "Where the fuck are we going?"

She pulled her elbow from his grasp and sat back on her haunches.

Luq looked down. He adjusted the heavy skates, panting. "I was heading to San's. There's no telling if Jewel will come through here."

Toni stood, her body rigid with fear. "So what's going on?"

"That guy that was eyeing you down at the P and W? He wanted to rob you. He was going to grab you when you came out the bar."

Toni began walking again, linking her arm through Luq's. "Okay. Let's go."

Luq could feel her rapid heartbeat as she leaned against him. He could feel her breath coming in rapid paroxysms from her nose against his arm. He tried to make light of the situation. "Hey, it's no biggie. You just have to stay out of sight for the night. It's not like dude is going to be gunning for you every night. He's so dumb he will have forgotten all about it by tomorrow. I hear his brain doesn't get sufficient oxygen because all the blood is needed elsewhere..."

Toni didn't laugh. "Wasn't that a line in *Daddy Was a Number Runner*?"

Luq stopped briefly to stare down in incredulity. "Wait a minute. You know that book? That is, like, one of my favorite books ever."

"Well, I wouldn't be bragging about that, but yeah, I read it."

"I know you're not trying to diss my book. What's your favorite, like, *Gone with the Wind*, or some shit?"

"Okay. It's going to be like that, again? More with the white girl jabs, but now it's the low key type jabs? I'm just saying your book was really just a rip off of *A Tree Grows in Brooklyn*, but with niggas instead of Jews."

Luq snorted. "That book wasn't about Jews. They were Catholics."

"Yeah, but a lot of what was going on described the Jews living in Williamsburg at the time."

"So you're a reader, too, huh? I wouldn't have thought."

"Why not? 'Cause I'm down here on the strip?"

"Well..."

"Ain't you down there, too?"

"Yeah, but I'm not doing anything. I'm just hanging out."

Toni laughed. "So am I. I'm just hanging out, too. It's not like it's a job or something. It's just something to do. Like smoking a joint or snorting crank. To take away the boredom. It's not like I love dick or something."

"So why do it then? I mean, why not just hang out? Why go off with guys?"

"I don't love dick. But I do love money." They both laughed. Their walking had slowed to a leisurely pace as they meandered down Chestnut Street toward San's house. "Money is power. The only way to get the things you want, and to get people to notice you, is to have enough money to get their attention. My mom kicked me out of the house when I was fourteen. I told her that her old man was raping me, and she told me to get the fuck out her house. She acted like she hadn't known before, but she knew. It started when I was twelve. But he would give me money to shut me up. And I would give that money to her. That would shut her up. She looked the other way because she wanted that money. Money is a way to get people to do what you want them to do."

"So who do you live with now?"

"I been hitchhiking around the country ever since I got kicked out. I started out in Ohio and went west. I lived in Vegas, Oakland, then went over to Houston, Atlanta, up toward Philly...that's where I met April. She convinced me to come to this buttfuck town. Guess it's safer than the cities. Can't make as much money here, but it's also a lot cheaper to live."

They walked past the front of San's house into the side alley, through the small yard, and sat on the back stairs.

"You don't have brothers and sisters?"

"Nah. It's just me. I lived with my grands for a little while. They actually raised me. When I was a baby, my mom left me on their doorstep. She was too busy in the streets to raise me. I went back to them for a little while when I ran out of money, but once I started messing around with black guys. Well, that was a no-no."

Both turned at the sound of a muffled skirmish coming from the doorway. Jonas opened the door, his eyes clotted with sleep. Seeing Luq, he approached and sat between the two of them, laying his head in Luq's lap and sucking his thumb.

"Hey, man. Santos here?" he removed the skates and chucked them on the concrete with a grunt.

Jonas shook his head.

Luq scratched his head and peered hard at Toni. "Okay. So money. But aren't you scared of going off with people you don't know, and with nobody having your back? You haven't heard about all those kids missing down in Atlanta?"

"Nah. What about them?"

Luq shifted his hips off the step and pulled a tattered piece of newsprint from his back pocket. He unfolded it, while Jonas attempted to see what the paper contained. Toni chuckled.

"You carry newspaper clippings around in your pocket?"

He laughed. "Listen, there's no telling what I have in this backpack. Books, cassettes, back up shoes, a seam ripper, to fuck up somebody that gets wrong. I'm a long way from home."

He leaned closer to Toni, who squinted, pretending to be able to see the newsprint without the eyeglasses left at home in order to increase her marketability on the street. Jonas jostled around on Luq's lap, bumping the top of his head into Luq's chin.

"Seven-year-old LaTonya Yvette Wilson was reported abducted June 22, 1980, from her home. This is one of many reports of missing children in the Atlanta, Georgia vicinity over the past year. Where this report differs from the others is that most reports involved young male street youth or vagrants. The similarity is that this child was also a resident of the low-income housing projects in the area. Wilson was reportedly seen by neighbor Gladys Durden being carried by an unidentified male through the back door of her parents housing unit at 7 am. She was wearing a slip and white panties. It was reported that the man was seen climbing into the window four times through the night. The unidentified man was then seen carrying LaTonya in his arms while talking to another black male in the parking lot before getting into a dark colored, late model van and driving off."

Luq finished reading in a whisper before folding up the clipping and replacing it in his back pocket.

Toni burst into laughter. "First of all, that is the most craziest sounding shit I have ever heard. Dude climbed in the motherfucking window four times and then carried this chick out on his shoulder and was in the parking lot just chatting with some other nigga? Does that sound real to you? These papers just put the craziest shit out, trying to get some attention."

Luq laughed, too. "Right? And why everybody black has to live in the projects? Are there that many projects out there in the world? I don't know one person living in the projects, not one. But every story you read or hear that has black people in it has them coming out the projects."

"Me neither! And trust me when I tell you, I know niggas..."

"Okay. Yeah, the story is crazy. But the facts are still there. The press never gets the details right when it comes to black people, 'cause they don't give a shit about the details. Most times there's the white people version, and then the truth, which you can sometimes get in bits and pieces through word on the street. But the facts are this girl was taken from her house by some man in a van. This isn't, like, something that happens once in a lifetime, you know? Black kids are being killed, or just disappearing every day all over this country, and nobody is even saying anything about it. They only saying a little bit right now about Atlanta because somebody is getting sloppy and these bodies are being found. And shit, everybody knows these old guys all over the country be luring kids into these vans that ain't nothing more than a whore house on wheels."

"Yeah. All kinds of shit going down in those vans, right?"

"Dion told me he got in this one van and there was already some naked girl strapped down in there, and he said it smelled like shit and bleach. He said he did a pirouette and hauled ass out of there."

Toni snorted. "He turned down some coins? I don't think so..."

"Now you know he don't do no type of seafood. When he saw snatch laid out on shag carpet, I have no doubt he was like, 'check, please!'"

They both laughed. "Right, right. Well, while all that is bad, there's two things that work in my favor: this ain't Atlanta, and I ain't black."

Luq glared at her. He was offended, but he didn't know why, since what she said was true.

132

Dion's Chinese flats slapped against the hard concrete as he passed the parking lot that housed cars for the lone apartment building along Lafayette Street. He dug into his jeans in search of a lighter, but the only item therein was a slim box cutter. Looking down the expanse of tarmac, he saw no cars or people about and decided to go up to the courtyard to see if anyone was hanging around up there.

He then heard a short, clipped hoot. He smiled, recognizing San's non-verbal trademark, and looked around, expecting to see him saunter around a corner. When San hooted a second time without showing up, Dion looked across the street at the trees and shrubbery of the Reading Railroad property, wondering if Santos was hiding over there.

Dion calculated whether he might have enough time to run across the street before whatever impending dilemma appeared, and decided not to risk it. He quietly meandered back toward the parking lot and squatted behind a parked car.

He didn't realize Melvin was standing behind him until he heard him laugh.

"Damn. You always in the same position," he bumped his crotch into the back of Dion's head. Dion jumped up and walked out into the light as Floyd and Jewel came out from behind two other cars.

"What's up, guys? I was hiding from my cousin; he's down here looking for me..." Dion assessed the scene: if any of these three were down here alone, he would have had a better chance that minimal violence would occur. All three of these guys were known to periodically come downtown, late night when few witnesses were around, to get their dicks sucked and then follow up with a request for money for beer and cigarettes. But that was only when traveling alone. When they were together, their agenda was entirely different.

Wilding out they called it; just hanging out on a weekend night, looking to get into some mischief. Taking some money. Looking for some dumbass girl from school, trying to get her to hang out and drink a little beer so they could sneak a little pussy, snatching an old woman's bag, throwing rocks at a faggot, stealing bikes, whatever.

Across the street in the brush, Santos cursed to himself. This dumb bitch had walked right into their hands. Now he would have to come out. He rose and jogged across the street toward them.

Dion had his change purse splayed open for all to see. "I told y'all I don't have no money. I just got down here. If y'all come back in a few, I can break you off..."

"Shut the fuck up!" Jewel snapped. "You full of shit. How you gonna have money in a few? Broke ass faggot."

As Santos neared the tableau, something about the position of all four boys jogged a segment of his memory. He was suddenly not standing on Lafayette Street. He was back in sixth grade, in Gotwals Elementary.

He had skipped out while Miss Cook's back was turned toward the board so that he could catch a quick smoke in the boy's room.

"You full of shit. Broke ass faggot." He recognized Jewel Caroll's voice reverberating off the white bathroom tiles as he entered the boy's room. He slowed down, staying behind the metal partition between the door and the stalls so that no one inside the bathroom could see him.

He could hear wet noises. The sound of someone sniffling back tears, along with another, more carnal wet sound, and laughter. "Eww. You crazy, Jewel. That's some nasty shit."

Jewel laughed. Santos recognized the other voice belonging to Floyd. He slowly peered around the partition. He saw the rotund body of Dion, his gray pants bundled about his feet, with Jewel, Floyd, and Melvin surrounding him. Floyd was laughing, his face a mask of vitriolic glee, as he pressed a pair of nun-chucks between Dion's exposed ass cheeks.

Jewel had his large appendage exposed from his fly, inserted into Dion's mouth, and was lightly slapping his face while he pushed himself further and further into Dion's mouth.

"What you gagging for? You like this shit don't you. Running around here saying you a girl and shit..."

Melvin laughed and unzipped his pants. "Let me get some too, man."

Dion flailed behind him, pushing at the nunchucks, and Floyd punched him in the back of the head. "Git your dirty ass hands off my shit, man. You know you like this shit, faggot ass."

From his post behind the partition, Santos swung out a leg and kicked at the door, while banging his fists on the wooden barrier, shouting, "Dr. Joseph's coming!"

The boys quickly scattered, tugging up pants, and pushing Dion to the ground, who scrambled for his clothing as he struggled to stand. As the group rushed around him, Santos stepped into the room. His eyes burned with tears as he locked eyes with the boy on the floor of the bathroom.

Now, although a few years had passed, years that had developed into a friendship, this particular moment showed how little had changed for both of them. Dion had been shipped off to a school for behaviorally challenged students, and Santos had just gradually stopped attending school until both parents and school board eventually lost interest in their truancy.

Santos searched his mind for a plausible story as he plunged into the scenario, yelling out his name.

"Dion! We got get going. Libby is up at the cut looking for your ass. He's heading down now."

Dion tried to navigate around the clutch of boys, but Floyd flung an arm against his throat, pinning him to a parked car. Another boy grabbed his clutch and dumped the contents on the pavement. A smattering of objects tumbled out.

Jewel grabbed the neckline of Santos shirt and yanked him against the same car.

"Bullshit. Nobody's going nowhere until somebody comes up off some money. I know you got some money, faggot."

Jewel reached a hand into the tight pocket of Dion's denim shorts, ripping fabric as he searched.

Dion whined. "Come on, Jewel. You know if I had it, I'd give it to you. I gotta get out of here before Libby gets here. I'm not trying to get locked down tonight."

Santos grumbled to himself in fury. He reached into his back pocket and flashed a ten-dollar bill. "Here, this is all I got."

The money acted like a lure. All attention turned to Santos. The boys formed a clutch around him, and Dion darted past and ran around the corner of the nearest building.

"You got more than this, motherfucker. Give that shit up." Jewel maintained his hold on Santos' collar.

"Yeah," piped Melvin. "I know you don't want your ass kicked."

Santos looked beyond the group and noticed Dion peeking from around the corner. "Now hold the fuck up. I told y'all that was all I got. Now let me the fuck go. I know if you put a fucking hand on me, my brother will handle this shit. You know it too."

"Yeah, man," Floyd reminded them. "That's Nini's brother. He already on my ass for owin' for that half ounce we ain't paid for yet."

The boys did not want to look easily cowed, so they gradually let him go, nudging him and kicking at him while muttering under their breath about not catching faggot motherfuckers down here again, lest they get fucked up.

Santos brushed off his pants and sucked his teeth. "Yeah. Right. I hear you."

He rounded the corner, and both he and Dion raced up the street. "You fucking bitch! You just gonna leave me the fuck out there to fight your battle."

"Oh girl, pay it. I knew you could handle it. If it got out of hand, I would have come back."

SANTOS

A large box fan stood vibrating in the doorway, blasting humid air into the tiny room. Santos pulled a kitchen chair into the cross breeze from the backyard into the kitchen, positioning it close enough to his bed so that he could rest his feet upon it, allowing Jonas to lay his head across his brother's lap while his body hunkered under this wool blanket.

Jonas' sweating head felt like a lava rock in Santos's lap, overheated, as it was, because of the blanket. He marveled at the boy's ability to sleep in such humid weather. It was so weird to him that the only way that Jonas could sleep was underneath a pile of thick blankets, even in this weather; like he had to hunker down under the blankets and make himself a tiny little ball.

Santos was so uncomfortable that he wanted to nudge the boy's head off of his lap, but he knew this ritual was the only way to get him off to sleep. His stomach gurgled and lurched. Jonas turned restlessly, looking up at him with dark, hollowed eyes. Jonas' fingers clutched together into a claw and gestured toward his mouth.

"I know you're hungry. Nothing here to eat. Just go to sleep, I'll get us something tomorrow morning, promise."

Jonas moaned angrily and pitched to the other side of the bed.

"If you sleep on your stomach it won't feel so empty. And your stomach pains won't be so loud."

Santos got up and clicked on the tiny black and white television on the dresser. He turned the volume loud so that it could be heard above the blast of the fan. He smacked at his arm, smashing a mosquito nourishing itself on his undernourished blood. Mosquitoes were hurtling into the room through the open door, but Santos chose intermittent bites to stifling heat. He walked into the kitchen and rifled through the trash can, moving debris aside and going deeper. He found an old corn can, took it to the sink and rinsed it off, peeling off the Libby's label under the hot water, rubbing it until all the glue was removed. He then dried the can on the side of his striped t-shirt. Beneath a pile of take-out menus in the utility drawer, he found duct tape and scissors. He knew without looking that he would not find any construction paper, so he looked at the backs of the menus until he found one that was blank on one side.

Back in his room, he heard the small little slurping sounds that told him Jonas had gone off to sleep. He noticed a white lump sticking out of the hem of the blanket and his heart began a rapid thumping against his ribs. He rushed over and moved back the blanket to confirm his fears. He wondered where the pillow had come from. Jonas must have been rummaging around upstairs and found the pillow in Gloria's room.

He gingerly slipped it from beneath Jonas' head, holding it against his chest as he looked at his brother's tightly curled hair. No pillows. Jonas knew that. Santos always threw any pillows he found into the trash. Ever since the night he had come home, many, many years ago, when Jonas was just a baby and found Gloria standing over his crib with a pillow pressed against his head.

He had rushed into the room with his head low, aimed at Gloria's gut, taking her down. He still remembered the sound she had made as the wind left her diaphragm; phsssh!

Santos shook his head to rid his mind of that night. He sat on the floor with his can, scissors, and tape. He opened up the Times Herald newspaper, searching for the advertisement he had seen earlier.

He looked up, squinting at the tiny TV screen that shifted from newscaster to crime scene, with the words 'Atlanta, Georgia' emblazoned at the forefront.

Atlanta is suffering abnormally frequent occurrences of violence against their youth of late. Earlier today, seven-year-old LaTonya Yvette Wilson has been reported missing from the bedroom apartment of the subsidized home of her family.

What makes this disappearance different from the other occurrences in the area is that Wilson has been witnessed as being abducted from her home. She is also one of the few victims that are female. Most of the males missing have been identified by neighborhood sources as vagrant or boys with 'street smarts,' seasoned to the life on Atlanta's gritty streets.

Wilson was abducted by two men from a second-floor window of Apartment 7 in 2261 NW Verbena Street of the Hillcrest Heights housing project, wearing a slip and white panties. A witness claims to have seen a man climb into the Wilson's bedroom window four times. This same witness saw the man leave through the back door, leaving the door ajar. At that time, he stood in the parking lot talking to an unidentified man while holding the victim in his arms.

Another witness claims to have seen a late model panel van with two males and a female hanging around near the back of the Wilson apartment. He heard a commotion coming from the Wilson apartment that he says, "sounded like someone was getting a whipping." Then he heard the victim's mother yell, "Stop!"

Police have no leads at this time.

Santos crossed the room and clicked off the TV. He walked to the door facing the alley and closed it, moving the fan to the side. He stood for a moment in darkness before hitting the light switch, turning on the overhead lamp.

He heard the sound of gravel crunching in the alley and peeked through the blanket tacked over the window. A blue van meandered slowly past the gate and rolled to a stop. Santos reached out and clicked the light off. Footsteps padded across the stones. He sighed in relief as he recognized Dion's flatfooted walk.

He opened the door as Dion walked up the steps. "What you doing?"

"Nothing. Why?"

"Cootie's looking for another person. He wants a girl, but Linda ain't home. So, he gonna have to take what he can get."

Santos wondered why Dion was whispering. He looked beyond his shoulder out at the blue van. He could see nothing through the smoked glass of the van's windows. "White Girl ain't downtown?"

Dion sucked his teeth. "Bitch, he don't want no white cunt. Besides, White Girl's too old. He wants some tight snatch."

San barked out a laugh. "Well, white, or black, young or old, tight or loose, bitch, snatch ain't what I got..."

"Chile, four fists locked tight and closed eyes, and boyfriend better make the best of a bad situation. You coming or what?"

Santos leaned against the door frame. His stomach gurgled hungrily. He looked back into the room at the TV. "Nah. I can't."

"What! Come on bitch, stop playing. You gonna make these coins or what?"

"I can't get out, bitch. My mom just got back tonight, and she's running me ragged."

As soon as Santos brought the image of Gloria into Dion's mind, he began to head back toward the van. "Okay, girl. Gotta swirl."

Santos watched him sashay back to the van before closing the door. He went back to his can on the floor, holding up the strip of paper he had cut out from the newspaper: A large picture of Jerry Lewis smiled out above the words, please give, Jerry's Kids.

He wrapped the paper around the can and held it up against the light. This would work. He hoped.

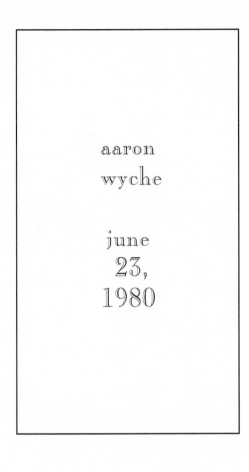

aaron
wyche

june
23,
1980

SNEAK ATTACK

Luqman was sitting on a bench in the courthouse lower pavilion, beneath an ornate lamp in order to take advantage of the light it offered. He was leaning against his canvas backpack for comfort, trying to read *A Tree Grows in Brooklyn*. He needed to verify whether Toni's accusation of pilfering was legitimate.

He heard a familiar hoot, and tucked his book into a side pocket of his bag, turning as an unidentified object sailed past his face and landed on the concrete at his boot. He bent down to pick up the Chinese slipper and flung it back in the direction from which it had come. It hurtled toward Dion's face, who dodged behind Santos with an over-the-top scream. Santos shook him off with annoyance.

"Don't hide behind me, you black bitch. You threw it!"

Dion picked up the shoe and placed it back on his foot, walking closer to Luq. "Bitch, that shoe almost hit me in my face. And here I am, beat to perfection and you trying to fuck up my paint job."

"Beat to perfection?" Santos barked. "Bitch, you look like you put that blush on in the dark."

"Yeah," Luq chimed in. "You don't look beat. You look bludgeoned."

Santos laughed venomously. "Here you go with those words again. What is bludgeoned?"

Jonas made a grunt of annoyance, tugging his hand free from Santos' grip, and walked over to lock hands with Luq.

Dion said, "If you carried your ass to school, perhaps you would know what it means, Miss Thing. But instead, you spend your days hiding out at the library, slicing pictures of Marilyn Monroe out of all the books. Aw, look at how Jonas and Luq are bonding. It's like Mary and Jesus. Bitch, what voodoo and trickery you doing on that child to get him to run to you like that?"

"Fuck you," said Santos.

"What's he cutting pictures of Marilyn Monroe out the books at the library for?"

"Who you asking? I guess he's trying to make his room look like yours...."

"By defacing public property? Interesting. Anyway, where is everybody headed?"

Dion took a small comb out of his purse and scraped the sides of his hair back. "If by everyone, you mean Miss Dion, I am heading around the corner to visit this fat, grisly monster I know. She just opened a sneaker store, and I try to support beasts in their endeavors."

They all began walking in the same direction, back out of the pavilion and onto Main Street.

Santos said, "You mean Miss Roger's Sneak Attack? Chile, that business is dead in the water. Don't nobody go there to buy those high ass bobos. That place never has a single customer!"

"I didn't say business was booming, did I? That's why the fat bitch needs support. Moral, that is. I wouldn't be giving her a dime of my coins."

Luq was impressed that Dion was friends with someone that was running their own business. "And this is her business? She's not the manager or something like that? How did you meet her?"

"You know the fat bear that does security at the library? It's her store."

Santos doubled over with laughter. "Bitch, that is the third time you called her fat. You don't have to keep emphasizing that the bitch is big. We get it."

Dion put an innocent hand to his chest. "I'm not emphasizing that she's big. SHE is emphasizing that she is big, by being a fat greasy bitch. I'm just letting y'all know her tea."

Luq was confused. "The guard at the library? Wait, that's a guy...?"

Dion huffed in exasperation. "Chile. Will you catch up? You are acting as dingbatical as Santos, right about now."

"Are you calling me dumb, fucking bitch?" Santos demanded.

Dion again feigned innocence. "Oh no, chile. What makes you say that?"

By this time, they were under the awning of the darkened façade of Sneak Attack.

"It's closed, bitch," Santos said. "I told you this place gets zero business. Wasting my time..."

Dion's voice was sing-song as he tapped a yellowed fingernail against the glass window. "I can see why you gravitate towards Marilyn. You may not be blonde, but you are not too quick on the uptake, are ya, hun?"

Luq commented on Dion's tapping on the door. "Damn bitch, how are you able to make such a loud noise with your fingernails, it sounds like a door knocker."

"Those aren't fingernails, Luq. Look at how thick and yellow they are. Those are fucking talons. I think they glow in the dar..."

The door swung open with an overhead bell chiming minutely. Before them stood a short brown-skinned man wearing a large V-necked t-shirt that barely covered a large belly. He had an unruly beard and mustache and dark piercing eyes that quickly but efficiently assessed each boy before he spoke in a low-pitched rumble.

"What's up?"

Dion breezed past the doorway, with Santos and Luqman following behind. "Hey, Walt. What's going on?"

The man closed the door, speaking while still facing the storefront. "Nothing much, nothing much. So who we got here?"

Luq noticed the sound of the bolt of the door clicking true and looked over at Santos, who was smirking while staring pointedly at Walt's bulging waist, and flat backside, encased in too-small acid washed jeans. Santos elbowed Dion in the side and nodded his head toward the eggplant shaped man. Jonas stood very close to Luq, so much that Luq had to make a concentrated effort to keep his balance. He patted the boys shoulder reassuringly.

Dion spoke with a voice of cultured derision, only noticeable to the other two from years of familiarity. "Those jeans are fierce. They Vanderbilt?"

Now Luq began smirking too, while San leaned against Dion in derision, before quickly returning to attention when Walt turned to face them.

"Fuck naw. These Wranglers. My girl bought this faggot ass shit. Stonewash. You like them?"

"Oh yeah. All the young trade is wearing stonewash. They make you look thinner."

Walt preened. "Yeah? I thought so, too."

"Well anyway, we stopped by to see how the new store is going." Dion looked around expansively at the shelves along the walls. There were a few bleak sets of Adidas lining some of the shelves.

Luq squinted through the unlit interior, wondering how this place was selling shoes when there were approximately four pair on display.

"Oh, we good, man. We good." He looked at Santos. "Hey, I know you, don't I? Ain't you Nini's brother?"

Santos nodded.

"How he doing? He still with that fine ass Muslim bitch?"

Santos sucked his teeth. "That fat bitch ain't going nowhere. She in love with the dick. Even though he beats her ass like a runaway slave."

Walt laughed. "Well, sometimes you gotta fuck a bitch up to let her know you care. Man, you call that fat. You young cats don't know what it's all about. All that there is some cushion to keep you comfortable while you taking care of that pussy right..."

Dion huffed. "Well I know one thing for sure and two things for certain; I did NOT come here to discuss snatch. I'm starting to feel sick on the stomach."

Walt laughed. "I keep telling you; you need to broaden your horizons. It's okay you like boys, but you need to be about more than sucking some dick. Get you some pussy, too. And man, don't nothing feel like some young boy pussy. These young boys that ain't had no pussy yet. They all horned up with nowhere put it. You get they dicks hard, and you can talk them out giving up the ass."

Walt brushed past them, deliberately rubbing against Luqman and sitting on the wooden bench at the center of the room. "Why you think I opened this store, man?"

Dion reached into his clutch for a cigarette and lit up with a flourish. Walt continued, "Added to my part-time job coaching at the high, I just tell the young bucks to come by so I can hook them up with the right sneaks to make they game tighter. Take me some booty, give them a pair of sneaks I got for twenty-five wholesale, we golden. And ain't nobody telling nothing, 'cause I got that ass. Now you, the young bucks talk about you because they got you to suck they dicks. If you suck that dick while you finger the booty, get them hot, then, bam, flip 'em over and before they know what's what, you done eased the dick inside, ain't nobody going to be telling shit. Trust, man. I got this situation assessed."

Santos' eyes grew wide with wonder. He lowered himself beside Walt. "Wow. I never thought about that shit before. Then, you got it all over these motherfuckers out here."

Walt nodded. "I'm trying to tell you."

Dion made a sound of disgust. "No, thank you. I can't speak for her, but I am a LADY. I'm not about to be putting my fingers in no trades dirty, unwashed ass. I do not want no salad dressing on my fingers. I don't like Seven Seas, okay?"

"But you okay sucking a dirty ass, unwashed dick. Man, how you sound?"

Santos laughed. Luq leaned uncomfortably against the counter, not making any effort to enter further into the store.

He stooped down and began to tie the laces on Jonas' shoes, just to have something to do. The movement drew Walt's attention.

"And you, my man. Why you so quiet over there? You a virgin or some shit?"

Luq felt his face redden in embarrassment as Dion and Santos laughed.

"Bingo," said Santos. "We call him tighty mighty."

"Or the Pre-Jesus Mary."

Walt eyed Luq's thin arms, the musculature of his neck extended from the huge collar of large t-shirt with The Clash emblazoned on front, his cropped blood red linen pants and drooping yellow socks. "Yeah, when I saw you at the library I said to myself, 'who is this flaming queen?"

San laughed again.

Luq pulled himself up to his full height, trying to ignore his heart hammering against his ribs, wanting to seem more self-contained than he truly felt. "What made you think I was a queen?"

"Yeah," Dion added. "She's not a queen. She's punk rock."

"Yeah, whatever. Same difference. My man's got on more eyeliner than Diana Ross. And you see how that arm be flailing out when he walks?" Walt snorted in derision. "I'm just telling you what these niggas out here on these streets are saying. I don't knock nobody. But y'all got to know how that world works and thinks, so you can know how to hustle your way in it."

Luq looked out toward the windows facing the street in time to see Toni walking past on the steep incline of Dekalb Street. "Hey look."

San sucked his teeth. "That bitch."

Dion said, "Who, White Girl Toni?"

Walt said. "Don't bring that white bitch in here. I don't have no time and no tolerance for no white woman antics."

Santos laughed, "I feel you. Anytime she's around everything got to be all about her situation."

"That's all white women," Walt said. "It's her world."

He brought his focus back to Luq. "I don't see you around here much. Where you from?"

"King of Prussia..."

"Oh shit. Well, that explains it. Maybe that's your deal. You might think you a rich white woman."

"White Girl Luqwoman!" Santos chimed.

"All right, knock it off, bitch," said Dion.

"I'm not saying you got anything to be embarrassed about. Like I said, virgin booty is worth some money." Walt stood and approached the boy. In his nervousness, Luq didn't notice Jonas backing into him, stepping on his feet. "Nothing in the world like it. So fucking tight and warm. Holding your jawn just right. You looking for a nice new pair of kicks, my man? I got you, right here. Your friends just need to chill out here for a few, and you and me can head to the back room. I got it all nice and set up back there. Some soda, TV, tape deck; you like Teena Marie? Barry White?"

Santos elbowed Dion, watching Walt rub his protruding belly.

Suddenly, Jonas began to emit a high pitched, unmelodic keeling from high in his throat. He pressed further into Luq, so much so that Luq felt a sharp pain in his navel, as Jonas seemed to pitch back against him and launch forward into Walt, bringing the point at the top of his head directly up into the man's navel. Walt gasped in shock as the wind was knocked out of him.

"What the...?"

Jonas began screaming and flailing his limbs. Santos and Dion jumped up from the bench, and San rushed over and put his hands on his brother's shoulders. Jonas shook him off and turned to press his face into Luq's torso, throwing his arms around him with a low moan.

Luqman spoke, his voice quivering. "It's okay."

He patted the boy's head and pushed him toward the door. "I'll just take him outside for some air. We'll go see what's going on with Toni. And catch up with you two up in the courtyard when you're done."

Santos nodded, taken aback by his brother's refusal of his attention in favor of Luq's. Luqman tried to grasp Jonas' hand, but the boy refused to let go of him, so he had to meander toward the door while within his bearhug. The door chimed tingled as his flung it open and shut, and moved to the sidewalk.

Dion noisily opened his clutch and dug out a cigarette. "Girl, that was dramatic. I need a goddamn cigarette. That child got my nerves all in a tizzy!"

He lit up and began to inhale aggressively. Santos walked over and snatched the cigarette from his mouth and began to inhale, himself.

Walt was sweating profusely. "What you bring that retard here, for, anyway? I told you to bring over some of your friends for me to check out. That boy is a kid."

"He's not retarded. He was born with a veil on his face," Santos said.

"Well, whatever. He too young. I ain't no child molester. You think I'm a pervert or some shit? You ain't getting no kicks for that shit."

As the element of what Walt was saying began to play out in his mind, Santos turned toward Dion with incredulity.

"Hold up. So trickin' now your side hustle? You trying to pimp?"

Dion shrugged him off with annoyance. "Bitch, please. Walt just said if I knew any people that might be down for some new kicks, to bring them by. I thought y'all might want some sneakers..."

Santos could do no more than stare at Dion in disbelief. Then he snorted derisively. "You are too many things."

"Oh, chile, pay it. You in, you in. You don't want to; you don't."

Walt came over and lowered his bulk gingerly to the bench, wincing at the dull pain in his stomach.

Well, you two can still get some sneaks. Y'all out there on them streets all the time. Y'all are magnets. The young heads flock to you. Next time I take the van down to Philly, y'all should come with me, see what boys is interested. Much as Dion like to suck on a dick, you can prime these dumb motherfuckers for the taking. I'm telling you. Anytime you can get them primed for me to get some ass, I'ma break you off. You down?"

"For some city dick? When we going?"

Santos said, "I ain't trying to put none of them dirty motherfuckers in my mouth, but I'm down too. If I can watch you bust them motherfuckers in the ass."

Dion laughed. "I forgot to tell you. This bitch is a freak. She likes to hide and watch what's going down."

FLUKEY LUKE

As soon as they reached the sidewalk, Luq looked up the hill toward Airy Street. There was no sign of Toni. He held Jonas' hand and trotted up to the narrow intersection of Penn Street, thinking she had perhaps dodged in there, but she was not there either. Luq was confused. As slowly as Toni was known to walk in high heels, it would have been impossible for her to have reached a location beyond his eyesight within such a short passage of time.

He shrugged and continued west on Penn. He could take the side entrance through the courthouse and just wait for Santos and Dion in the Pavilion. There was no way that he intended on returning to the sneaker store. He was actually glad about Jonas' weird little freak-out having taken place. It removed all the attention away from where Walt seemed to have been intent on taking the conversation. Luqman had no interest or desire concerning sex. His knowledge of the mechanics came from reading trash novels that his mother left around the house and the sex education class conducted in his freshman year at school. In his eyes, that was more than enough information to tide him over for now.

Luq did not really see himself as lacking any sexual awareness. Dion and Santos talked about their exploits frequently enough that he considered himself to be rather knowledgeable. He just did not want to have to think about the specifics of what actually happened during 'the act' when it concerned himself as the party engaging.

He was thinking about going off to college when he graduated in 1981, at the age of seventeen: a full year ahead of everyone else in his class. Of course, he did not intend to go off to college a virgin. He had every intention of engaging in sex before that time. The only question was with whom. And would it be a boy or a girl? He really wasn't particularly committed to either party, just that he get it done so that he would not be subjected to the taunts that he currently endured from his two friends as being the only one who had never been molested or accosted by an adult. He was starting to think that maybe he was asexual. Why is it, he wondered, that he was the only person he knew that had never been propositioned by an adult. Was he that ugly? He had always been taunted in junior high by Heidi Blob, who would scream, 'bye, ugly boy!' as he got off the school bus. Maybe he was just not the sort to garner much attention from adults.

Now that he had been subjected to some of that attention, by Walt, he decided he much preferred to be the sort that did not.

As he and Jonas walked up the marble staircase, he rumbled around in his backpack and dug out a piece of hard candy. He gave one to Jonas, who hungrily unwrapped the red cellophane and popped it into his mouth.

It was beginning to get cooler, and the air was no longer as humid as it had been earlier. This was the time of day that Luq enjoyed most. The quiet lull that seemed to exist right before the hectic work day gave way to the hustle and confusion of night: when the children of the night started to trickle onto the streets. Before everyone became rambunctious and combative. Before the alcohol and drugs, clouded perception. Before sexual appetites became heightened, and people grew more demanding, more voracious in their needs. The needs that had been suppressed during the day, and would later jettison out into the universe with animalistic intensity.

Luq found himself back in front of the very same bench he had been sitting on earlier when Santos and Dion had approached. He sat down rummaged in his bag for the book he had been reading. Jonas hopped up onto the bench with a ladybug perched on his outstretched hand. He watched as it meandered about on his fingers, stopping to rest on his dirty thumbnail. He laughed delightedly.

Luqman looked toward the sound of squeaky, metallic wheels.

The old bum was pushing a shopping cart full of bags and dented cans toward them. Luq briefly wondered how the man got the cart up the stairs to the courtyard.

The man looked up through rheumy eyes as he approached. He had the remnants of a cigarette clutched between his chapped lips. He came to a halt before the two boys. Jonas turned his hand over so that the ladybug could navigate along the palm of his hand, and looked up curiously, his nose crinkling at the smell of urine and sweat.

"Got a match?" the man asked.

Luq dragged a hand through his stiff hair and nodded. He opened his knapsack and rooted around in the bottom. The sound of loose change and metal emanated from within. He came out with a piece of cinnamon candy. "Want a cinnamon drop?"

The man nodded and extended his hand. Luq looked over at Jonas. "You want another piece?"

Jonas nodded. "Yeah."

After handing him a piece, Luq again reached into his bag and came out with a small Bic lighter. He handed it to the man, who braked his cart onto the grass and sat beside them with an agonized grunt. He lit his cigarette between moist sucks on the cinnamon drop, then handed the lighter back, his bony arm flaring out close to Jonas' face.

"Thank you."

"No problem." Luq tossed the lighter back into the bag and once more searched for his paperback.

The man tilted his head up toward the trees and blew out a stream of mentholated smoke, savoring a taste that he had not had on his palate for months. He looked down at the meandering ladybug, marveling at the sounds of delight emanating from the boy.

Jonas briefly shifted his attention from his hand to the man. He looked up at him, shook his head once, blinked, then re-focused on the antics of the ladybug.

"This your little brother?" the man asked.

Luq brought his feet up onto the bench and cracked open his book, looking down at the pages rather than at the man. "Yeah."

The man watched him for a second, drawing hard on the cigarette. He looked at him while speaking in a low voice.

"I was born with a caul on my face, too."

Luq barely paid attention to the man. He flipped a page, searching for where he had left off earlier.

Suddenly, the ladybug fluttered into movement, buzzing her wings and rising into the air. Jonas gasped noisily, both dismayed that she was leaving and awed at the sight of her in flight. The man watched the look of joy on the boy's face.

"Here's the thing about having the gift. Some people look at you like you a monster or a freak, a retard even. You got to stop listening to what other people try to make you and not lose track of the voice that guides you. Ain't nothing more than intuition, really. Everybody got that. But we got it stronger than most until all the name calling make you stop paying attention to your voice."

Luq put his book down on his lap and looked over at Jonas, who had stopped looking at the insect and was nodding his head at the man.

"Don't stop listening to that voice. That voice will save your life. I didn't listen to mine. Let myself go to that doctor's office for those treatments even when my intuition told me wasn't no good coming from a buncha white men in white coats telling me they wanted to help me. Let that longing for the long green stand in front of good sense. Lost my family. My health. Good common sense. Everything."

He looked at the boy and briefly rubbed his head. "You know what I'm saying to you, young fellow?"

Jonas nodded. "Yes."

The man nodded back satisfactorily. "Good. Good. Name's Silas. What they call you?"

"Jonas."

The man then looked expectantly at Luq.

"Luqman."

Silas stood and reached around in one of the bags in his cart. "Nice to meet you both."

He turned toward Luq with a yellowed and torn fragment of newspaper and handed it to him. "Read this when you get time. Read it to the little man here, too. You might think he too young to understand, but he smart. Smarter than everybody knows."

He shuffled Jonas' hair, grabbed the handle of his cart, and ambled off.

Luq gingerly unfolded the paper clipping, trying to ignore the thoughts of bugs and dirt that entered his head, as Jonas moved closer in an effort to see the paper.

First to grab their attention was the bold headline above a grainy photograph, reading; *Killing for a Good Cause: The Tuskegee Experiment.*"

anthony
carter

earl
terell

july
6,
1980

july
30,
1980

DION

Dion sat in his bedroom, on a large canopy bed with light green skirting. A large plastic Tupperware bowl sat before him, from which he noisily ate potato chips, watching a Shirley Temple movie. He wiped the oil from the chips from his fingers onto his red and white checked blouse and reached up to re-do a loosened box braid.

He sang loud and off-key, attempting to outdo Shirley's rendition of "The Good Ship Lollipop" with a gospel-tinged version of his own until a loud banging on the wall convinced him to shut up.

The sound of the door chime caused him to jump from the bed, adjusting too-short cut-offs with a brief tug to remove cloth from his rear, then he sashayed down the carpeted hallway and down the ornately banistered stairs. The bell chimed again as he approached the oak double doors of the foyer.

"I'm coming! Hold your jock, would you?"

He hurled the open the door to a squat well-muscled pair of swarthy delivery men. "Hello, gentlemen..."

Both men paused, giving a surreptitious assessment before one harrumphed. "Thomas?"

"You got it."

"We got a call for a pick-up of a mahogany armoire."

Dion moved aside, nodding his head. "This is the place, fellas. Come on in. It's right here in the living-room. We got it all ready for pick up. You have the check, right?"

The men moved briskly into the common area of the house, then came up short. There was a very ornate, but faded Oriental rug marking the center of the parquet floor, and a few palms in the corners housed in hand-painted ceramic pots. Heavy velvet drapes hung from valanced cornices over the windows of leaded glass. There was a large console television between two windows, faced by a burgundy wingback chair. The only remaining object in the room was a large, hand-carved armoire that was wrapped in bubble wrap and a hauling carpet, and tied with a heavy rope.

Dion held out an unmanicured hand, snapping his fingers for the check that had yet to be dispensed to him. "Come on, guys. Time is money. The check?"

"Uh. Sorry, but I think we are going to need a signature."

"Of course, of course. Do you have a pen?" Dion snapped.

"We gonna need signature from an adult..."

Dion huffed angrily. "Seriously?"

He spun on his slippered heels and stomped up the stairs while yelling ahead of himself. "Mommy! Can you come down here? Mommy!"

The two men looked at each other and shrugged, laughing, as they gave one another a pound. There was much shuffling and slamming of doors heard from the floor above, and the sound of someone shouting 'wetback' and 'jackass,' before discordant steps were heard descending the stairs.

Both men removed their hats when Dion re-entered the room helping a thin woman in a silk robe into the room. Dion held her up with one shoulder pitted under her armpit, while her opposite hand held onto a silver cane. She looked at them with large hazel eyes. Although she appeared weakened and frail, the men were able to see the great beauty that had once been there. It remained in the set of her high cheekbones, her regal stature, the fringe of her dark lashes and the remains of her waist-length auburn hair that contrasted with the caste of her olive skin.

Marie inhaled a labored breath to propel her voice. "Gentlemen, you have payment from Mr. Havisham for me?"

Dion smirked as one of the men hopped superciliously forward, practically bowing in his haste to accommodate the woman. Dion was used to the reaction his mother elicited from people, particularly from men.

"Yes, ma'am. Right here. We were just saying that we needed to get your signature before taking the piece of furniture. You know, it is a good sum of money. We wanted to make sure that an adult had approved this exchange. You know how kids are these days..."

Marie snatched the paper from him in mid-sentence.

"No. Actually, I do not know how kids are these days." She reached out a hand imperiously.

Dion barely suppressed a laugh as he noticed the man's hands trembling while he handed her a pen and watched her hastily scribble onto the clipboard. He nodded to her and smiled.

"Thank you, Mrs. Thomas. We'll get that taken care of right away. Thank you for your business..."

Marie grabbed her cane and whispered, "Take me back up."

She turned away from the men, her business with them completed, and mother and son headed back up the stairs while the men began to maneuver the armoire onto a dolly.

By the time they reached the top of the stairs, Marie was drenched with sweat, her arms trembling with the exertion of navigating both walking and interacting with people. Dion provided most of the labor of the walk down the narrow hallway and into his mother's room at the far end.

The door banged back against the wall, and Dion practically dragged the heavily breathing woman to the four-postered bed piled high with linens and pillows. He lifted her onto the yellowing sheets, tucked her into the comforters, and held out her breathing mask to her. Marie took heavy gasps of the oxygen and fell back gingerly, semi-reclined. Dion rushed into the powder-room, returning with a washcloth and basin of cold water.

He sat on the bed and applied to moistened cloth to Marie's forehead, reaching up to smooth stray lengths of hair from her face, stroking her hair while making consoling noises.

"You okay?" He applied the cloth to the back of her neck. Marie leaned forward gratefully, nodding her head.

"Yes, sweetie. Fine."

He shushed her. "Don't talk. Breathe."

Their heads turned as they heard the front door slam shut.

"Those assholes."

Dion looked around at the gilded picture frames spread throughout the room. Photos of his father hung from walls, rested on the dressers, the night-stands. This room, along with his, were the only rooms left in the house unmolested. The other rooms were virtually eradicated of all significant furniture. Any pieces of value had been gradually sold off. The armoire had been the last item that was worth any saleable value, sold off piece by piece through the last four years to pay off debtors, ameliorate hospital tabs, obtain medications in the hopes of staving off the ravages of cancer that relentlessly devoured Marie's organs.

"Mommy. Don't you get depressed with all these pictures of Daddy all over the place? Why don't you just leave out one picture? We could probably get some money for those frames. They look like real gold. Are they?"

Marie looked at him as if he had lost all remnants of sanity. "These are all I have left of your father. They don't depress me. They lift my spirits. They remind me of better times."

Dion looked at the large ten by twelve hanging close to the bed. Delbert Thomas beamed the megawatt smile that had initially drew Marie's attention at an Army/Navy dance in 1972. Delbert had been on leave during the Vietnam War. He had looked so handsome, his deep chocolate skin against the muddy green uniform, contrasted with teeth so white that he looked as if he had walked out of an ad for the Saturday Evening Post. If the Saturday Evening Post had ads featuring black men.

Over the years they had learned to ignore the stares, the whispers about how she had betrayed her race by marrying a dinge. They had been rapturously happy.

Her parents had immediately disowned her. When she told them she was pregnant but had not yet married, they had been horrified, insisted that whomever this man was marry her forthwith. When they saw his smooth black face, they were beyond horrified; they were silent.

They silently closed the front door in his face. They silently walked up the stairs. Marie's mother silently packed her bag while her father silently beat her with a strap, until Delbert kicked in the door, rushed up the stairs and knocked him to the ground, carrying his sobbing fiancé from her childhood home for the last time.

Although they silently hung up the phone each time that Marie attempted to call them, she was confident that they would eventually come around. Each month, as her belly swelled larger and larger, she would attempt to call her parents. Each month, the phone was hung up with the same finality as the month that had preceded it.

When she gave birth to Dion, a large, bawling, ten pounds of overindulged access, she had gotten photos taken by the best photographer in Norristown, dressing her baby in frilly pink clothes and piercing his ears with silver studs. She sent the largest copy through the mail to her parents with a simple note: your grandson.

The package arrived back at her doorstep one week later, stamped; Return to Sender, package refused.

For the next nine years, each year, on Dion's birthday, Marie would pack up the latest school photograph and mail it off to Henry and Lilly Narberth. Every year it would return with the same stamped message: Return to Sender: package refused.

Despite this, Delbert and Marie were happy. They bought a house through the G.I. loan. Delbert got a job at Alan Wood Steel, and Marie worked part-time as a librarian. They lived a quiet existence on a quiet street off Elmwood Park, indulging their roly-poly child with everything that he requested. Marie baked cakes and puddings, pies and cookies, feeding the gaping hole left by her parent's abandonment to her child instead.

As Dion grew rounder and rounder, the children's taunts grew aggressively more mean. The taunts turned from verbal to physical: tripping, throwing rocks, and then finally to fists. Dion learned how to fight back. His bulk gave him an advantage. Soon the physical assaults diminished, as the children in the neighborhood became aware that they could not best him physically.

Then, one day, Dion announced that he wanted to be a girl.

Accustomed to indulging their beloved child, Marie and Delbert were unperturbed with this turn of events. When he asked for blouses to replace shirts, they relented. When he wanted to replace Spiderman and Superman with Barbie, they relented. When he wanted to replace his bunkbeds with a canopy, they agreed, but with one caveat: pink was a no-no, but any other color would be fine.

They were all satisfied.

Until 1976. Delbert, a member of the American Legion, went to the annual convention, this time in Philadelphia, at the world-class Bellevue Stratford Hotel.

A week later he returned home, coughing up blood and unable to breathe. Marie was in a panic. She took Delbert to a hospital and would not leave his side. She asked Delbert's sister to keep Dion while she tended to her ailing husband.

Even though Carol had never been particularly fond of the white woman that had married her brother, she adored her nephew and took him in without question.

One week after returning home from the convention, Delbert was dead. Reasons, unknown. Thirty other conventioneers were also dead, while hundreds of others that had participated in the convention had also fallen ill from some unknown pathogen. Doctors were at a loss when explanations were demanded. Some said a new strain of swine flu. Others hypothesized about some bioterrorism on the tail end of the war. No one knew anything definitively.

Officials from the Department of Health and the Centers for Disease Control interviewed, but gave no answers, swabbed mouths, took blood samples from family members; from those that came within proximity of the sick, and then retreated back to Washington, D.C.

Dion reached up and removed the picture from the wall, placing it in Marie's outstretched hands. Marie lovingly dusted the motes clear with the sleeve of her robe.

"Your father always made sure we were well taken care of. He was a great man."

Dion nodded, looking off at the other pictures. He didn't remember his father as particularly great, or particularly bad. He mostly remembered a stiff pair of trousers attached to a low, booming voice, either coming home at the end of the day or rushing off at the start. When he was not working, he was out with the American Legion at some event or another, while Dion and Marie spent their free time filling the empty spaces of their home with furniture from Main Line antique shops, or buying frilly clothing from Sears, or Strawbridge and Clothier, or Gimbels.

"It's that damn VA that screwed us over." Marie gasped. "Your daddy thought we would be okay. That we'd have his veteran's benefits if he passed on. Little did I know that the only benefit they would approve was you getting SSI benefits, and that tiny widow's pension, not even enough to live on, to pay a mortgage. That Legion turned out to be a crock of shit. Taking dues and never giving out a red cent. I told him that they were just taking his money. They didn't really want black folks in there. But you know your daddy. Always wanting to think the best of people, always thinking men have the best intentions..."

Marie snorted, "That, really, was his biggest downfall."

Dion rolled his eyes and stood up. Marie clutched the picture to her emaciated breasts.

"Okay, Mommy. We are fine; you know this. We got the check for the armoire, and you know that agency keeps sending us money for incidentals. We're good. I'm going to go down and make you a bite to eat."

"I'm not hungry."

"I know. But you should try to get a little down. I'll fix you a nice fruit bowl. Don't that sound nice?"

Marie reached out and grabbed his wrist. "You're not going out, are you? I told you, I don't want you leaving this house."

Dion gingerly removed her fingers from his wrist, smiling falsely. "Mommy. Didn't I just tell you where I was going? Why would I be going anywhere? Here, why don't you take one of these pills, you haven't had one all day. You've got to take care of yourself."

He reached amongst the many amber shaded medicine vials and tapped out a tablet into Marie's hand, then turned to the bathroom to fill a glass with water. This was their daily routine. Since Delbert had died, Marie was terrified of going out of doors, refusing to take care of errands, doctor's appointments, insisting that Dion stay inside.

The only way that Dion was able to get out was to feed her sleeping pills. Once Marie drifted off to sleep, he was free to leave the house and try to make money so that they could stave off the onslaught of debt that deluged them; a seeming avalanche of never-ending demands for remediation.

Summer was a far more lucrative time for Dion to make money, so he tried to be as productive as possible through the summer months, heading downtown as soon as the dinner hour passed, working through the night until the beginning dregs of sunlight began to show. If he took advantage of the increased opportunities that summer allowed, he was able to stockpile enough for them to eke through the winter season.

Telling his mother that they were given monthly stipends from a local charitable organization seemed to satisfy her. Every now and then, if things got really bleak, he'd ask Luqman, who'd give him enough for a few groceries, all the while yammering about it being a loan and wanting to be paid back, but he never asked for a payback after the money was given. Or he could go over to Aunt Carol's for dinner and ask to take a plate home for his mother. Aunt Carol would huff, and then pack up enough food to get them through a few days, by which time some other strategy would present itself, getting them by.

Dion sat on the edge of the bed and watched Marie take a few bird-like sips of water. She set the glass on the bedside table, reached out for Dion's head. He allowed her to press his head on her chest, listening to the patter of her heart. He closed his eyes and rested against the radiant warmth of his mother.

"I love you," she whispered.

He whispered back, "I know."

SANTOS

He stood before the full-length mirror nude from the waist up. He turned on the tap full blast and grabbed a wad of paper towels from the dispenser, releasing a generous dollop of pink hand soap, then applied to his sparsely haired armpits. The sound of gushing water reverberated from the indigo tiles, surrounding him in resonance.

He imagined himself at an ancient bath, or in a hidden cave beneath an Amazonian waterfall in the rainforest. The reflection staring back at him from the mirror did not please him. Ribs pushed tautly against his brown skin. His pallor, usually reflective of light, was dull and ashen. His hair was lank and listless. His cheeks were sunken. He was hungry.

He had only been able to eat a few nibbles of food for the past few days, stockpiling whatever was available to make sure that Jonas was able to eat. His stomach rumbled discontentedly. He cupped his hands and swallowed a few mouthfuls of water to silence it.

There was a firm tap at the door. Santos quickly dried himself, shrugged his t-shirt over his shoulders and walked toward the door. "Just a sec."

Ordelia's brow furrowed slightly. He appeared slightly flushed when he opened the door. "You've been in there for quite a while, my dear. Are you all right?"

He nodded, smiling as he entered the waiting room, squeezing pasts the woman's hips. "I'm fine."

"Well, my dear. I don't know why you are here. You know you do not have an appointment scheduled for another few weeks. And we are very busy here getting things in order. You know we are relocating to another area, don't you? Combining some of our operations, Detroit, Oakland, Atlanta, Chicago..."

Santos cut her off disinterestedly. "Yes. I know I'm not scheduled."

He peered up at her. "I was hoping you might be able to see me sooner. I could really use the money, now. And, um, my family was going to be spending the next couple weeks visiting folks in North Carolina, so I wouldn't be around, and I didn't want to miss treatment."

Ordelia squinted astutely. She was aware that the boy was lying. According to his historical information on file, he had very limited extended family contact. That was one of the criteria for acceptance into the study. She looked upon his unkempt appearance, the beseeching in his eyes, and nodded.

"Okay, my dear. I think we might be able to squeeze you in. Come with me, and we'll get you some orange juice and a donut."

Santos smiled with relief, following the undulating mounds of starched white scrubs.

JONAS

I was hungry. But this hungry don't feel like the other hungries. Those hungries was always for short time; then San would find us some bread, or cereal, or raviolis. I liked cereal best. Especially Cap'n Crunch with crunchberries. And I could wait until the milk is nice and pink, then drink it out of the bowl till my tummy gets filled up.

But this time my hungry gets real big. And San don't come home with Cap'n Crunch with crunchberries, or even Oodles of Noodles, his favorite cuz he can make it bigger when he just puts in more water or puts in some cheese curls and eggs. This time, San comes home with empty pockets and a bag of Colt 45, and a mean face. This time San gets mad and punches me and says that it's my fault that he is hungry and I don't make him get hurt because he is right, it is my fault. If I wasn't here, San could eat all the food by himself, and he won't have to take a small bite and then give the rest to me.

After San hits me, I cry, and that makes San cry back. He goes to his room and gets the corn can he covered with a white man's face called Jerry's Kids. The can has a hole in the top. San digs in his pockets and finds two pennies. He puts them in the can, and they go thunk. He says this will get us some food and he leaves the house. He yells at me to don't go no fucking where or he will break my arm, and he slams the door so Gloria will be mad, only she's not here. If Gloria was here, then my tummy won't make noises.

I goes upstairs and walk to Gloria's bedroom. It smells like funny cigarettes and old red flowers. I pull the chair from the corner and drag it to the closet. I climb up and take her favorite dress off the hanger. It smells like old red flowers too. Gloria calls it Tea Rose.

I carry to the bed. It smells like when mama is hanging the clothes on the line, or scrubbing the steps. I fix the dress to lay the way she stands when she is dancing to her favorite Nat King Cole song that's a Spanish word. I go back to the closet and take out the high red shoes with the flower on the toes that she calls her go dancing shoes and I put them at the bottom of the bed, under the bottom of the dress. One foot is kicked up like when she does a swirl. I go to the dresser and take the picture of her smiling nice and bright. This is a picture when she was a skinny girl. Back on the island. I go into the drawer and take out her black stockings. I line them up out of the bottom of the dress and curl the toes into the red shoes. I put her picture at the neckline of the dress.

I stand back and look at the bed. It's not right. I move one shoulder down. I don't know what is not right.

I smell the air. Then I go to the window and push it open. The hot breeze pushes past me, making the sheers flutter out onto the bed, over the dress. I walk back around and look again. The smell of mama moves off the wind and goes inside me. This is right. I close my eyes, and I think really hard.

STATE OF THE NATION

If I think really hard I can make things happen. I did it before, with Uncle Nash.

This time I wish for Gloria to come home.

But when I open my eyes, she not there.

THE SEER

She was a tiny woman. She peered up at Gloria through eyes that were so cloudy the color could not be determined. She was stooped over a carved oak cane, hovering in the doorway like some ancient entity.

"Gloria?" It didn't really sound like a question as much as an accusation. She did not bother to wait for a response, but turned on her sandaled heel and re-entered the sanctuary, with cockleshells and amber beads swinging from strands of gray hair banging melodically.

Gloria collected herself and trailed behind the woman, through a narrow, labyrinthine passageway, passing a small living area whose doorway was covered by a sheer burgundy panel. They entered a room that was empty save a monstrously large hutch filled with debris, and a low slung table with two chairs. A squat candle trembled a tenuous light from the center of the table, fighting a futile battle against the darkness encouraged by the heavy drapes drawn across windows.

The crone waved a red painted talon at the chair, bidding that Gloria sit first.

Gloria set her bags on the floor and lowered herself to one of the chairs. The woman stood above her, staring expectantly. Gloria looked back, on the cusp of becoming indignant, then remembered the routine. It had been a long time since she had visited a precog. Her last visit, in fact, had been when she had been forewarned of giving birth to a child with a caul on its face.

She reached into the neckline of her shirt-waist and removed a bundle of bills, studiously counting out the agreed upon amount and spreading it out in the center of the table, on the woman's side of the candle, before returning the remainder to her bodice.

Satisfied, the woman trundled over to the table and sat. She peered at the bills, doing a fleeting addition without touching the money, and then rose again, going over to the hutch and removing a few items. She placed two more candles on the table and lit them, humming an old spiritual as she waited for the smoke to meander through the room.

When satisfied, she reached out her hands, palms up, toward Gloria, who slowly placed her own within them. They felt cool and leathery, like a well-loved but seldom used purse. One that had cost a lot of money and so was only taken out on special occasions.

The woman began to recite the Lord's Prayer in a low timbre. Toward the end she seemed to slow it down, drawing out the words. She then made a slight movement of her hands, indicating that Gloria should recite along with her, so they made another round of the verse, Gloria's accent adding mellifluous accompaniment.

When they finished, the woman looked at her expectantly.

"Tell me what you want."

Gloria breathed out. She looked down at the table, then reached down to her handbag and rustled around in her bag until she found the needed item, placing a torn page from a local magazine before the woman.

The woman watched her, then looked at the paper on the table.

Donald Wayne Thomas, the appellant, was sentenced to death today in Georgia, Fulton County Superior Court of the April 19, 1979, murder of Dewey Baugus, a nine-year-old child.

On April 11, 1979, Dewey Baugus and a playmate left his mother's home on Primrose Circle in Atlanta to go to a ball game. After the game, the two children separated to return to their respective homes in the early evening darkness. This was the last time the victim was seen alive.

The appellant, a 19-year-old male, lived at a rooming house on Primrose Circle. Linda Cook, the appellant's girlfriend, had stayed with him for approximately a week during the time in question. The appellant had kept her locked in the room when he was not there, with a bucket he provided as her only toilet facility. Linda Cook testified that when the appellant returned to the room on Friday, April 13, she noticed that he had a lot of blood on the front of his pants. The appellant took her to the railroad track behind Primrose Circle and showed her the body of the victim, lying face down, and told her that he had killed the child by beating him with a stick and choking him. In her presence, the appellant rolled the body over. Telling her that he had to make sure that he was dead, the appellant then jumped on the neck of the victim.

Thereafter, he threw the victim's body in the bushes. Thereafter, they returned to the room, where the appellant removed his pants and hid them behind the house. That same day, the appellant, again in Linda Cook's presence, admitted the murder to his stepfather, Enzor Lowe. However, his stepfather testified that he did not believe him because the appellant was grinning about it.

On April 19, 1979, Calvin Banks discovered the body of the victim when he took a shortcut on his way back from applying for a job at the Dolly Madison Cake Co. When the body was discovered, it was partially decomposed, and the pants the victim was wearing were pulled down to mid-thigh level.

"I'm worried 'bout my children," she stammered. "Bodies turning up missing all over this country, babies being killed and tek from they houses. Police doing nathan. I work a long way from home. Can you give me somet'ing tek care of my babies while I'm not home."

The woman watched her. She slowly let go of Gloria's hands and picked up a deck of cards, which she spread before her. "You pick three cards from anywhere. Then pick a card from the front and one from the back."

Gloria bit her lower lip and pondered the cards. Slowly, she picked the cards as instructed and handed them over to the woman, who laid them in front of her with a loud thwack.

She then removed from her lap a small leather bound bible. "Open."

Gloria inserted a fingertip into the pages and flipped the book open.

The woman leaned forward and read the passage that added up the sum of the numbers on the cards. "You will build a house, but you will not live in it. You will plant a vineyard, but you will not even begin to enjoy its fruit. Your ox will be slaughtered before your eyes, but you will eat none of it. Your donkey will be forcibly taken from you and will not be returned. Your sheep will be given to your enemies, and no one will rescue them. Your sons and daughters will be given to another nation, and you will wear out your eyes watching for them day after day, powerless to lift a hand. A people that you do not know will eat what your land and labor produce, and you will have nothing but cruel oppression all your days. The sights you see will drive you mad. The Lord will afflict your knees and legs with painful boils that cannot be cured, spreading from the soles of your feet to the top of your head."

Gloria looked at her with terror and confusion. "The fuck does that mean?"

"If you worried about your babies, go home and take care of your babies. A child can't be safe without they mama to watch over them. Go home."

Gloria snorted with derision. "I can't tek care of dem without money, and me job is here."

The woman snorted back at her. "What job you got that can't be found closer to home? You a doctor? You do open heart surgery?"

She reached out her palms again for Gloria to lock hands with her. Gloria acquiesced reluctantly. The woman began a low pitched murmuring, which slowly morphed to a keeling moan. Still holding onto Gloria, the woman jerked in her seat, her face contorting as if she were struck by a blow. She suddenly released Gloria's hands as if they were scalding hot.

The woman's voice is barely a whisper. "Why are you here, child?"

Gloria looks alarmed. "I...I already tell you..."

"You not here 'cause you worried for your babies. You scared," the woman hissed. "You scared of that baby. You want for me to give you something to take care of him."

The crone stood up, her shadow casting long and towering on the wall behind her. "I don't do dark work here. You hate that child for showing you something you already knew in your heart all along. You don't need to fear him. He can't do nothing to you. You need to protect him. He ain't nothing but a baby. A baby needs they mama. Go home. Watch over them. I see death. Watch over them."

Gloria lowered her head to hide the tears falling. The old woman was right. She could not forgive him. She hated him.

UNCLE NASH

Santos walked down the alley abutting his home, sidled along the narrow pathway and opened the gate to the backyard. The can he had rigged to resemble a donation container for muscular dystrophy jingled in his hand. He walked onto the sloping back porch and sat at the ledge. He removed the false bottom on the can and shook the change onto the porch. He counted out the money that he had collected before the police had chased him away from the courtyard, where he had positioned himself all morning, accosting passerby for donations for 'Jerry's Kids.'

He mumbled a low expletive. Eight fucking dollars and seventy-six cents. That was the result of six hours standing in the hot sun in shoes so worn down that the heat from the pavement burned through and scorched his feet. Tears stung the corners of his eyes. He didn't have any other ideas of how to get together money. The check he had been given by Miss Purchase had barely lasted a week, after buying weed, cigarettes, bread, lunchmeat, and some soup, he was back where he had started.

He stared down the end of the walkway, to the charred remnants of what had once been a lean-to tool shed, where they had stored the push-mower and trash-bins. It was now no more than a smoky sculpture of black wood, with a surprisingly intact roof.

Santos remembered when the shed had been a source for acquiring money. Back when he still lived with them, Uncle Nash would spend time in the shed smoking large, foul-smelling cigars and drinking from big bottles of brown liquor, sitting in a lawn chair listening to some obscure, static-y jazz station on a transistor radio.

The first few times had happened in the house. When Gloria drifted off to sleep, Nash would hover at the doorway of Santos' room, quietly smoking a cigarillo until the smoke, and the dim light from the hallway nudged Santos awake, after which, he would approach and sit on the bed, whispering coaxing words and offering gifts.

At first, Santos had been terrified, but the sensation of Uncle Nash's hand rubbing his chest through his t-shirt, the sweet smell of his cognac laced breath as he neared; making more promises, the warmth of his full lips near his ear had all felt good. After the first few times, Santos found that he like the way it made him feel.

He also had to admit that when Gloria swore at him, called him a dumb ass faggot, disappeared for days without leaving enough food for him and Jonas to eat, he felt a little better when he glared back at her, knowing that he had a secret that she knew nothing about.

But Jonas knew that she did know. Just like Jonas knew what was going on the entire time. He stayed snuggled down beneath the bulk of his bedclothes and was sure to keep his breathing at the even pace that evidenced sleeping to the two copulating shadows on the bed next to his, but he watched. In horror.

Jonas knew that Gloria knew. He could see it, the change that happened the day after Uncle Nash first crept into their room. He could see it in the change in her eyes when she looked upon Santos in the morning, and in the increased look of desperation in her eyes and her movements whenever she interacted with Uncle Nash. If he made a demand, Gloria jumped to appease him much quicker. If he commented that the dishes were not done, or that dinner was not seasoned quite right, she sprang into action to make him happy. Her appearance became a weaker version of herself: her dresses became shorter, the necklines deeper, her lip rouge grew more virulent and her perfume more cloying.

The move to the toolshed was a natural transition. Uncle Nash spent most of his hours there, away from Gloria's desperation, enjoying his manly interests. When Santos was in need of spending money, or a new pair of sneakers, or attention, he would saunter down to the shed and make the scowl on Uncle Nash's face disappear.

But Jonas had decided Uncle Nash needed to go. From the time of the first night that he had crept into their room, Jonas watched him, thinking about what he could do to make him disappear.

The solution came gradually, and naturally.

It had always been easy for Jonas to change his voice to sound like Santos over the telephone. He would just speak in a louder, more clipped tone, cutting his words off before they became sing-song. As long as he didn't have to talk for too long, he could fool people. He knew he couldn't trick his older brother, Nini, but he thought he could get away with fooling Yasmine.

The toolshed locked from the outside, with a clasp and padlock. When Jonas saw Santos wandering down toward the shed from the vantage of the rear bedroom window, he picked up the phone and called Nini's house. Luckily, Yasmine answered.

He kept it brief, speaking only two staccato sentences and then hanging up the phone. He then unplugged the cord so that she could not call back.

When Gloria walked past the window, she noticed Jonas outside squatting by the old toolshed but paid little attention. He usually went down by the shade of the maple tree there to play with his toy soldiers, tossing them repeatedly at each other in scenarios of combat.

The precision of perfect timing was the element that Jonas could not control. It was fortuitous for him that it all seemed to fall in to place at just the right time.

When the first screams began, Gloria wasn't certain what she was hearing. When she absently walked toward the rear of the house to try to determine what the sound was, a loud banging erupted from the opposite end of the house. She walked toward the front door, from where a rapid-fire series of banging came.

She opened the door, and Nini and Yasmine spilled inside in a flurry of questions and movement. "What th' hell's going on?"

Her oldest son was a lean copper colored thirty-one-year-old full of outlying elbows, knees, and feet. "Why you call me, for? Why ain't you call the ambulance?"

Gloria stepped away from them, confused.

Yasmine said, "San called and said you had fallen off the stairs and was passed out. What happened."

By this time, the screams had become loud enough for Gloria to know without a doubt that they were screams. And that those screams were coming from Santos and Nash. She turned and ran towards the screams, Nini and Yasmine right on her heels.

They barely noticed Jonas standing off to the side of the maple tree. The sight of the toolshed engulfed in flames diverted all attention. Nini gave a brief yelp of surprise. Gloria outright screamed and dashed toward the door to open it, but it would not budge. From within, the door trembled as the inhabitants of the toolshed hammered against it. Yasmine rushed back toward the house and scrambled for the garden hose attached to a rusted spigot.

Gloria tried to remove the unlocked hasp of the padlock, but the heat singed her fingertips, making her yell in dismay. Nini grabbed the axe leaning upon the trunk of the tree and frantically hammered at the lock. Three panicked blows and the door gave way.

Santos, wearing a pair of dirty underwear and a t-shirt rushed out and into his mother's torso. Everyone began to talk at the same time, asking what had happened. Yasmine released the handle of the hose, releasing a spray of water that she aimed at the base of the fire, which seemed to primarily be at the outside threshold of the doorway. Nash rushed out, unclothed, holding his garments in front of his nudity and cursing furiously.

It took a moment for everyone to collect the disparate images of the tableau. As the tale began to become decipherable, the cacophony of questions lowered to a low murmur. Then, Nini grabbed the other end of the axe and rammed the handle into Nash's teeth. Nash screamed, loud and perilously, as the sound of gristle and broken porcelain crunched in his ear. Nini jumped on him and began to throttle his throat.

"You fuckin' faggot ass pervert! I'll fucking kill you."
Gloria turned and pushed Santos away from her. He fell over a root, and she jumped on him in fury, thrashing her hands at him and screaming. Jonas screamed and rushed over, jumping on her back and yanking at her braids. Santos recoiled a knee and connected to her diaphragm, screaming back at her.

Once she was sure that the fire was subdued, Yasmine threw down the hose and ran over to grab Nini's shoulder. "Nini, stop! Leave the motherfucker alone. You want to go back to jail?"

Nash stood, cursing, streaming blood from his traumatized mouth. He jerkily kicked into his pants, mumbling about getting his boys to come down from Chicago and blowing up the whole town.

"Shut the fuck up," Yasmine said.

Gloria rolled off Santos and lay on the damp dirt. Santos sat up, Jonas sitting in his lap while sobbing inconsolably. Nini, walked over toward his mother, screaming. "So you got the same shit going on here as always, I see."

Gloria slowly rose to her feet. Yasmine approached and put a hand on Nini's arm. "Don't do this, babe. Let's just go," she whispered.

"When Yasmine told me you were knocked out at the bottom of the stairs, my first instinct was to let you stay there and bleed out. I don't want nothing to do with you and this shit you got going on here."

"What you talkin', boy? What happen here ain't my fault."

"It's not? You been letting motherfuckers stay with you, fucking your little boys since I was five years old. Just so you didn't have to sleep in a bed by yourself."

"You lie," she hissed.

"You pimped me out. Now you doing the same shit again. That's why I walked out this house when I was fifteen. You're sickening. Pretending you don't know what's going on. If you stayed the fuck around you would know what's happening under your own roof."

Gloria began to sob. "No, son. Listen."

She reached out for his hand. Nini yanked his hand back, and spit at her.

Everyone gasped. Nini turned and headed back toward the house. Yasmine rushed after him.

Shaking his head free of the demons of past events, Santos scooped up the coins he had spread out on the porch and replaced them in the can. That was the last time that Jonas had spoken to him. That was also when Santos, without requesting permission, moved his meager belongings out of the room he shared with his brother upstairs, and into the tiny mudroom behind the kitchen.

As far as he knew, Uncle Nash had left that very day. He did not collect his things. His threatened "Chicago posse" never showed, nor did he ever return for his possessions. After a week passed, Gloria piled a neat pyre of items in the backyard and set them ablaze while sucking fiercely on a cigarette.

Just then, from inside the house, Santos heard a bunch of commotion. He grabbed his can of change, stood up, and walked into the mudroom. Jonas, who had been asleep on the bed, had risen to a seated position at the sound of the noise. He sat motionless on the bed, his face ashen and clammy, his eyes large and unreadable. Santos walked through the narrow rooms to the living-room, where his mother stood with a collection of suitcases and a short, balding man.

Santos watched her warily.

Gloria smiled a bit too broadly. "Hi, darlin'. I'm here. This here's Uncle Bill."

The man, chewing aggressively on a squat cigar, charged forward with his hand outstretched. He grabbed Santos' hand, although he had not offered it, and pumped it up and down furiously. "Hi, son. Uncle's not necessary. Just call me Mr. Bill."

DAVID JACKSON AMBROSE

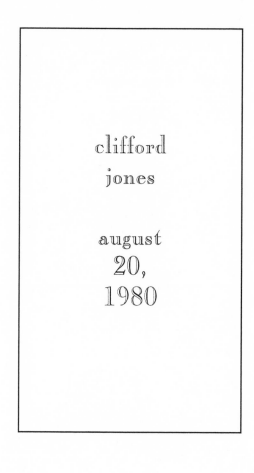

clifford
jones

august
20,
1980

WALT'S SNEAK ATTACK

The three of them stood in the tiny vestibule before a dirty white door. Santos and Luqman glared at Dion with hostility. Dion returned their looks with one of total innocence, smiling in a cloyingly sweet way that telegraphed to them that he was fully aware of why they were annoyed.

Santos mumbled 'black bitch' repeatedly under his breath, while Luqman shifted impatiently from one bondage boot to the other.

The door to the apartment cracked open, and a very dark colored woman pushed her curly head out.

"I'm sorry, y'all," her Bronx accented voice was deep and low, unsuccessfully attempting to mimic a feminine register. "Miss Tiffany is getting dressed. We'll be out in two shakes."

All three of them jumped slightly as the door slammed shut.

"You black bitch!" Santos snapped. "We already been waiting out here in this stinking ass hallway for fifteen minutes."

Luqman looked at his outsized watch, hanging loosely on a bony wrist. "Actually, it's been twenty-three minutes..."

Santos barked a laugh. "Thanks, Mother Time!"

"Well, what's the problem, bitch?" Dion asked. "Y'all act like it's my fault that the bitch is in there washing her pussy, or whatever the fuck she needs to do to get herself street ready."

Luq said, "I don't know why you came to get them, anyway. Miss Karen is always ready to get out, but every time we come by here, we have to wait for eons so that Tiffany can get herself up in yags. Why's it take so long to toss on a wig and jump into a funky dress, I'll never know."

Dion said, "Well, it's easy for Miss Karen. All she has to do is put on that same red punk-rock skirt she wears whenever she goes down to the beat, and some red heels. There's no need to put on any makeup, all the paint at M.A.C. won't distract from the fact that Miss Thing looks like a Doberman."

"Keep your voice down!" Santos whispered. "Miss Tiffany is from the Bronx, bitch, and you know she has no problem slicing a bitch up with the blade she keeps down in her titties."

Luqman said, "So what you saying? That Miss Tiffany needs time to put on her face? That child is just as ugly as Miss Karen, so you trippin'."

Santos said, "But, you know, Miss Tiffany had the operation, so she needs more time to get herself together, right? Miss Karen is just a dragon."

With their mouths hanging open, both Dion and Luqman stared at Santos disbelievingly.

Santos looked back. "What?"

"This child is so goddamn dumb, Luq. What is wrong with her?"

"He's just gullible. I mean, that is what Tiffany told us. That she got the operation done in New York and then moved down here with her cousin Karen. Why shouldn't we take her at her word?"

"Because we got eyes!" Dion screamed. Then lowered his voice back to a whisper, lest Tiffany overhear them. "How's this bitch think that Miss One is real fish? That face is harder than Dekalb Pike."

All three of them muffled laughter.

"Hold up," Santos said, "you mean she's a dude?"

Luqman preferred to give Tiffany the benefit of the doubt. "Well, you know, maybe she don't have the money to 'mone."

"Girl, if you don't have the money to 'mone, what she out on these streets for? If you can't do the whole kit and caboodle, then don't get a vaginal installation, 'cause you are not going to be fooling the trades, okay? They are going to be spooking you from the gate, and you are going to get bashed too lovely!"

"Only this bitch is from the Bronx, so she ain't featuring a bashing, okay? That bitch will fuck a dude up like she's trade," said Santos.

"Be – Cause – She's – A MAN!" Dion hissed.

All three of them laughed, then stopped abruptly as the door once again opened.

Karen squeezed through the narrow opening of the darkened apartment. Dion immediately began to knife her fingers through her curls. "Bitch, this hair is sitting! Did you curl it yourself?"

"Mmmm hmmm. You like?"

"Yaas, bitch. Work!"

Santos snapped, "You just wanted to run your hands through it to clock whether it's a weave or not..."

Karen cooed, "And it's not."

She flipped her head down and shook her hair to confirm its authenticity. "Listen, my sister says she can't make it tonight. She just got too much to do to hang out. So it's just me and y'all."

Luq said. "She's not even wearing stockings. You have some beautiful legs."

This infuriated Dion, who prided himself on having the best legs in town. He huffed in agitation and lagged behind to watch as the rest of the crew walked toward the door. "Miss Karen, are you kidding me with that walk? That's the most ridiculous walk I've ever seen. You can't be cunt walking like one of the Philadelphia Eagles!"

Dion slammed the door behind him, the laughter of his two friends the response he had intended to elicit. "No, for real. How you gonna be cunt like that? I want to know?"

It was early evening. Darkness had fallen. Traffic driving along Dekalb Street was minimal enough for them to feel safe walking a main thoroughfare with a boy passing as a woman.

"So where we going?" Santos asked. "It's too early to be heading to the strip. Ain't nothing popping yet."

"Let's go see what Miss Rogers is doing," said Dion. She don't live too far from here, and it's on the way to the strip, so..."

"So you still trying it, huh?" said Luqman.

Dion batted innocent eyes. "Trying what?"

"Taking people down to that perverts so that you can get broke off some change," Luq snapped. "You know what I'm talking about. Don't act stupid."

"Yuck." Santos piped in. I wouldn't pull his pud with garden gloves on. She look like she stank down in the cat area, too."

Luq said, "Let me make this clear to you so you stop wasting your time. There is no way I'm about to do anything with that creep, okay? So you can just stop."

Dion's response was totally unctuous. "No way, chile. I wasn't even thinking along those lines. I just thought it would be worth a kee-kee to see her fat ass pumping around her apartment in boxers and ruby slippers, okay. I would never pimp my cousin or my sister."

"Give me a break."

"And besides. She keeps a well-stocked liquor cabinet and some bumping ass weed, so I thought we could go soak up her shit before we hit the strip."

"Did you say liquor?" Santos quipped hungrily. "What types of liquor she got, girl?"

"I knew that would get the attention of the alcoholic in the group. All types, sweetie: Miss Thunderbird, Miss Irish Rose..."

"You know Wild Irish Rose is my shit. Let's go!" Santos began to walk a bit quicker.

Dion responded. "And besides, Miss Karen never met Walt. She might be interested in what's going on."

Luq said, "So you pimping out Miss Karen. See, bitch, we going to have to give you a pimp name; like Silky or Luscious."

"Ain't nothing luscious about that bitch," Santos said, "or silky. I say we call her Cotton or Gabardine."

Luq laughed. "What about Polyester ? Or Carpet Fibers?"

"Yeah. Polly! Hey, Polly! What hos you got in the stable tonight, Miss Pol?"

"So anyway, Miss Karen..." Dion huffed, ignoring them and linking arms with Karen. "How you been doing, girl?"

"Polly want a cracker?" Santos continued.

Luq countered, "You mean Polly want a dollar. No matter whose ass she got to pimp, she bout that lira."

In an effort to ignore them, Dion began to sing loudly. Knowing that Karen patterned her appearance after, and worshipped Donna Summer, he sang "Bad Girls," and Karen began to sing along with him.

Luq rolled his eyes. "Okay, so now we have to sing a song about prostitutes? Great."

"I know, right?" Santos began to counter that song by singing the chords of "Knee Deep" overtop of them.

"What's wrong with Donna Summers?" Karen asked. "Donna Summers is the number one singer in the world right now. The *Bad Girls* 'alblum' is a winner from start to finish."

"There's nothing wrong with Donna SUMMER." Luq's inflection attempted to correct Karen's mispronunciation, eliciting snickers from Santos and Dion. "The ALBUM is good. But does everything always have to be about money and sexing? Shit."

"Okay, Miss Virgin is getting sensitive," Santos snarked.

Karen said, "Well it's not really about ho'ing. It's about surviving out on these streets. It's universal. Donna Summers is a role model. She used to be a man living in Germany with her lover, and then she got the change and moved to America, and started living her true life as a singer. That's what the whole album is about..."

Santos' brow crinkled in consternation. "Are you saying Donna Summer is a dragon?"

"No, chile. She's a real woman."

"What are you telling me, right now?" Luq screamed.

Karen continued, oblivious. "Did you ever look at her pictures? She always got on a banging ass wig."

"That's your evidence?" Dion quipped. "Black women been wearing gildas since they been able to snatch the manes off lions and the tails off horses. Girl, please."

As if not hearing them, Karen went on, "Look at the neck. Look at the shoulders. Don't no real fish got shoulders that big."

"Yup." Dion mocked her. "Look at the feet, chile. When'd you ever see feet that goddamn big on cunt? I think you right, Miss Girl."

"Yup." Karen nodded her head.

"Well, go 'head, Miss Donald Summers. I ain't mad at you. Do your thing, girl!"

The three boys laughed, Karen unaware that she was the butt of their joke.

Dion began to sing the stanza from a Stephanie Mills song. Everyone joined in, each attempting to be heard over the others:

Don't be afraid, no
I'm waiting just for you,
And if it takes you all night long
I'll see you through.
Keep on dancing, you can do it
It's non-stop now.

A car full of screaming youth drove past, and a bottle hurtled toward the pavement.

"Fucking faggots!"

Everyone dodged toward the far side of the curb, with the bottle shattering into shards against Luqman's leg.

"You all right?" Dion asked.

"Yeah. It missed."

Karen said, "See, we should have taken the side streets."

"They ain't no safer," Santos countered. "Niggas is everywhere."

"White niggas, too," said Luqman. "And they are way more dangerous than black ones. Y'all hear about all those boys gone missing in Atlanta?"

Santos huffed. "Here he go again. Talking 'bout those missing queens down south. This bitch is obsessed with those girls."

"Damn right, I am. I'm scared as shit. And y'all should be, too. People are just being snatched off the street, in broad daylight, too!"

"For real?" said Karen. "I ain't heard about that. Here in town?"

"And who said they was queens?" Luqman ignored Karen. "Didn't nobody say they was gay."

Dion said, "Come on, chile. They been talking about seeing those girls jumping into vans, and riding around with corny-ass looking white trade. If they ain't queens, they damn sure is jumping for coins. Just like what's going on here and everywhere else where a girl such as myself is trying to earn a decent living. That's why I keeps my box cutter tucked firmly in the crack of my ass, for emergencies."

Santos laughed, "Good place for it. How you going to leap into action and be Wondercunt when you are sitting on the weapon."

Luq said, "Not only that, if it's stored in her snatch, it will have fallen in far too deep to get to during the emergency, so she's fucked."

By this time, they had reached their destination; a narrow set of cement steps that hovered in the corner beside a Chinese restaurant storefront.

Dion banged on the door and gave a hoot up to the bay window on the second story.

Santos spoke in a low register, "Bitch, just so you know, I ain't trying to get into no shit with that greasy bear, either. So you are on your own. That motherfucker look like he stink. And besides, he knows Nini, too. I don't want no bullshit."

Dion looked through the window of the door and saw a pair of legs descending from the second-floor apartment located atop the restaurant. "Oh, bitch, bye. Stop acting like you all above the fray, and things. Walt told me you sucked his dick before, for ten dollars, mmkay, so don't do it."

"Okay, I maybe tasted it once or twice, but that was a one-time thing."

Luq looked repulsed. "How is once or twice a one-time thing? Can somebody tell me that?"

"Tasted is right. As little as his dick is, a taste was all anyone could get."

Dion flashed a huge smile as the door opened and his tone change from scorn to outsized solicitousness. "Hey, Walt. What's doing?"

He began to saunter into the doorway, but Walt raised a meaty hand and blocked him by the neck. "Who's the homey wearing the skirt?"

"Oh, that's my good, good girlfriend, Miss Karen. She's good people..."

Walt shook his head. "Nah. I can't have that kinda shit going down over here. You gone have to roll, my friend."

They all looked uncomfortably at Karen, who grinned and rummaged in her bag for a cigarette. "Hey, no problem. I got better things to do. I'll see y'all when you get downtown."

With that, Karen was off down Cherry street.

They followed Walt up the narrow staircase, all the while, Walt was complaining about Dion having the audacity to bring a boy in a skirt to his front door, on Cherry street, the most notorious street in town, where people were sitting out on their stoops looking for information to spread around town. During his diatribe, Dion was subtly pointing to the rolls of fat that were undulating up the stairs above them and elbowing Luqman and Santos so that they'd notice.

When they reached the apartment, Santos immediately began to scan the meagerly furnished interior in search of a liquor cart. "So, Walt. Got any refreshments? I'm parched."

Walt cocked a brow at him. "Parched? Motherfucker, you better drink your spit. What you think this is, Joe Brown's Bar?"

Dion chimed in. "That's not very hospitable, when we came here to see if you wanted us to ride down North Philly with you to see what's popping."

Walt absently scratched at his belly. "Oh yeah? Cool. He sneered at Luqman, "The virgin coming, too?"

"No," said Dion. "She ain't going. She's just with us for now. I thought you could use Karen. She got a nice body. The boys might have liked her tea..."

"You crazy? We going down to the heart of the hood. Them boys would fucking murder that faggot. Bringing your fruity ass is risky enough, but you flamboyant enough so that we get the message across."

Santos barked laughter, "Fruity!"

"Sit yo' ass down, man, and stop acting so silly," Walt told him. "Let me go get my boy to come down with us. He in the other room with some punk, but I'm sure he down to go to North."

He yelled toward the furthest interior of the apartment. "Yo' Chicago! Come out here for a sec', man."

The three of them looked at one another quizzically.

Chicago walked into the living-room, barefoot and wearing a towel around his torso. He had a cigar gripped between his teeth. Sweat slowly descended from the tightly coiled hairs on his wide chest. He eyed the boys astutely, nodding his head at them. "What's up?"

"Got some company to ride down North with. You coming."

Chicago sucked his teeth. "Ah, man. You know I got company. Let me take care of that, real quick."

At that moment, an extremely thin male entered from the back. He was the color of melted chocolate, wearing snug denim shorts and a loose t-shirt. His straightened hair was pulled back from large doe eyes into a tight ponytail.

Santos recognized him as someone that he had gone to school with. "Hey, Lonnie. I ain't seen you in a minute. What's been up."

Lonnie looked lazily toward him. The delay in recognition relayed that he was under the influence of some chemical. "Oh, hey Santos. You still at the high?"

"Yeah, you graduated, right?"

"Fuck yeah. Two years ago. Couldn't wait to be done with that shit. And live my life."

"So what you doing, now? You still dancing?"

Lonnie sucked his teeth. "Nothing, man. That dancing shit was for the birds."

Dion said, "So, you living your life doing nothing? That's fierce, girl."

Santos shot him a venomous warning look. "I like your hair. What you got, a Dark and Lovely?"

Lonnie ran a limp wristed hand across his well-oiled head. "No. This is my natural grade. You know my grandmom was Indian."

Luq snorted. Every person in town claimed Indian ancestry.

Santos noticed that the back of Lonnie's head was shaved up to the crown. "So why you cut it off in the back like that?"

"I created that look. That's so my ponytail would be longer."

Dion gaped at him. "So you gave yourself a receding hairline in reverse, so your ponytail could be longer? Huh. That's different..."

Lonnie let out an overly loud, braying laugh. "Who's your friend, he's really funny."

Chicago irritably broke into the fray. "So they was thinking about going down to North Philly to see what's what. You down?"

"Nah. I can't be gone that long. My mom would flip."

Santos tried to convince him. "Come on, man. I really need to get some extra money."

"Oh, you need money?" Walt asked. "This shit ain't going to get you no real money. If you trying to get some money, you need to get with these white dudes I know. They hold this thing like every three months or so, faggot in a box."

"What!" Dion yelled, incredulous.

"Two faggots get in a ring and fight it out. No gloves, no rounds, just go blow for blow till one can't fight no more. The winner splits the nights' take with the guy that sets it up. You can clear, like, a thousand dollars."

"And fuck up this face?" said Dion. "I think not. This is how I make my money."

"A thousand dollars?" Santos speculated. "No shit?"

Walt ignored Dion. "Anyway, get with me later, if you down."

Chicago said, "So, uh, before we go, I was thinking maybe we could all do a little something here first. So I can see what we working with."

Walt nodded his head. "Sound like a plan to me."

Santos immediately grabbed his stomach. "Okay, can I use your bathroom right quick? I gotta go."

Walt pointed him in the direction of the bathroom. As Santos walked down the hallway, Luq grabbed his bookbag and stood up. "Well, I'm off. I'll catch you when you get back."

Walt put out an arm to block his path, his eyes scanning the length of his body. "Why don't y'all head to the back, while I talk to your cousin real quick before he leaves."

Luqman felt a sense of the surreal envelope him as Walt propelled him with a hand at the shoulder. Had Walt moved him toward the bedroom, he would have put up more of a fight, but since he guided him into the kitchen, Luq felt a bit less panicked.

Santos suddenly came out of the hallway from the bathroom. "Not feeling too hot, guys. I'ma hafta catch up with y'all later."

He brushed past everyone and headed to the front door.

In the kitchen, Walt demanded that Luq unbuckle his pants.

"What? No, I got to get doing."

Walt's voice was smooth, but there was a tone of steel beneath. "Come on, man. I know you don't fuck around, yet. I just want to see what's going on. Ain't nobody going to hurt you."

Luq walked toward the doorway, but Walt blocked his path. "I can't let you leave till you do me this favor. No harm, man. You a beautiful dude. I just want to admire all of you, that's all."

Luq looked overhead at the fluorescent lights, tears burning his eyes as Walt tugged at his belt buckle. He felt his pants being pulled down and hovered his arms in front of his groin. Walt brushed them aside, and lifted his large shirt, breathing lightly.

"There. That wasn't so bad, was it? Pretty. Real nice..."

Luq yanked his pants up, and rushed out of the kitchen, heading straight toward the door. Dion rose from the sofa, following his cousin. "Well, I'm going to have to take a rain check, too. I'm not going down to the city by myself."

Walt countered. "You sit your black ass down. You ain't alone. Lonnie will go down. He ain't got no choice. Just sit tight right there, and I'll go tell Chicago to move his ass."

Dion nodded reluctantly, hearing the door slam as Luqman rushed out.

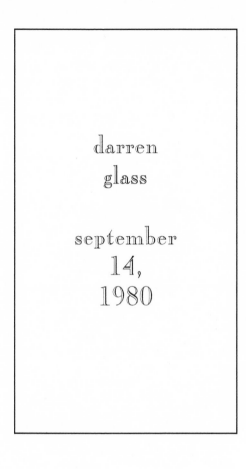

darren
glass

september
14,
1980

GLORIA

Santos sat at the kitchen table smoking a cigarette. A large trash bag sat at his feet. He looked across the table at Jonas, who was sitting on another trash bag, as if it were a beanbag chair. Jonas looked back with a blank expression.

"No! I don't want his faggot ass here!" Nini yelled. "You spread your legs to have him; now you want me to raise him because he kicked your new mans' ass?"

Santos blew out a plume of smoke. Yasmine stood at the sink, her hands wet with dishwater.

Gloria's voice was strident but confident that she would get her way. "I did all I can wit' the boy. I raised him. Him wan' go to school. Don't bring in no money. Don't I deserve some happiness after raising you kids?

Nini looked quizzically. "You fucking joking, right?"

Yasmine tried to be the voice of reason. "How we expected to feed that boy? He eat like a full grown man. You expect us to take care of that ourselves?"

"I'll send you money every week."

Nini looked at Yasmine, close to defeated. "What about Jonas?"

Gloria sighed. "Me keep 'im with me. That's the baby."

"You mean he got a social security check." Santos quipped. Gloria moved aggressively toward him, and he stood, in preparation to retaliate.

Gloria stopped in her tracks. "You see what I mean. Look at him, ready to fight him mama like she a stranger inna street."

As it dawned on him that Gloria intended to take him with her, Jonas threw himself on the floor and began to scream at the top of his lungs, clinging to Santos' pant leg as if it were a life raft.

Gloria glared at him, totally void of maternal instinct.

"Why don't you let the both of them stay," Yasmine whispered. "You know Jonas will die without San."

"Besides, you gonna leave him at the house so the same shit can happen to him that happened to us? I don't think so." Nini snorted, snatching the cigarette from Santos' mouth and toking it himself. "At least this way, we sure to get some kind of payment."

Everyone in the kitchen took turns glaring at one another.

LUQMAN

Luqman lay on the Oriental rug, facing away from the large console television, watching the screen with his eyes straining to see beyond his forehead, at Joan Crawford pantomiming her way through the life of Sadie Thompson in "Rain." It was pantomime because he could not hear the sound, due to Dion's need to have the radio blaring, seemingly at all times.

Dion yowled the chords of "Aladdin's Lamp," by Teena Marie, while also trying to mouth the words contained in the letter with a giant gold header emblazoned with a crest and Pittsburgh School of Design at the top.

Toni was sprawled perpendicular to Luq, with her stiffly sprayed head resting on his torso, reading Luq's copy of *Interview* magazine, while also admiring Joan Crawford's heavily maquillaged visage. "How did they get the movie stars' skin so smooth back in the thirties? I would kill for that make-up job."

His eyes never left the paper, and his voice sounded distracted, as he continued to read the contents of the letter in his hand. "You serious, bitch? You already paint your face so pale you look like a zombie. Now you want to be beat so that you look like the zombie of a masculine 1930s movie star? You'll never pull like that. Who's going to be pulling up wanting a dead body to jump in their ride?"

Before she could respond, Dion spoke to Luqman. "My God, this is awesome. You got accepted to the fashion design program. Why aren't you excited."

Luq continued watching the movie. "I am excited. I guess."

"Isn't this the school you wanted to go to?"

"Sort of. I really wanted F.I.T., but there's too many murderers and perverts up there, so I settled for applying to Pittsburgh."

"Bitch. You sound retarded. There are murderers and perverts right the fuck here. Probably next door."

"And in Pittsburgh, too," Toni added.

"What Aunt Carol say? Is she happy for you?"

"She said I better find a job up there because she doesn't have money to send to me."

"You always have a job." Dion snorted, "She don't give you money NOW."

"I'm kind of scared, you know. I never been away from home before. Not like that. And with all those killings going on in Atlanta...I know this is not Atlanta, but not being around people I know, that's got my back. I should have gone up to visit the place first, I guess. I wish I could do that before I commit to going."

"Why can't you? I understand about being a little leery. Hell, I'm worried every night I step out that door that I might not make it back. But you can't let that stop you. Hell, bitch, you got to become a famous fashion designer so I can move into your penthouse and be your publicist. Didn't we always talk about me working for you? Yes, bitch! I will come in each morning with my hair snatched up into a topknot, eyes beat for the gawds, in a tight pencil skirt, and six-inch stilettos, yaaas!"

Luqman laughed at the vision. "Bitch, you too bald-headed to even be bottom-knotted, let alone top. And a pencil skirt? So you want to drive away all my goddamn customers? And where you going to find a stiletto in a size sixteen wide?"

"Why couldn't you schedule a visit, now?" Toni asked. "I'll go up there with you. We could take the Greyhound. It'd be a couple hours' ride. It'd be fun.

"Seriously? You'd do that?"

"Why not? I lived there for a little while, so I can show you the spots to go."

"That is so awesome."

"So it's settled," Dion said. "You will set up a visit with the school. Miss Toni will go up with you to make sure everything is copacetic, and our new life will begin."

Dion folded the paper and placed it back in the envelope, handing it over to Luq.

"Since Miss D is going to be your publicist, I guess I will have to be your personal assistant. I can help you buy fabrics and give input on designs."

"You?" Dion's voice cracked, incredulous. "Give input on designs, Miss Thing....?"

Luqman intervened before things took an ugly turn. "What about Santos. What job would be left for him?"

"For real?" Dion asked. "Since this bitch is so well versed with taking shit that don't belong to her, she might as well be your security detail."

"Ha! That'd be perfect. Except he'd be stealing my shit, so what would be the point?"

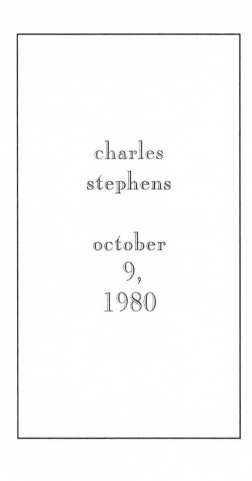

charles
stephens

october
9,
1980

ATLANTA

It had not taken long for Santos to unpack his belongings. Nini and Yasmine had set up a cot in the only vacant room in their modest rowhome for Jonas' use. Yasmine washed and folded the moldy smelling clothing in the trash bag, and folded them into the warped dresser jammed into a corner of the room.

Santos had been relegated to the unfinished basement, a damp, cavernous space filled with overhead pipes and unpredictably erupting mechanical devices that mysteriously (to him) kept the house supplied with heat, water, and plumbing. Nini communicated to him that he would be using the basement by standing by the door to the cellar, which stood off beneath the stairs leading to upper levels, inside a nook of the large kitchen, by wordlessly pointing, and tossing his bag of clothing down the steps, and then mumbling something about not bringing no faggot ass niggas in his house at night.

Santos was rather happy with his new digs. The basement gave him a degree of privacy. The location was rather cool on sweltering days. The space was large, with lots of crannies that he could partition off with curtains into different 'rooms.' He designed a makeshift apartment by segregating different areas with curtains, lodged his mattress onto a few jutting pipes to create a platform bed, and critically surveyed the peeling cement walls to determine the best locations for his pilfered collection of movie star photos.

The best reasons that he liked being located in the lower-most portions of the house were; Nini vindictively thought of it as a punishment, but it was an advantage. The basement had a door that lead to the backyard, which allowed him to come and go without having to explain himself to anyone, and the close proximity to the phone hanging on the kitchen wall allowed him to dash up the stairs whenever it rang, getting him there before anyone else had the chance to answer.

Oddly enough, Luqman seemed to be excluded from the 'faggot ass niggas' designation. Despite his spiked hair, eyeliner, and huge pants painted with large dandelions, he seemed to meet with Yasmine's approval.

He, Santos and Jonas were sitting in the basement, reading from *Ebony* magazine while lying on the bed. They all looked up as they heard the doorbell ring, then went back to their activities.

Jonas was adjusting the colors of a Rubik's cube, grunting confusedly. From upstairs, they heard the door open, and Yasmine speaking animatedly. Other, lower voices responded to her, and the sound of hard-soled shoes, at least two pair, reverberated from the wooden floors above.

Luq read the article from the magazine aloud.

"Late in the evening of October 9, twelve-year-old Charles Stephens had gone missing. He was found murdered the next morning on a hillside. Stephens had died from suffocation from an unknown object. At the crime scene, the evidence has been found to be inconclusive, due to contamination by the Atlanta Police Force throwing a blanket over the corpse in an effort to cover his nude body.

An un-named drug dealer reported to area police the day after Stephen's body was discovered. He told police that on the same day of the disappearance, he had gotten into the car of a client of his to sell drugs. When the drug dealer looked into the back seat of the car, he saw a young boy lying lifeless with his head turned towards the trunk and wrapped in a sheet. When he asked about the boy, the driver of the car became angry and told him the boy was merely doped up and passed out.

Police have interviewed the man in question, a known pedophile with a history of offering money to young boys with whom he could have sex. Police have determined that the allegations are unfounded."

They heard the front door slam and footsteps moving toward the kitchen, then down the stairs to the basement. Yasmine entered the room with a shadow following her on the stairs. A grizzled old man descended to the landing. Jonas twitched his nose at the smell of sweat and wet wool.

Yasmine smiled tentatively. "Hey, y'all. This is my father. He's been missing for a while. A long while. The police found him, after all this time, in Norristown, of all places. He's going to be staying here for a minute until we find somewhere for him to go."

Santos was astounded. "Flukey Luke? Flukey Luke is your dad?"

"Silas," Jonas whispered.

Santos and Yasmine stared at Jonas with their mouths agape.

Silas walked forward with a large grin, patting Jonas on the shoulder. "How you been, little man? So, you family? Ain't that nice."

"When'd you start talking?" Santos asked.

Jonas shrugged, engaged with his Rubik's cube. "I always talked. I just don't talk to people that call me retard."

Silas nodded his head and reached out to shake hands with Luqman. "How's it going there, young fella? What you reading?"

He took the magazine from Luq's hands, lowering himself to the bed while ignoring the look of disgust Santos aimed at him.

Yasmine put her hands on her hips and sighed. "Well, I'm going to leave you down here for little bit, while I call Nini. Let him know what's going on. Then I'll draw you a bath and fix you something to eat. How's that sound?"

They all ignored her, as Silas began to read. Yasmine brushed her hands together and walked up the stairs.

Mothers of the murdered and missing children of Atlanta have banded together to form the Committee to Stop Children's Murders (CSCM) as a support group. In light of the fact that the death count continues to escalate, and police response has been minimal thus far, CSCM have begun to lobby as a political force working to pressure city officials to more thoroughly investigate these tragic events, hopefully to track the perpetrators and bring them to justice.

On the heels of the discovery of the skeletal remains of LaTonya Wilson, missing since June 22, 1980, Atlanta officials have established a task force, which has begun to investigate the possibility of a serial protagonist that is targeting impoverished street vagrants within a very specific location.

"Well, that's good, right? They finally will try to find out who is doing this shit, right?" said Santos.

Luq said, "I guess. I didn't know the mothers had banded together to try to get the cops to DO something."

Silas closed the magazine angrily. "Don't be fooled, young fellas. You see they are talking about one man doing all this by themselves? That's how white people change what's truth and make their own version of the truth."

"How's that?" Luq rose from the bed and walked over to the table against the other wall. He grabbed the box of Cap'n Crunch and took out a handful of cereal.

"They trying to say that one person has killed all these kids. One person, even though they are not all being killed the same way. Serial killers follow a pattern. Some of these kids been raped, some not. The two girls they found were tied to a tree. None of the boys were. Some had their throat cut, some strangled, others just beaten. So, now, instead of taking the time to investigate each murder and trying to pinpoint who, where and why these kids been killed, they will just lump them all together and look for one man. A scapegoat."

"You think?" Luq asked. "You're right about serial killers having a pattern. I read about Charles Manson and that Bundy guy. They did what they did the same way every time."

"This how the white man makes his own truth. You read that paper I give you?"

"What paper?" asked Santos.

Luq nodded his head. "So doctors lied to all those farmers? Told them they were giving them treatment for bad blood, and really, they were letting a sexually transmitted disease make them even sicker?"

"Who says this? What doctors?" Santos asked.

"This happened to you?" Luq asked.

Silas nodded his head. "It's still happening. The government made them put a stop to the studies not too long ago. And then they made a payout to the folks that was still living, or to the families of the ones they watched die. I didn't trust that shit, by that point. I figured if I went in to collect my money, what's to stop them from just killing me off right there on the spot? So I packed up my shit and got out of town. Been roaming around ever since. I knew my daughter moved up to P.A., but it was never my intention to let her know I was close by. If I hadn't been picked up by Norristown cops, I wouldn't be here right now."

"Medical experiments...?" Santos asked absently. Jonas dropped his cube and watched his brother closely.

"You might think all this talk is too much for the little one to hear. But we not like white people. If we tell our youngsters that the world is a great place and that the police are here to protect you, all y'all will end up dead in the streets. The cops aren't here to protect you. They here to protect the world FROM you. 'Cause they convinced the world that we all criminals; ain't got no value. The things you kids need to know is different from what little white kids need to know. You need to know how to conduct yourself in public, and in front of the police. You need to know what to do to keep yourself safe on these streets, 'cause in this world, black bodies are vulnerable. I'm here to show you how to survive."

From upstairs, Yasmine's sing-song voice rang out. "Pop, your bath is ready."

The old man struggled to rise from the bed, nodded to the boys, and meandered up the stairs.

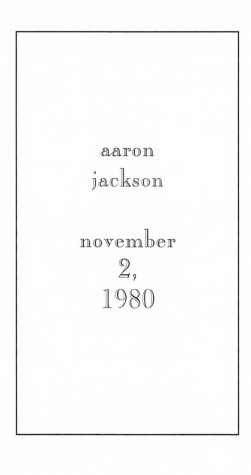

aaron
jackson

november
2,
1980

SNEAK ATTACK

"Put on your big-girl panties, bitch," Dion admonished, looking through the front door window to Walt's apartment. "I'm just going to pick up these coins he owes me. We won't be here long. Besides, it's not like I'm going to let the gorilla rape you, or anything."

Luqman crossed his bony arms and glared at him. Walt flung open the door and immediately turned to head back up the stairs, talking on the phone. He pulled the long cord after himself. They followed him up the stairs. Dion once again pointed out the undulating rolls of ass fat. Luq did not find it very amusing, this time.

Walt hung up the phone with a loud bang. They heard a deep voice swearing from the rear of the apartment. "Y'all picked a bad time to stop by, man. Chicago is flipping the fuck out."

As if in confirmation, there was a loud crash from Chicago's bedroom. Dion and Luq jumped.

"What's up?" Dion asked.

"Y'all remember that punk from the last time you were here? Lonnie?"

Dion sucked his teeth in disdain.

"Yeah. Well, Chicago had this very expensive nugget ring on the dresser, and later on, after we got back from the city, he noticed that it wasn't there. We looked high and low for that ring and couldn't find it. The dumb ass must've taken the shit while they was handling business."

Luqman and Dion exchanged wary glances. Dion cocked an eyebrow at him but kept his voice at an excessively even keel, which was to warn Luq to keep neutral.

"You lying? Who would be dumb enough to take shit from you? Especially when they come here on the regular."

Walt corrected him. "Oh, he ain't steal shit from me, let's be clear. He stole that shit from Chicago. Had it been me, that faggot ass be dead in the water right now. Chicago called him not too long ago to come over, so he can get his shit back."

As if on cue, the doorbell chimed. Walt smirked and skulked off to answer.

When they were alone, Dion turned to Luq and spoke very slowly and deliberately, sweat bursting onto his brow. "Be cool. If we run out of here like we crazy, they gonna know we know something. So we got to sit up in here for a few and act real cool until it looks like we can roll out with no problems. Do Not Say Shit. You got me?"

Eyes large with terror, Luq nodded. "San couldn't have taken shit. He left out of here before I did."

"Didn't I say don't say shit!" Dion hissed. "Of course the stupid bitch took it. She got sticky fingers. And she need money, too? She'd steal the shit stains out your drawers if she could take it to the pawn shop for money. Now be chill. Be cunt. Follow my lead."

Dion elaborately spread himself out onto the velour sofa, crossing his legs and digging in his bag for a cigarette. His shaking hands belied his calm demeanor.

Luqman sat beside him, attempting to stop the tremors that assaulted his limbs as Walt and Lonnie entered the apartment.

Lonnie smiled and waved at them. "Hey, guys. How you doing?"

"Hey," Dion responded. Luq sat silently, staring.

Walt said. "Chicago's in his room. You can go on back."

As Lonnie walked out of the room, Walt went to the stereo and turned the radio on, turning the volume very high.

Walt then yelled, "Be right back."

He went to his bedroom, and there was a loud crash. Luq sat stiffly, hugging himself as more sounds erupted from the rear of the house. Suddenly, they heard Lonnie screaming, and the wet sound of flesh being hammered.

They could hear Lonnie begging in a high pitched voice. "I swear, man! I didn't take anything! Stop, please!"

After another loud crash, Luq began to cry. "We can't just sit here. We have to stop him. Maybe if we tell him, we can get it back from San..."

Luq stood up and began to walk toward the screaming noises. Dion lunged for him and grabbed his arm.

"Do you think that's what's going to go down if you go back there? You think that crazy nigga is going to put a halt to that ass kicking and listen to you try to bargain with him? He will just start kicking two asses instead of one."

"Well, I can't sit here and listen to this. I'm leaving."

He ran toward the hallway. Dion ran behind him.

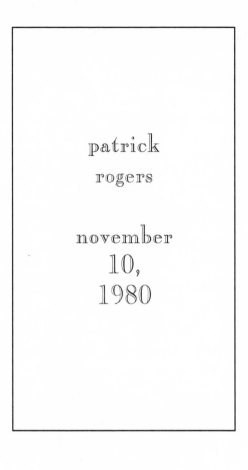

patrick
rogers

november
10,
1980

LUQMAN

The Norristown Police Station was an impressively columned marble structure located on a secondary road in the center of town. In order to access the administrative office of the station, however, one needed to bypass the main entrance, walk through a narrow side alley to the rear parking lot, and ring the bell beside the gray steel door with a small glass window protected with wire mesh, located at head level.

Luqman pressed the buzzer for the third time. He leaned against the wall and huffed in annoyance.

A voice squawked out of the speaker with static-filled authority. "Yeah?"

Luq lowered his head so that his mouth was about one inch from the speaker. He struggled to mask the sound of annoyance that he felt from his voice. "Hi again. Um, I've been waiting to have an officer take down my report of an assault. I've been out here for, like, twenty minutes now. The officer said he would be right out."

"What assault?"

"I witnessed a kid getting beaten up by this man that lives at 822 Cherry street a few days ago..." Luq looked up at the sound of electronica activating. The camera above the door blinked to life, aiming down at him.

"How old was this kid?"

"I don't know. Nineteen? Twenty?"

"Sex."

"Huh?"

"What is the gender of the alleged victim?"

"Oh. Uh, male."

"Do the two individuals involved cohabitate?"

"No..."

"What is the nature of their relationship?"

"I don't know. What do you mean?"

"Are the individuals involved engaged in a relationship of a sexual nature?

Luqman paused. "I...I don't know...."

The voice cut him off. "Hold on a sec."

After waiting for another five minutes, the voice returned. "What are the names of the individuals please."

"I don't know their last names. But I have the address where it happened."

"Okay. Thank you. We've taken your information. Thank you for your time."

"Don't you want my name?"

There was no response. Luq stood there staring at the dirty gray box. He shrugged and walked out of the parking lot, through the alley and up the steep incline of Airy Street toward the courthouse. At the intersection, a hulking black Cadillac zoomed by him. He thought the vehicle had cut him off a little earlier in the day. He paid little heed, as vehicles were known to circle this radius of town, on the prowl for working girls.

When the car circled again at the lower side of the courthouse, as he crossed Main Street to get to the train station, Luq strained to see if he recognized the driver. The darkened glass obscured identification. Luq had decided to go home. He was exhausted by his fruitless encounter with the police. He just wanted to go home and rest, start reading his new book. He was so tired that, instead of walking, as he would normally have done, he intended to take the bus, and he cut through the foliage below Lafayette Street to get to the Reading Railroad station.

While standing on the platform, the black Cadillac sped up the incline and parked. A lean man with a shaved head wearing a white button-down shirt and black pants climbed from the car and rushed over to Luq. It seemed to Luq, from the proximity that the man stood to him, that he knew him, but his face was unfamiliar to him.

"What you doing?" he asked.

"On the way home." Luq assumed the man had seen him out and about with Dion and Santos and was confusing him with one of them.

"Take this walk with me real quick." He jerked his head toward the underpass that linked the eastbound train access with the westbound.

"Nah. I got to get home." Although he denied him, Luq considered the offer. With the thought that he would be going off to college when he finished his senior year, he had determined that it would be a good strategy to lose his virginity. He had grown weary of being the butt of jokes based upon his lack of sexual prowess. He did not want the same reputation to follow him to Pittsburgh. The problem was that whenever he reached a scenario of potential interaction, his stomach became so upset that he ended up denying any continuation to fruition.

The man grabbed his arm and gently but urgently pulled him toward the darkened underpass. "Won't take long. Come on with me."

He tried to control the wild tremors that began to impede him from walking in his usual manner. He silently allowed himself to be led down into the cool underbelly of the station, which reeked of stagnant water and vagrant piss.

Once they were located at the center of the tunnel, the man frantically unzipped his pants and pulled his appendage from the fly of a pair of brilliantly white boxers. The sight of uncircumcised evidence of the man's arousal created a turmoil of confusion in Luq's stomach. The man placed the palm of his hand behind the boy's head and pushed on his neck, down toward his angry, insistent penis.

Luq struggled free, placing his hands on the man's loins to push himself back to an upright position. "Sorry, I can't..."

Before he could finish speaking, his head did a sudden quick jerking motion, before he saw a brief flash of red that then faded to blue. He wasn't at first certain that he had been struck across the temple, until the man struck again, a blow to his cheekbone that turned him from facing the black pantlegs toward the entrance to the tunnel.

Luq quickly turned back to the opposite entrance and ran to get out of the enclosed space. After the moment it took to tuck himself back into his pants, Luq heard hard soled shoes echoing after him, and angry yelling reverberated along the concrete walls.

A sense of fear mixed with that of outrage for having had his person violated. Luq paced along the length of the black

Cadillac, picking up a large cinderblock lying against the station house. The man came to a halt.

"You better not. I will fucking kill you."

Luq weighed the options and made a decision he raised the block over his head and brought it down into the windshield with a scream of rage. He then ran toward the exit and down the stairs.

Once in the shadows offered by the stairwell, Luq stopped to catch his breath, listening for the sound of footsteps behind him. Hearing none, he waited. He then heard the sound of a car door slamming and an engine roaring to life, tires squealing on tarmac. When he was certain that Cadillac had left the parking lot, he backtracked up the stairs and raced through the underpass, using the cover of the foliage to stay hidden, lest the car zoom down Lafayette street. He rushed up the hill of Airy Street, knowing that the one-way street would take a while before the Cadillac made the circuitous route toward Airy. He rushed through the courthouse courtyard, and up the stairs to the upper level, where he sat upon one of the stone benches encircling maple saplings, and rested his head in his hands, taking large gasps of air.

A hand grasped his shoulder, and he leaped up with a shout.

Startled, Toni screamed too. "What!? What's wrong?"

He turned to look at her, standing in a defensive stance against his antagonized response, and sat back down, crying uncontrollably.

She sat beside him, pulling his head to her shoulder as he continued to sob, talking through gasps for air.

While Luq told her what had happened, Santos and Dion approached from the opposite end of the courtyard.

Dion reached into his bag to be sure his box cutter was among its contents, then said, "Okay, let's go down. We will sit down there all night. You let us know if this motherfucker shows up. We all ready?"

Everyone nodded stoically. Toni pulled a handkerchief from her purse and handed it to Luq. He wiped his face, stood up, and they all headed back down toward the transportation center, one silent, focused entity.

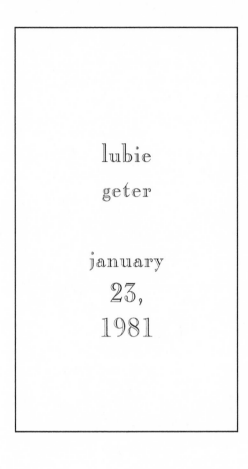

lubie
geter

january
23,
1981

SANTOS

The two of them sat in the back room of Walt's Sneak Attack. Walt was on the showroom floor, demonstrating a few pair of basketball shoes to a customer. Since the customer was not just a minor, but included parents, he had warned Santos and Dion not to leave the storeroom until he returned to let them know that it was all clear.

Dion was smoking a cigarette, and staring at Santos with disbelief. "Why would you do that? That's crazy, to me. You going to let some queen go to town on your face for some little bit of change?"

"You call a thousand dollars a little bit of change?"

Dion laughed. "Come on, now, bitch. This dumb blonde routine was cute for a little while, but now you are starting to be an embarrassment. Do you really think those slimy motherfuckers are going to be pulling in that kind of money by charging to watch a couple of faggots fight? And even if they did, you best believe that they will not be on the up and up with giving you your proper take."

Santos stood up and paced the small space of the room. "Maybe. But no matter what it is I need the money. You know how it is living with my brother? He don't feed me; he don't give me any money. I got nothing to eat. They call Jonas down to eat every evening and act like I'm not even there. I got no weed, no cigarettes, no beer..."

"That's tragic, chile." Dion chirped insincerely.

Santos glared furiously. Dion went into his bag and extended a hand with three ten dollar bills. "Here you go. If you needed some money, why didn't you say something before? You know I wouldn't see you go hungry. You could have even asked White Girl."

Santos took the money with a look of gratitude, tucking it into his tight yellow jeans. "Thanks. I would rob banks before asking that white bitch for her help. Anytime she does you a solid; you best believe there's something in it for her. She slimy."

"Girl, she white. Of course, she can't be trusted. Just take the goddamn money and fuck her. She ask you to do something you look at that bitch like her pussy stink." Dion then lowered his voice, looking toward the doorway to be sure Walt wasn't coming. "And I guess robbing a bank wouldn't be much of a stretch for you, after snatching Chicago's ring, now would it? How much you get for it, you treacherous bitch?"

Santos' voice rose two octaves. All the evidence Dion needed to know that he was lying. "What ring? I don't know what you're talking about."

As Santos batted his eyes in a display of innocence, Dion scornfully blew a tuft of cigarette smoke in his face. "Bitch, bye. Who you think you talking to. How much?"

"Couple hundred."

"You know Miss Lonnie got beat like a dark-skinned field hand for that shit, right? Chicago fucked that bitch up," he laughed savagely. "Then fucked her up. If you know what I mean."

Santos laughed. "Fuck that tired bitch. I don't give a fuck about her and her lying, putting on airs ass. She probably had that ass kicking coming for something, anyway, so it was her just due."

Dion fanned smoke fumes out of his face. "You a shady bitch. Sha-dy...Well anyway, I know that money I gave you wasn't much, but I hope that, and your ill-gotten gains, will persuade you not to do that stupid ass faggot in a box shit."

Walt entered the room as Dion said the last part of his sentence. "Man, mind your business. Don't be trying to talk my boy out of doing this shit just because you too punk-ass to do it. That's good ass money, and you know it."

"I don't know shit. But I know one thing for sure and two things for certain: ain't going to be no winners with a bunch of crackers paying to watch two black faggots beating on each other. I'm not feeding into any type of bullshit like that. And anyone that does is addlebrained."

PITTSBURGH

Luq lie on a narrow bed snug against beige concrete walls, reading a newspaper article. The sound of water reverberated through the room. He looked around. While the room was somewhat small, barely accommodating the three beds that were placed as far from each other as the space allowed, the two full-length windows stretching from floor to ceiling brought in the light of the sun, giving the illusion of more space than actually available. Two dressers and a small wooden This End Up closet were also taking up space along the walls alongside each respective bed.

Luq thought, when he moved here in the fall, he would choose the stand-alone closet rather than one of the dressers. That way he could hang his clothes so that they would not wrinkle, and the shelving at the top would give him a place for a few folded items, too. He would definitely need some sort of temporary crates or bins for socks and underwear. He wondered why the room only included two monstrous wooden desks. One would think that a place of higher learning would think that desks were more important to provide its students than containers for clothing.

Toni popped her head around the corner, her hair wet and lank from the shower. "Did you bring shampoo?"

Continuing to read, Luq nodded, "Check my bag."

She walked out with a towel wrapped around her torso and rifled through his bag. "I love Pantene, great."

Luq had been relieved to find that the dorm rooms had private bathrooms. One of the things he had been dreading most about considering living on campus had been communal showers, which had been a constant source of dread at high school. The taunts, the towels snapping, the loud abrasive macho posturing. He had coped by using the strategy of late arrival. If he arrived just five minutes after the scheduled start of gym class, he could rush into the locker room and pretend that he had changed there, all the while wearing his gym shorts under his pants.

The people at Pittsburgh School of Design had been very nice. When they saw that he had appeared for his tour with a companion, they had cordially set the two of them up in a dorm room and then proceeded to deposit Toni in the room while they accompanied Luqman to a pattern making class, a hat making class, and a jewelry design class.

Luq had been somewhat relieved that the administrators had taken him to tour without Toni. He had expected that she would have worn clothing more befitting of interacting with school officials, but she showed up at the bus terminal in Philadelphia with her platinum hair teased out into stiff curls, and wore an off-white synthetic dress intended to give the illusion of silk, cut low in the front, with deep draping, and black high heeled shoes.

Luq could tell Toni had attempted to tone things down. The dress was more sedate than what she usually wore. The length was respectably knee length, and she wore flesh-colored pantyhose, and only her lips and eyelids held colors from lightly applied make-up. She had forgone the aggressively applied swaths of color usually applied to her cheekbones that were her interpretation of Kim Alexis', but her heavy-handedness made even her attempts at subtlety not-so-subtle.

Toni entered the room in a beige bra and panties. She rummaged through her bag on one of the beds and took out a blow-dryer. "Where's an outlet?"

"By the desk, is one."

Toni made the pretense of looking, then said, "Where? I don't see it."

Luq rose from the bed took the blow-dryer from her hands, plugged it into the wall, then set the dryer on the desk and pulled out the chair so that she could sit down.

"Thanks." She clicked on the dryer, flipped her head upside down and began drying her hair. Luq went back to the bed and continued reading.

Luq had enjoyed the six-hour bus ride to get to Pittsburgh. He liked driving across the expanse of Pennsylvania, seeing the different ways that people lived. The farmlands, the bucolic small town vistas, the mountains, the dirty but bustling cityscapes. He also enjoyed talking with Toni about their hopes, their aspirations, the events of their lives. He liked the stops, where he could get off the bus and briefly explore places that had only been names on a map, before now.

Toni had proven to be a competent educator, giving him advice on proper traveling etiquette. Keep your bag on your person at all times. If you rest, at the most, put your bag on the filthy terminal floor, but rest your feet on top, or put the bag in the crook of your knee so that you feel if someone tries to move it, if you happen to fall asleep. Do not make eye contact with bums that approach, or with the smooth-talking men, who might be trying to make a sexual transaction, but who may also just as likely be attempting to get you to an isolated place in order to rob you. If you go to the toilet take your bag into the stall with you, and keep the bag strapped in front of you because stealthy thieves might reach over the top of the stall while you urinate and steal something of value from one of the zippers before you even become aware of it. Instead of spending your quarters for ten minutes of television, sit in an empty seat next to someone that is already watching the TV hooked to their seat and watch it for free. Always sit as close to the cashier's booth as possible. That is the location where the least violence will take place. Keep your money tucked in a place of limited public access: your shoe, or sock, or your underwear. Put a few dollars in your pockets so that you can reach it without having people seeing you go into your real stash if you need to buy a snack or magazine, or pay for some other incidental. Do not talk to anyone. The nicer they are, the more respectable they look, the slimier they probably are. Do not trust a white person unless they are wearing official garb, and even then be wary. Black people are honest about their shit. If they want your money, they will ask if you have a couple dollars. If they want sex, they will ask for sex. If they are looking for drugs, they will ask you if you know anything about it. But white people are not as forthcoming. They will act officious and focus on rules and laws to a degree that seems maniacal, but that is a distraction to make you feel off kilter. Meanwhile, they are picking your pocket, or backing you into a corner so that their crony can hit you over the head.

Luq had stared at her. "But you're white...right?"

Toni had laughed. "That's why I know. There aren't many people that are going to tell you like I'm telling you. When it comes to the races, there's black truth, and there's white truth. But when the two are interacting, there seems like there's a different interpretation for truth, that's totally different for each side."

Toni turned off her hair dryer, shaking out her hair. She then searched for her curling iron and plugged it in to allow it time to heat up.

Luq asked himself why she had not plugged both appliances in at the same time. That way, by the time she had dried her hair, the curling iron would have been ready. This was the thing that annoyed Luq about Toni. He wondered if this were a thing for all women. He remembered always waiting impatiently for his mother to finish getting ready for church while he and his siblings sat in uncomfortably fitting ties and starched clothing.

Whenever the gang made plans to go into the city, he always had to convince Santos and Dion to wait for Toni, who could be counted on to be at least one hour behind schedule, while they all waited for her to apply and re-apply makeup, and to get her hair just right, even though, to them, it always seemed to result in the same fried, electrified appearance.

Luq would try to justify the wait by pointing out that women had more to do, what with hair and makeup application, but Dion had scoffed.

"Do you see how flawlessly this face is beat? And this hair is coiffed for points? So, bitch, don't give me that shit about her needing more time to get it right. It'd be one thing if she came out here, and it was right, but girl, it be dead wrong, each and every time!"

"What?" Toni asked. "What's so funny?"

"Nothing," Luq replied. "Hey, listen to this:"

Public concern continues to grow concerning the series of child murders. Police have begun making appearances on the evening news to report on the status of their investigations. They have begun to seek consultation from psychics in an effort to come up with leads, and to seek consultation from experts from other cities. On January 9 of this year, two more children's skeletons were discovered, but evidence has been contaminated by FBI and police officers securing bones from different crime scenes in the same bags.

Fulton County medical examiner R.E. Stivers has threated to sue the Atlanta P.D. and the FBI for tampering with a crime scene, as they recover more teeth and bones from the site currently under investigation.

Although several suspects have been questioned, no arrests have been made. Police agree that at least some of the murders are linked and hypothesize that there are several sets of killers. They also still suspect that some of the murdered children may have been killed by the usual people who kill kids – their own parents, as many kids from poor black environments who turn up missing, are often runaways or victims of their own parents.

The Committee to Stop Children's Murders representative Camille Bell, formerly of '60s civil rights organization SNNC (Student Nonviolent Coordinating Committee) blames both classism and racism for the marathon of official apathy. According to Bell, "It takes a lot to get people concerned about a child out of the ghettos. The feeling of the middle class, who cops and bureaucrats tend to be, is, 'These people don't care about their children, so why should I?' But a lot of these ghetto people care deeply. Their kids are about the only things they have in the world.

Luq folded the paper neatly. "So this has me thinking about what you were saying on the bus; about different realities, different versions of the truth for whites and blacks."

"What about it?"

"Well. These kids seem just like us. Some of them go off with adults; some don't. Some of them live in houses; some live in apartments. But the papers say they all have been kidnapped out of the projects. We don't live in projects. We don't live in the ghetto. We don't have a lot of money, but that doesn't mean we live in the ghetto."

"Yeah? So? Do you think the news is saying they all are from the ghetto to make black people look bad?"

Luq's forehead crinkled in thought. "I don't think it's that. I think maybe the CSCM might be making things worse. I mean, I think they are needed. Nobody would be doing anything about trying to find out what's happening down there without the CSCM, but I think they are maybe distracting attention from the truth by putting their own truth over top of the real story. So that would be sort of like what you are saying about a black truth versus a white truth."

Toni curled another piece of hair, watching him. "I don't get it."

"Black people talk about ghetto. But they don't always mean that you're poor or living in the projects. They are talking about how you grew up, who you know, who you hang out with. It's all a small group of families and friends that you maybe knew all your life."

"Socializing and stuff?"

"Yeah. Who you socialize with. And if they all live in a certain area, that's the ghetto."

"But when they say ghetto to white people, they only see it as a bunch of niggas in the projects living on welfare, drinking 40-ounces, beating up their wives, selling drugs…"

Luq laughed. Toni laughed along with him. "You can be middle class and still be looked at as ghetto. I'm not poor. My mom and stepdad work, we live in a good neighborhood, I go to school, have a job, on my way to college. If I turn up missing tomorrow, the papers will say that I am a poor nigga that was known to go off in cars with men in nondescript vans. That's the other thing the papers are going out of their way to avoid explicitly stating. They are hinting around about these guys going off with other guys so that it all appears shady, but they refuse to state that homosexual shit is going on. They don't want to turn off their readers by bringing in the stomach-turning faggotry that is obviously jumping off down there, like it is every other town where there are fucking perverted old men trolling for young boys. And girls."

"I see what you're saying. But if the papers are making these kids looks sleazy anyway, why would they take care not to paint them as gay?"

"Well, painting black kids as sleazy, and telling everyone that they are all poor project dwelling nobodies is the typical story we all get of black people, so that just feeds the stereotype, and people will buy that. Literally. But if you start talking about dick suckers and ass fuckers, well, the 'middle class' white readership may not be so anxious to buy the paper to read about that. That's disgusting."

Her hair fully curled, Toni fluffed it up with her fingers and shook her head wildly. "I think I get it. Like, for me, when I'm around you guys, I talk in a different way. I use more slang, curse more. That's how I fit in, show you guys I'm just regular people, just like you. But if somebody white overhears us talking, they think we don't know how to talk proper English, that we are stupid or street people."

"Yes. It doesn't matter where you live. You have just changed perceptions or altered reality. Now white people think you aren't like them. It doesn't matter where I live, as far as they're concerned, I come from the projects. Even though we don't have any project in King of Prussia, there's these apartments down on Prince Frederick Road. They all think that since I'm black, I must live at Prince Frederick apartments, and Prince Frederick apartments are subsidized housing, for poor people.

"That's why I say CSCM is trying to get people that don't care to take some action, but the only way they can do that is by lying. The only way white people might give a shit about us getting taken off the streets and killed is to paint us in the way that white people expect us to be, that might make them more sympathetic. So we all poor, dumb ass little niglets."

Toni moved from the chair, sitting next to him, laughing. She took the paper from his hands and started to read the article.

Luq continued, "God forbid that it's faggots getting murdered. Police won't do shit about that. So CSCM won't even mention the gay stuff most of these guys been doing, that will make their agenda harder."

"Obscuring truth..." Toni whispered. "And the dumb ass police are going to confuse CSCM advocating for a link in the murders and make it about trying to find one perpetrator, even though these murders are not following one pattern."

"Right! So instead of giving each kid the individual attention that might find the real killers, and give us a real answer, they're going to try to lump everybody together, just to shut up complaints, and we won't ever find out why this is happening, not just in Atlanta, but everywhere."

Toni lay back against Luq's stomach, absently reading the article. "So, as a gay person, does it bother you that the papers don't say whether these guys are gay?

"I think if there are kids that were killed that are gay, it should say so because maybe that has something to do with why that person has gone missing. But I'm not gay."

Toni sat up and turned to look at him. "What do you mean you're not gay."

He shrugged. "What do you mean, what do I mean? I'm not gay."

"So, you're straight?"

Another shrug. "I don't know."

"Bisexual?"

Luq vehemently shook his head. "That's just what people say when they don't want to be called a faggot. I haven't slept with anybody. Male or female. So I don't think of myself as anything."

"But you let Dion call you 'girl' and 'bitch' and refer to you as 'she,' and all that crap. If you're not gay, why do you let him get away with that?"

Luq laughed. "Who cares? That's just the way Dion talks. It doesn't bother me that he calls me 'girl.' He's not really calling me a girl. It's more like he's filling in his sentences. You know how valley girls, like, say like, while they think of what else to say? It doesn't mean anything."

"But it does. It's just like you say, with CSCM referring to those kids as living in the ghetto, so when people hear Dion calling you bitch, they automatically think you're gay."

"That's not my problem, that's their problem."

Toni was silent for a moment, pondering what Luq said. "Well...because, let's say, God forbid, you turned up missing, right? Then if you are described as gay, but you're not, that makes the investigation focus on false information, right?"

"Hmm. I guess you're right."

"You've never been with a man?"

"I tried. But I couldn't go through with it. It skeeved me out. It felt sleazy and gross."

"What about a woman?"

"No."

Toni moved closer. She touched a fingertip to his face, brought herself closer, and lowered her lips to his. Her breath was warm and sweet. "How does that feel?"

He whispered, "Nice."

She kissed him again. This time, she tentatively pushed her tongue into his mouth. He followed her lead and pushed his tongue into her mouth as well.

The warmth of her breath on his face, smelling of toothpaste with a faint hint of cigarettes felt good to him. The warmth began to emanate into his loins. He felt himself responding to her. She gently took his hand and guided it to the swell of her breast. It was firm but spongy, like a pound cake. Luq took initiative of his own and brought his other hand to her other breast. She blinked rapidly, looking briefly into his eyes to gauge what he was feeling. If he looked panicked, she would stop. His eyes were closed.

She moved the length of her body alongside his, turning to face him. She reached out to unzip his pants and began to massage. When he reached his own hand into her panties, he hesitated in surprise at the wetness there. It repulsed him, but the light moans that came from her throat, indicating that he was doing the right thing, excited him and kept his erection turgid with self-confidence.

She looked at him once more and asked him if he were okay with this. He nodded passionately.

She reached over to the desk and turned off the lamp.

terry
pue

january
23,
1981

SILAS

He had sat in the park for the past several months. He had sat there whether the sun blazed so unmercifully that it caused white spots to dance before his eyes, or the rain pelted through his clothing, soaking through until he quivered uncontrollably. He sat there from sunup to sundown. He would not leave unless the police chased him out. From this elevated perspective, he watched the travelers of the Norristown High Speed Line, coming and going. Some obliviously reading newsprint, others watchful for taxis and connecting modes of transport.

He had always left with disappointment coursing through his blood.

This day, however, was not like those days. This day, what he had sought for all the previous months showed itself to him.

And he followed her. He followed the familiar but changed luxurious hips as they undulated along the sidewalk. He watched the regal bearing that was markedly slower, less regal, assaulted by the passing of time and gravity. He followed, watching the hair that had been full and vibrant, that had caught the light, now turned gray and catching light through artificial chemical effects of hair dye.

He was sure to lurk in the shadows, lest she spot him in the reflection of a storefront window as she paused to admire a pretty dress or a display of wigs. Lest he be spotted by the regularly roaming squad cars that crawled along the thoroughfare in search of male black bodies to interrogate.

As a light rain began, Ordelia Purchase reached into her clutch for a rain bonnet to put over her head, and rushed the last few paces to the door of the Regional Health Initiative, unlocking the door and rushing inside just as the rain began to pour down in a flurry of cacophony.

He stood beneath a majestic oak tree. He did not notice the rain drenching his tattered clothing. He reached inside his coat to reassure himself that the weapon he had carried with him remained secure in his waistband.

FAGGOT IN A BOX

Luq quietly descended the cellar stairs from the backyard entrance. He opened the door, hearing Sharon Redd bleating "Beat the Street" from the turntable inside. He charged into the room in a fit of anger, looking around.

Dion sat on the bed thumbing through a hand-sized *Jet* magazine. He looked up briefly. "Hey, bitch."

"Where the fuck is Santos?" he asked, still looking around for him.

"Beats me. I've been waiting here for the past hour, and he hasn't shown."

"That record playing is my record! I've been looking all over for that record at home. He fucking stole it the last time he was at my house."

"Oooh. For real? Well, you know the bitch got sticky fingers. This song is fierce, though."

Luq snatched it off the turntable, searching for the jacket. "Where's the fucking cover? See, that's the other thing. The bitch can't even take decent care of shit!"

"Hey, did you see this? Frank Sinatra and Sammy Davis Jr. are performing a benefit concert in Atlanta to raise money for the investigations into those murders."

"Frank Sinatra? Sammy Davis Jr? Who the hell wants to see those old farts? What about Shalimar, Prince, Grace Jones?"

"Girl, don't nobody want to see her bony ass up on stage in her panties, or that dyke crawling around with a record on her head. They trying to raise coinages, okay?

"Well, I'd much rather see any of them than that one-eyed fossil singing about the candy man. Isn't that song about a pedophile?"

Dion laughed uproariously. "Don't get me to lying. It would totally make sense, though."

They looked up as the door to the kitchen above opened. Jonas came down the stairs wearing a pair of blue pajamas, holding a Teddy Ruxbin. He looked at the two of them and walked over to the door to the outside entrance. He lowered himself to the floor and sat cross-legged, watching the door.

The door opened, and Santos rushed in. Luq gasped.

His hair was matted and filled with dirt. One of his eyes was swollen and blackened. There was a long scab running down the left side of his face, and his nose was twice its usual size, with a bubble of blood hanging from the nostril.

"The fuck happened to you?" Dion said.

Jonas stood up with a cry, holding his stuffed animal close to him. He did not rush toward Santos but stood watching him agitatedly.

Santos lowered himself to the bed and began to remove his shirt. His ribcage was blackened with bruising.

"Jesus," said Luq, approaching and helping to gingerly remove Santos' blood-soaked shirt. San's movements were slow and labored. It was obvious that his movements were causing him pain.

"What happened?" Dion repeated.

"Faggot in a box," Santos said.

Dion sucked his teeth. "So you went. Even though I told you what that shit was all about. Dumb ass."

Luqman picked up a towel from the table and went over to a spigot at the far end of the room.

"How much you get?" Dion asked.

Santos picked up a corner of the sheet covering his bed and tapped at the cut on his eye. "Three hundred."

"Three hundred! It's going to cost you that to pay Montgomery Hospital to treat you..."

"I'm not going to the fucking hospital. I'll be fine."

Luq approached and handed him the wet towel. Santos applied it to his wounds.

"Was it worth it?" Luq asked. "For three hundred dollars?"

"Damn right. Have you ever been hungry? Have you ever had to worry every day about survival, living in your own brother's house and he won't give you a fucking bite to eat? Have you?"

"I don't understand why Nini is so goddamn broke," Dion said. "What kind of drug dealer don't have no money, gets his lights shut the fuck off, and rides around in his bitch's Ford Festiva. Girl, Nini's hustling backward."

Luq said, "You know what, San? You can save all that shit for somebody that doesn't know any better, okay. Don't give me that shit about survival. What dumbass runs out to buy weed and beer when they only have fifty dollars to get through the week? Who buys fucking cigarettes instead of food when they are always claiming to be freaking starving? And since you have decided not to go to school, and you are so worried about survival, how about you get a job instead of these simple ass hustles; pretending to collect donations for muscular dystrophy, fighting some other dumbass in an abandoned factory for a bunch of anonymous white niggas that think you are retarded for knocking the brains out of each other, robbing people that are supposed to be your friends. You're lazy, is what you are. My house has food half the time, more times than not our electric or phone is getting cut off, but you don't see me stealing from people. I got a job. It might not pay three hundred a pop like getting the shit kicked out of me might, but it's steady, and it's safe. And when I'm hungry, I have the money to buy food to feed myself, because I didn't blow it on fucking weed!"

"Fuck you!" Santos rushed up from the bed and charged at Luq. He raised a fist and cuffed him across the chin.

Jonas squawked and leaped on his back. Luqman recoiled in shock, then pushed San, who fell against the table, knocking the items onto the floor. "No, fuck you, dumb bitch."

Jonas was swinging angrily at Santos. Santos swatted him aside angrily. "Now you got my own brother taking your side against me."

Dion said, "Because he can spot stupidity, too. Sit your ass down. You know everything he said to you is right on the money, so don't get stupid. Because if you hit him again, I'm going to have to get involved, and you don't want the three of us kicking your black ass, I know."

Santos stood and went back to the bed, sulking. "I didn't know everybody thought so little of me. I didn't know you all think I'm just a stupid idiot."

Dion sucked his teeth. "Chile, yes you did. We ain't ever kept it a secret."

curtis
walker

february
19,
1981

WHITE GIRL

Luq was tired. He normally would cut back the hours he worked at the telemarketer when the school year began to work only alternate weekends. But now, since he would be heading off to Pittsburgh after graduation, he was trying to save as much money as possible. His mother had made it clear that there was no possibility that the family would be sending money to him. It had also been made clear that the trip up to school to move in his belongings would need to involve public transportation because going to school for fashion design was considered a folly. It was not a real education. One that would result in a respectable job in, say, accounting, or computer programming.

These things were not surprising to Luq. He had known from the time he made the initial inquiries into design school that there would not be much support from home.

He sat on the rear of the bus reading *Once Is Not Enough*, heading home from Montgomery Mall. The bus was somewhat empty, the way that he liked it. The fewer travelers on the bus, the less likely that someone would pay attention to his shaved temples, his spiked hair, his outlandish clothing. He could just relax and read his book.

Whenever the bus stopped, he would briefly look up from his book to see who was boarding, just to do a quick assessment of any potential troublemakers, so he noticed when the bus stopped along its route to allow a thin blonde woman and her daughter board, but he did not really pay attention to them, as they registered as non-problematic.

But as the two were talking, and Luq overheard their tones above the din of the bus engine, the melody and stops and starts of one of the voices tugged at his consciousness. He looked up to get a better look at the couple.

The older woman did not look familiar, but looked familiar in that she had the look of the typical suburban mom: highlighted hair pulled into a sedate bow at the nape of her neck, frosted lipstick, excessively lean, wearing a pseudo Chanel suit with a white Talbot's bow blouse, and a stocky one-inch heeled shoe. The girl talking to her also had her hair pulled into a navy bow, although her hair was dyed a brighter blonde hue. Her make-up was light; a bit of liner and lip color in a slighter stronger hue than the older woman. She wore a loose beige blouse and tie-dyed tapered jeans from The Limited, and a pair of powder blue Converse high tops, with brightly colored orange socks spilling out of the top.

Luq rose uncertainly from his seat and approached. "Toni?"

The girl looked up, her eyes wide, blinking fast. "Oh, hey. What are you doing here?"

"I work near the mall. What are you doing here?"

"Uh. I live in Lansdale..."

The older woman smiled. "Cheryl. Who is this? Is this a friend of yours?"

He was confused. "Cheryl?"

The woman reached across the girl, extended her hand. "Hello. I'm Mrs. Sandusky, Cheryl's mother. It's nice to meet you. Cheryl never brings any of her friends around. I was beginning to think she was living a double life, was a secret agent or something!"

The woman brayed. The girl laughed uncomfortably.

"Mom, this is, uh, Luqman."

Luq returned her handshake. "Nice to meet you. You say you're Ton - - Cheryl's mother?"

She nodded excessively, as she stood up. "Nice to meet you too. Our stop is coming up. Why don't you come over for dinner? It would be wonderful to get to know one of Cheryl's friends. She's such a loner. Always stuck in the house, reading a book, about the adventures of made up characters when she should be out in the world creating her own life. We'd love to have you. Her father will be coming home from work soon. I'm sure he'd be happy to meet you, too."

"That sounds really nice, but I'm afraid I can't do that today. I just finished working, and I'm really beat. But I would love to take a rain check."

"You work, too? Well, that's wonderful. Maybe you could help our Cheryl here find a job. She hasn't had any luck finding work since she graduated three years ago, and it's really frustrating her. Cheryl, give this nice young man our address so that he can join us for dinner, and I want that to be soon, you hear?"

Luq nodded. The woman brushed past them and carried her bags to the front of the bus to wait for their stop. Luq stared at the girl in confusion.

"So, Cheryl, huh?"

She laughed uncomfortably. "It's a long story."

"Can't possibly be as long as the one you told me. About being thrown out of the house, hitchhiking across the country, eating out of dumpsters, surviving on your wits."

She stood and gathered her things. "It's not like I expect you to get it. I wasn't just running around outright lying to people...."

"What do you mean, Cheryl. That's exactly what it is. Even your name wasn't real. So I don't really know you at all, right. Everything you've ever said was to game us. I told you about every part of me, we all did, and we thought you were doing the same. But what you were doing was feeding us a hard-luck story that you thought niggas like us would need to hear. That the only way to fit in was to be some unwanted, cast aside creature, right? Because that's what you think of us. That's what we are to you. So you just became one of us, instead of being yourself."

"Well it worked, didn't it? Do you think you guys would have accepted the corny ass white girl that lives in the 'burbs? That's never done anything in her life but go to school and read a book. That goes on family vacations. That lives at home with both her mother and her father."

Luq cut her off. "Yes. Because despite what you believe, that's who we are too. We aren't vagrants and street people. We haven't done anything in our lives either, except go to school, or read a book, or go on family vacations. Look at the way you're talking now. Even that was a put on."

She scoffed. "And yours wasn't? Look at how you're talking, now. It's not the same as when we hang out. You are just as phony as me."

"But I didn't lie about who I am. You know my name. You know where I live. You know me."

"You didn't lie? Are you gay or straight? What are you?"

"That's not a lie, Toni! I told you the truth."

Mrs. Sandusky approached inquisitively. "Is everything all right, you two?"

Luq nodded his head.

Cheryl said. "Yes. Everything is fine."

"Well, this is our stop, dear. We've got to go."

Cheryl looked at him as she passed. "I'll call you."

He just looked at her. "I guess you were right, what you said about white truth and black truth. Little did I know that you were backing me into a corner so that I could get knocked over the head."

SILAS

His sleep was restless. The thing that he kept on his person, the thing he intended to use to vanquish Ordelia Purchase lay beneath him, between the mattress and box spring. As he lay above it, the convolutions of his harried mind seemed to intuit the dark intent emanating from the thing, disrupting his usually unencumbered sleep.

In his mind, he sat on a smoothly stained teak bench. The sun dappled warmly through oak leaves, giving the pollen that danced before his eyes a somewhat tinged scent. He wore a voluminous cloak of dark wool, with many pockets. He had been sitting on this bench all day. Just as he had sat on the days that preceded it. Waiting. Watching her comings and goings. Becoming familiar with the pattern of her work day. Memorizing which days averaged more visitors and which days averaged the least. Which days she closed early and which days she closed late.

He sometimes stood under the shade offered by the large pine tree by the rear window, near her office, and watched her in a more relaxed state than her public persona. Kicking off her white shoes and rubbing her swollen feet through orthopedic hose, taking a tube of hand cream from a desk drawer and kneading a dab of ointment onto hands that he remembered as lean and elegant; now truncated and arthritic.

On the days that she stayed late, he watched through the window, at the end of the day, when she loosed her hair from the severe coils anchored at her nape, and let it fall, long and voluptuous, to her shoulders, running a wide-backed brush through it, before she leaned back against the leather chair and closed her still-wondrous green eyes for a brief nap.

Silas lay in the bed looking at the ceiling. He turned to his side and saw the boy sitting across the room, in his own bed, watching him.

He sat up, swinging his feet from the bed into his slippers. He rubbed his eyes with a gnarled knuckle and watched the boy.

Jonas said, "Will you stay home with me, today?"

"I can't do that, little man. Got something to do."

Jonas watched the old man's light changing from blue to red.

DAVID JACKSON AMBROSE

joseph
bell

timothy
hill

march
2,
1981

march
12,
1981

LUQMAN

Luq tried to keep all of the tips in his head when he went to the Greyhound station. He purchased a round trip ticket to Atlanta with the return date March 13, following the All-Star fundraiser for the missing children. He had called CSCM and been informed that there were daily searches of designated areas, efforts to assist the police with locating any evidence to help with ongoing investigations.

He figured he could volunteer to do that on the Friday before the concert.

He had asked for permission to spend the weekend at Dion's. Once his mother gave her approval, he asked to go there Thursday following school, telling her that he would go to classes Friday directly from Aunt Marie's house.

That Thursday, he told Dion his plans: if his mother contacted him during that weekend, he would just tell her that Luq had stepped out and would call her back. Luckily, Aunt Marie was usually too medicated to hear, let alone answer the phone. So Thursday after school, Luq headed into Philadelphia and purchased his tickets. He would miss school Friday. He knew that his school would contact his mother the following week about the unexcused absence, but he figured that the thing would be done by that time, and he would just take whatever repercussions resulted.

He didn't reserve a hotel in advance. But he had three hundred dollars securely lodged in his tube socks, which were reinforced with a second set of slouchy socks, and his cuffed ankle boots. He remembered to keep thirty dollars in his pants pocket for incidentals so that he would not be observed going into his stash. He remembered to stay close to the ticket window while waiting for his bus. He remembered to save his own money by looking over the shoulder of another traveler that was watching television at their seat. He sat with his duffel bag tucked securely under his arm while watching the motley crew of bleary-eyed travelers: mothers screaming at children, shadowy men wearing filthy fedoras roaming the perimeter, so smooth that they seemed to float rather than walk. No one paid the slightest attention to the boy with clothing too big for his skinny body. His hair was devoid of its usual spikes. He had shorn it down to a quarter of an inch, totally bald on the sides, in an attempt to fit in.

When the route number for his trip was called out, he stood in the haphazard line waiting to board, handed his bag to the conductor, watched him toss the bag into the belly of the beast as if he were throwing rats to a boa constrictor, and boarded the bus. He hunkered down into a window seat near the back of the bus and opened his copy of *If Beale Street Could Talk* to keep him company.

THE BEAT

Santos sat on the cement stairs of the service entrance to the Fraternal Order of the Elks, leaning on a large boom box. Cars trickled down Swede Street, stopping at the traffic light, where it t-boned Lafayette Street, where Dion stood, pigeon-toed, wearing a dark pair of basketball shorts and a thin tank top, waving obnoxiously at every car whose occupants had the nerve to stare at him.

"Hey. How are you? Welcome to Norristown, county seat of Montgomery County, and things," he would scream.

Santos laughed, "What are you, bitch, the welcome wagon?"

"Bitch. I am the first lady of Norristown. That's the gag, okay? I own this city."

Or at least this corner."

"Ooh, bitch, turn that up!"

Dion had already started gyrating his hips and dipping his torso, as Santos increased the volume to hear Phyllis Hyman singing "You Know How to Love Me."

"An oldie, but a goodie, honey. I never get tired of this song." He screamed along with Phyllis, "You and I together, will stand the test of tie-i-me!"

Just then, a large dark Cadillac stopped at the light. The passenger side window slid down, and Dion tried to peer inside, unable to see the driver. Dion shouted a greeting as the car turned the corner. "Come back around."

Santos turned the radio volume low and approached Dion.

"Didn't Luq say that the guy that he had that run in with was driving a black Cadillac."

Dion was looking up the street distractedly. "Mmm hmm."

"Well then, what you telling dude to circle around for?"

"Girl, Luq don't know these streets. I can handle myself."

"I don't think you should take any chances. It's not like he's the only trick that will be down here tonight."

"How do you know that?" Dion asked. "It might be."

They both watched as the black Cadillac circled the block and slowly approached. "Even so, it's a bad idea."

Dion shook his shoulders, as if channeling a new personality, and approached the passenger side window, raising his voice a few octaves. "Hey, what's what?"

The voice from inside said, "You want to take this ride?"

"Sure. I know a place."

"I know a place, too. Bridgeport."

"Oh, no. I don't leave town. I know plenty of places right here."

"Bridgeport." He insisted.

Dion paused to consider his options, then shrugged and opened the door to hop in. Just then, an object sailed past his head, landing on the windshield. Santos threw an open bottle of soda at the car, which splashed all over, shattering on the glass and causing it to splinter.

"What the fuck!" the car jerked as the man slammed the gears into park and hurled open the door.

Dion looked over his shoulder in confusion and began to run across the street into the dense fauna of the railroad property. Santos grabbed his boom box from the stairs and quickly followed.

Over his shoulder, Dion screamed. "Bitch, what is wrong with you! That shit could have gotten in my hair!"

They raced over to the underpass of the Reading Railroad, the strategy being, that if their pursuer followed them there, the underpass allowed them to see him enter on either side, and they would be able to escape by going through the opposite end.

They stood in the center of the tunnel, gasping to catch their breath.

"Bitch. You fucking with my money, now. What you do that for?"

"You won't be making any money if you get killed, will you? You should at least be safe out here."

Dion was incredulous. "I should be safe? Me? Who the fuck was it that fought somebody while people watched so you could get a little bit of money, and I don't mean Joe Frazier. And how much money did you really get? You didn't get the amount you said, I know."

Santos mumbled, "They didn't pay me yet."

Dion's eyes grew wide as saucers, "Did Not Pay You Yet? So when are you expecting it? Is the check in the mail, you dumb bitch?"

"Stop fucking calling me dumb! I'm sick of that. You ain't no smarter than me. You are out here hustling just like I am, so what makes you so smart. Just like Luq said that I could get a job, why can't you get yourself a real job, where it's safe, and you don't have to worry about being taken off these streets?

"Safe? What safe? It doesn't matter if I work for SmithKline or I stand out here sucking dick, I'm not safe. You think all those kids in Atlanta was prostitutes? Some of them were just regular students, going to the store and shit. We ain't safe no matter what we do. I can work at the goddam bank and be going to my job and just turn the fuck up missing, and who would give a shit? Who's looking out for my safety? And what kind of job can I get, looking like this? Am I supposed to cut my hair, wear and shirt and tie, try to walk like trade, so I fit in? I don't want to live a life where I have to pretend to be something I'm not. At least down here, I don't have to lie about who I am."

"Y'all talk about me hustling up coins and then wasting it on reefer and beer, but what makes either of you any better? Luq has a job, big fucking deal. All he does is spend his money on stupid ass clothes and books. Clothes to try to look like some kid from London, books to read about shit he ain't never going to get. And what do you do with your money? You're just like me, buying weed and cigarettes."

"You don't even know what I have to do. You don't even know. And how do you know Luq can't get the things he reads about? They are dreams. Don't you have dreams?"

"Do you?"

Dion paused to think about it. "I do. Lots of them."

"Well, then that's what makes you and me different. Even if you dream, when you least expect it, something happens. Like you go to the store for your grandmom, and you never come back. And then the cops find you strapped to a tree with somebody's dirty underwear stuffed down your throat."

LUQMAN

By the time he called home, Carol was already aware that something was amiss. Monday morning, when she picked up her office extension and heard her son's voice, she had already been contacted by Upper Merion School District, informing her that Luqman had been absent from class today, as well as Friday.

Once she accepted the charges, hearing the tremulousness of uncertainty in his voice exacerbated the fear that had been welling inside of her all morning, and she unleashed it by yelling into the phone.

"Where the hell are you? Atlanta! How did you get to...what on earth are you doing in Atlanta?" She listened. Her hands trembled. She removed an earring from her ear and replaced the receiver to her ear. "You've...lost all your money? Well, where have you been staying for the past three days?"

He stood in the phone booth, among a bay of booths lined along the perimeter of the Atlanta bus station, with his foot pushed against the accordion doors to keep the skulking shadows roaming outside from opening them to beg for money.

"I've been sleeping at the bus station. I walk around during the day when security chases you out. But I've been helping with search parties."

"What happened."

He spoke through tears. "I don't know. When I got here, I went to a motel for a place to sleep, but when I got there, my money was gone. I fell asleep on the bus, but I don't know how anybody could have gotten to my money. I mean, I would have felt it."

"And your clothes? They stole your bag, too?"

"I don't know. My bag was missing when they unloaded."

"Then how have you been changing, keeping yourself clean?

"I wash up in the restrooms here. I haven't been able to change my clothes. The search parties have sandwiches, soda. I eat when I'm there. But I can't get home. I have no money."

"Why haven't you gone to the police. You need to go to the police for help…"

"What police? Since when are the police going to help me? If I went to the police, I might not ever have been heard from again."

Carol wanted to tell him this was not true, but she couldn't. She thought about it for a minute. "Okay. Here's what I'm going to do. I will contact the Atlanta police. I will speak to the captain and get his contact information so that we have a name to refer to. Then I will call you back and give you his name, and you can report to him, or rather, I will have him arrange to pick you up, and I will be there as soon as I can. Give me the number."

He did as he was instructed.

"Do not move from that booth until I call you back, do you understand?"

He nodded as if she could see him, speaking through phlegm-filled sobs, "Yeah."

"Luq..."

"Yeah."

"Be careful."

She waited until she heard the line disconnect on the other end before she hung up. She then picked up again and dialed information.

SANTOS

He arrived early, before the offices of the Regional Health Initiative were officially open, hoping to catch Ordelia as she entered. He sat on the crest of a grassy knoll, the dew seeping into his khaki pants, watching as the old woman made her way down the walkway, the lamplights still beaming, despite the bright light of day, as they were set on a timer. He watched her reach into her large handbag to search for keys, her beautiful mohair coat flapping opulently behind her as she maneuvered the items in her arms to swing the door open. He laughed as she stumbled clumsily over the threshold and closed the door behind her.

From her inner sanctum, firing up her old, bulky Univac, Ordelia did not hear the outer door as it opened. She squinted at the green glow of words on the screen, tapping an inpatient fingernail on the desktop as the system keyed up.

Suddenly, her office door opened, causing her to gasp in surprise.

He smiled at her, but his smile seemed different than usual, less genuine, more urgent.

"We do not have an appointment set up for today, my dear. Why are you here?"

Santos stuck his jittering hands into his pants pockets and approached her desk. "Hi, Miss Purchase. I know we don't have an appointment set up, but I was wondering if you could maybe advance me payment now for our next appointment. I could really use the money..."

Ordelia cut him off, raising her hand to silence him. "Listen, I already forwarded money to you for an appointment that you never showed for. You know the program has folded. We don't have any further appointments to make. The initiative has moved its focus to another area of medicine. While we value your contributions, we have all the data that we need from you and the others that participated in this particular cohort."

She stood and approached him, placing a hand on his shoulder and aiming him toward the door. "I'm going to have to ask that you do not show up here anymore unless we happen to contact you. We have finished with you, okay dear?"

She did not wait for an answer, but pushed him out her door and closed it firmly behind him.

Standing outside her door, in the reception area, Santos cursed her under his breath, tears of frustration burning his eyes. He stormed toward the door, brushing past her coat hanging on the rack. He stopped and rifled his hands through the pockets. He smiled as he removed a small watch with a gold band. He put it in his own pocket, picked up the coat, and quickly shoved his arms into the sleeves, running toward the door as he placed the hood over his head.

The old man stood at his post beneath the old oak tree by the entrance, watching intently. He felt it in his bones. He knew that today was the day. He could not wait any longer. If he continued to delay, he knew, he would be influenced by the little boys' constant late night entreaties. When he saw her exiting the building, her hood pulled low over her face, the great coat swinging wildly as she almost ran down the walkway, he was confused that she was leaving so early in the day. He looked at the deviation in schedule as some sort of cosmic confirmation that the time was now.

As the form rushed toward him, he rushed toward it, reaching into his waistband for the cool metal handgrip. He did not think of himself in the present, but harkened back to his southern childhood, when hunting game was the only way to guarantee he and his family would eat, he eyed his target, peered through the guide, squeezed the trigger, aiming at the gut. His aim was clean and true. The figure fell forward without a sound.

The man approached, saw the figure struggling against the concrete. He aimed at the hood and squeezed again, the kickback burning up his arm, stinging his shoulder. He was out of practice.

He replaced the gun in his waistband and raced toward the back of the building.

ATLANTA

Carol Ettinger had come prepared. She brought with her to Atlanta generations of knowledge that had been passed down from her mother, and her grandmother, and her great-grandmother, back throughout time to the first arrival of their African forebears when they first stepped foot into the new world. What she brought with her was a thorough knowledge of the intrinsic micro-communications between the black underclass when interacting with the white dominant class. It was these micro-communications that had allowed certain people to survive while others met with acts of violence, or starvation, or early deaths.

She wore her hair in a subdued chignon, held with a Chanel hair clip, passed down from her grandmother, who had received it from the white woman that had employed her as a domestic her entire life. Her makeup was subtle but targeted to bring out the burnished hue of her flawless skin. Her nails were manicured and painted a comely peach shade. She wore a tailored suit, also Chanel, and carried a vintage Halston handbag.

All of these items had been selected strategically. As were her dark hose and sensible, well-shod feet, courtesy of Evan Picone. She had been taught well. She knew that when interacting with whites, first impressions were important. One must communicate an appearance that demonstrated an awareness for the finer things in life, but could not be ostentatious, lest you create a feeling of jealousy from the targeted party. One's manner must also be a subtle blend of respect and intellect, but with a hint of subservience intended to make the dominant class feel superior. One must show that they were aware of the power dynamics that not only formed this country, but that continued to undergird it even now.

Carol had come prepared. She brought with her a slim envelope of cash, an offering of her gratitude to the Atlanta police force (and Officer Justice in particular) for taking time from their most hectic daily routine to attend to her tattered, problematic child. As a back-up, in case the officer pretended to be offended by the cash offer and refused it on moral grounds, she had also stopped at an area boutique and purchased a cheese basket as well as the finest South American cigars available.

The two of them sat silently in the taxi on the way to Hartsfield-Jackson International Airport. Luqman, freshly showered and wearing new clothing purchased by his mother during her Atlanta gift purchasing expedition, looked sullenly out of the window. Carol looked out the window on her side of the cab. Her fingernails drumming on the console indicated belied the silence of the cab.

"Help me understand this. Help me understand why you would take all of the money in your possession and travel down to a place where they are murdering black children for sport. Because I do not understand that."

Luq was tired. It was evident in the lag of his voice. He spoke while continuing to watch the neverending expanse of roadway. "I wanted to help. I felt like if I wanted people to do more than what they were doing, I couldn't expect that unless I was willing to do more, too."

Carol laughed scornfully. "And what is it that you could have done to help? What can you do that the FBI and the police haven't been able to do?"

"I could care!"

She turned to look at him. His shoulders shook with fury and tears burned down his face. She softened her voice. "You're just a child, Luq. If you had turned up missing down here, I would never be able to forgive myself for letting you out of my sight."

"When am I ever in your sight, mom? When is that? You work all day; you go to church, auxiliary, bridge club. You don't have time for me. You don't even know what's going on with me."

This offended her. "What's going on with you? I don't even understand you. What is all this about? Hmm, Luq? What are you? This --- this hairstyle, these clothes, listening to this music that I don't know anything about, hanging in the streets with these, these...You're going off to a school I never approved of, to learn something that cannot possibly support you with a career. What is it that you are trying to pull with all of these stunts?"

He turned to her in fury. "I want to be seen! I want to be noticed. I don't want to be invisible anymore. The only time somebody notices us is when one of us turns up missing or dead. I don't want to be have to be murdered before anybody notices that I was alive."

She looked at him, tears coursing down her face.

Epilogue

AUGUST, 1981

They stood awkwardly amongst the chaotic atmosphere of the Greyhound bus station. His two duffel bags were on the floor at his feet. Dion stood with his hand on his hip, smoking a cigarette, looking off into the distance for the arrival of the bus, which had been announced five minutes earlier.

He blew out a tuft a smoke, looking at Luqman. "So Aunt Carol and Uncle Ambrose are going to drive up with your bulk stuff next weekend? You sure of that?"

He shrugged. "As sure as I can be."

They both laughed. The bus plowed into the station with a mighty roar. Dion lifted one bag and placed it around his cousin's shoulder. He looked at him with a thin smile. "You know I'm proud of you, right? You got to do this up right. Blow them the fuck away."

"Yeah. I know."

"Remember, you're doing this for all of us. For me. For San..."

Both of them were silent for a second, their eyes watering.

Luq lifted his other bag as people began milling around them to board the bus. "You know, you can do this too, right? You can go to school, be whatever you want to be."

He nodded. "I know. But who's going to take care of Marie? Right now, she needs me, you know? I'll get my ducks lined up. I sure as shit don't plan to be here forever. No, ma'am."

With an extra flourish that showed Luq his thoughts were preoccupied, Dion whipped a Newport from the pack tucked into his pocket and rummaged for a lighter. He then fixed his cousin with a piercing glare.

"Well, you should feel more at ease, now that they caught the killer down in Atlanta. I know that's way far from where you are going, but we were all feeling kind of noid while that shit was going on all this time. Girls just getting snatched up..."

Luq rolled his eyes and cut into Dion's dialogue with exasperation.

"Stop playing. You know that chile Alice snatched up ain't have nothing to do with those murders."

Dion blinked in false innocence. "What you mean? I thought it was a miracle, that as soon as those Hollywood people swooped in, bringing in all that attention, that Licia found the killer like that."

Dion snapped his fingers in Luq's face. Luq brusquely smacked his hand aside. "It's a miracle, all right. You seen that guy? She look as fruity as a can of Del Monte bing cherries. A music producer, auditioning those young girls so they could become recording artists."

They both laughed derisively.

"Right?" Dion smirked. "That's that samo that be going on up here. Some dude still in the closet driving around luring sissies back to they house to get they dick sucked. If she killed somebody, it would have been by accident 'cause her mommy was coming down the basement steps, and she was trying to keep the sissy quiet, or something like that. But ain't no way he killed all them kids. That's white people mess."

Luq nodded. "Of course somebody white did it. You ain't got to be an FBI agent to see that pattern. Same as it's ever been. White man killing niggas for practice, for fun. For entrance into some fraternal order. And the rest of white society pretends they don't know shit about it. That's willful ignorance. But I'm not afraid, anymore, to go off away from home."

Dion nodded with approval. "They gonna kill you. What goods being close to home or far away? So you can get your body decked out by Clifford Rose?"

They both laughed, the reputation of the local mortician and memories of appallingly made up corpses flashing through their heads.

Luq laughed. "No, ma'am. I'd rather be handled by an unknown. At least there's a chance he will make my corpse look a little bit like me."

As the last of the people began to board, Luq said, "Well, I better get going. Keep the goddamn phone bill paid, so I can call you."

Dion huffed, "Bitch, when do I get delinquent on my payments? You got the wrong doll. You take both these duffel bags on board with you, okay. And keep that money in your motherfucking draws. Do not go to sleep, got me?

Luqman laughed and suddenly grasped Dion in a brief, uncomfortable hug. "I love you."

Dion rolled his eyes, "Chile, please, all this drama. I can't..."

Before stepping away, Dion whispered, "Love you right back."

A girl holding a transistor radio walked past from another bus. "You Know How To Love Me" was playing. Dion walked away, waving at Luqman and yelling after the girl with the radio, "Hey, Miss Thing, turn that shit up, will you? That's my damn song!"

Luqman boarded the bus, found a seat in the rear, and lodged his belongings on the seat closest to the window with a hearty grunt.

Appendix

Baldwin, James. The Evidence of Things Not Seen, Bucaneer
    Books, Inc. Cutchogoe,
    New York. 1985

Bambara, Toni Cade. Those Bones are Not My Child. Knopf
    Doubleday Publishing Group,
    New York 2009

Bennet, Gillian and Paul Smith. Contemporary Legend: A
    Reader, Turner Patricia A.

The Atlanta Child Murders: A Case Study of Folklore in the
    Black Community.
  Routledge, New York. 1986

Byrd, Jerry and Doug Root. "Deaths Stir Fears Among Gays."
    Pittsburh Press, Sun. 24 October
    1982.

Heller, Jean, "Syphilis Victims in U.S. Study Went Untreated
    for 40 Years." New York Times
  26 July 1972.

The Imperial Night-Hawk. 29 August 29, 1923.
    @authentichistory.com

Killing   in   Earnest:
    http//www.crimelibrary.com/serial_killers/predators/Wil
    liams/earnest_3.html

McVeigh, Rory. The Rise of the Ku Klux Klan: Right Wing
    Movements and National Politics.
  University of Minnesota Press, 2009.

Rothman, David J. Were Tuskegee & Willowbrook 'Studies in
    Nature'? The Hastings Center
  Report Vol. 12, No. 2 (April 1982), pp. 5-7

Supreme Court of Georgia: (page 74) supreme-court-georgia.vlex.com/vid/Thomas-v-the-state

Timberg, Craig and Daniel Halperin, Tinderbox: How the West Sparked the AIDS Epidemic
and How the World Can Finally Overcome It. Penguin Group, New York. 2012

Tuskegee University Bioethics Center. Final Report of the Tuskegee Syphilis Study Legacy
Committee 1. 20 May 1996.

Wooten, James T. "Survivor of '32 Syphilis Study Recalls a Diagnosis." New York Times
27 July 1972.

Willowbrook Hepatitis Experiments. http://science.education.nih.gov/supplements/nih9/bioethics/guide/pdf/Master_5-4.pdf

.

Recordings

Springsteen, B., "Hungry Heart." perf. Bruce Springsteen. The River. Columbia. 1980. Vinyl.

Summer, D., "Bad Girls." perf. Donna Summer. Bad Girls. Casablanca. 1979. Vinyl.

Lucas, R., Mtume, James. "You Know How To Love Me." perf. Phyllis Hyman. You Know How To Love Me. 1979. Arista Records. Vinyl.

Hutter, R., Schneider, F., "Tour de France/Numbers." perf. Kraftwerk. Trans-Europe Express. EMI. 1977. Vinyl.

Bowie, D., "Ashes to Ashes." perf. David Bowie. Scary Monsters. RCA. 1980. Vinyl.

Robinson, S., "Ooo Baby Baby." perf. Linda Ronstadt. Living in the USA. Asylum. 1979. Vinyl.

David Jackson Ambrose spent his childhood dumpster diving for coverless paperback novels behind independent bookstores in West Chester, PA. He alternately immersed himself in the fictitious worlds of William Faulkner, John Steinbeck, Jacqueline Susann and Harold Robbins between stints of tadpole hunting and stealing fans off the trucks of the old Lasko factory.

He then progressed to adolescence writing comic books that featured his younger sister and brother, in order to keep them entertained while their mother worked as an accountant for Sperry Univac. During his teenage years as a student he wrote serial novels, whose chapters were circulated in the homerooms of Upper Merion High School. He also sketched abstract fashion illustrations that his psychology teacher analyzed as having been created by an individual with extreme body dysmorphia – who did not wish to see the world as it truly exists.

As a member of the Phi Theta Kappa Honor Society, David earned his B.A. in Africana Studies from the University of Pennsylvania, an M.A. in Writing Studies from St. Joseph's University, and received his M.F.A. in Creative Writing from Temple University. He has presented at the National Conference for Teachers of English, "Engaging the Marginalized Student," and has received honorable mention for his exploration of race and social work for the 2016 AWP: Intro Journals Project entitled, "There's A Nigger In The House." His short story, "Juxtapose," was published in the 2014 edition of the *Nota Bene* publication.

Keep up with David on social media on Instagram: @Davidjrhd, Twitter: @DJacksonambrose, and on the web at www.davidjacksonambrose.com.

CPSIA information can be obtained
at www.ICGtesting.com
Printed in the USA
BVHW03s2203280318
511866BV00001B/1/P